A Marvelous Murder

Praise for David S. Pederson

Fatal Foul Play

"The mystery was filled with plenty of twists and turns and kept me on the edge of my seat. The characters were complex and interesting, and David threw in plenty of relationship drama as well—and a budding new romance. If you are looking for a fun quick read that has almost as much gay romance drama as it does mystery, then be sure to pick up *Fatal Foul Play*."—*Lorie Lewis Ham, author of the Alexandra Walters Mystery series*

Secrets and Scandals

"It kept me hooked, waiting for what I knew would be a big moment when something suddenly happened and there would be a rush to uncover the truth. It really kept me guessing." —*LESBIreviewed*

Puzzles Can Be Deadly

"I have come to adore David's mystery stories, and this one did not disappoint...David writes fantastic mysteries, and this one had some really good twists...A most clever and engaging mystery that I thoroughly enjoyed."—*LESBIreviewed*

Murder at Union Station

"The story is full of engaging, lively characters...I also enjoyed the diversity in the novel, which one doesn't always find in historical fiction. It was a lot of fun to unravel the mystery of what happened...well-written, suspenseful, and smoothly plotted, and it kept me guessing until the big denouement at the end. It's a fast, enjoyable cozy mystery that I enjoyed."—*Roger Hyttinen (Roger's Reads)*

"Where this story really works is in the 1946 setting...I thoroughly enjoyed this mystery and look forward to the next one."—*Sinfully Good Gay Books Reviews*

"A Clever Murder Mystery. David always delivers an exciting story, always cleverly put together so I can never figure out 'who done it' until it is all pieced together by the detective…There is always an elegance and charm to the stories David writes, which makes them stand out."—*LESBIreviewed*

Murder on Monte Vista

"A great new mystery!…[T]he way everything is described really puts me in the moment. You feel a part of the story, and the way it is written, even though you know Mason is talking to another character, it's as if he is talking to you personally too, so it is so easy to become immersed in the story and really be a part of it. Most enjoyable, super exciting, and a series I cannot wait for more of! What a fantastic mystery!"—*LESBIreviewed*

Death's Prelude

"I highly recommend this story, introducing Heath and giving more insight to his past, as well as setting up the series nicely. The most fabulous thing though was seeing Heath blossom into the detective I met in *Death Overdue*, and I can't wait to read the next mystery he has to solve."—*LESBIreviewed*

Death Overdue

"Deftly drawn characters, brisk pacing, and an easy charm distinguish [this] winning follow-up to 2019's *Death Takes a Bow*. Pederson successfully evokes and shrewdly capitalizes upon the time in which his mystery takes place, using the era's prejudices and politics to heighten the story's stakes and more thoroughly invest readers in its outcome. Plausible suspects, persuasive red herrings, and cleverly placed clues keep the pages frantically flipping until the book's gratifying close."—*Mystery Scene*

"David S. Pederson never disappoints when it comes to twisted and suspenseful mysteries…I highly recommend the Detective Heath Barrington mystery series, and *Death Overdue* in particular is suspenseful and an absolute page-turner."—*QueeRomance Ink*

Lambda Literary Award Finalist
Death Takes a Bow

"[T]here's also a lovely scene near the end of the book that puts into words the feelings that Alan and Heath share for one another, but can't openly share because of the time they live in and their jobs in law enforcement. All in all, an interesting murder/mystery and an apt depiction of the times."—*Gay Book Reviews*

"This is a mystery in its purest form…If you like murder mysteries and are particularly interested in the old-school type, you'll love this book!"—*Kinzie Things*

Lambda Literary Award Finalist
Death Checks In

"David Pederson does a great job with this classic murder mystery set in 1947 and the attention to its details…"—*The Novel Approach*

"This noir whodunit is a worthwhile getaway with that old-black-and-white-movie feel that you know you love, and it's sweetly chaste, in a late-1940s way…"—*Outsmart Magazine*

"This is a classic murder mystery; an old-fashioned style mystery à la Agatha Christie…"—*Reviews by Amos Lassen*

Death Goes Overboard

"[A]uthor David S. Pederson has packed a lot in this novel. You don't normally find a soft-sided, poetry-writing mobster in a noir mystery, for instance, but he's here…this novel is both predictable and not, making it a nice diversion for a weekend or vacation."—*Washington Blade*

"Pederson takes a lot of the tropes of mysteries and utilizes them to the fullest, giving the story a knowable form. However, the unique characters and accurate portrayal of the struggles of gay relationships in 1940s America make this an enjoyable, thought-provoking read."—*Gay, Lesbian, Bisexual, and Transgender Round Table of the American Library Association*

"You've got mobsters, a fedora-wearing detective in a pinstriped suit, seemingly prim matrons, and man-hungry blondes eager for marriage. It's like an old black-and-white movie in book form…" —*Windy City Times*

Death Comes Darkly

"Agatha Christie…if Miss Marple were a gay police detective in post–WWII Milwaukee."—*PrideSource: Between the Lines*

"The mystery is one that isn't easily solved. It's a cozy mystery unraveled in the drawing room type of story, but well worked out."—*Bookwinked*

"If you LOVE Agatha Christie, you shouldn't miss this one. The writing is very pleasant, the mystery is old-fashioned, but in a good meaning, intriguing plot, well developed characters. I'd like to read more of Heath Barrington and Alan Keyes in the future. This couple has a big potential."—*Gay Book Reviews*

"[A] thoroughly entertaining read from beginning to end. A detective story in the best Agatha Christie tradition with all the trimmings."—*Sinfully Gay Romance Book Review*

By the Author

Heath Barrington Mysteries

Death Comes Darkly

Death Goes Overboard

Death Checks In

Death Takes A Bow

Death Overdue

Death's Prelude

Death Foretold

Mason Adler Mysteries

Murder on Monte Vista

Murder at Union Station

Murder at the Oasis

Puzzles Can Be Deadly

Fatal Foul Play

A Marvelous Murder

A Marvelous Murder

by

David S. Pederson

2025

A MARVELOUS MURDER

ISBN 13: 978-1-63679-798-4

This Trade Paperback Original Is Published By
Bold Strokes Books, Inc.
P.O. Box 249
Valley Falls, NY 12185

First Edition: June 2025

Credits
Editors: Jerry L. Wheeler and Stacia Seaman
Production Design: Stacia Seaman
Cover Design by Inkspiral Design

Acknowledgments

Thank you to my wonderful friend Lawrence Simon, who gave me a period newspaper that provided me with the surnames of Shufflebottom and Cobbledick used in this book. And thank you to my friend Sam DiTuro for providing delicious meals where things like this can be discussed.

And to Ted McLaren and Lara Cerri, without whom my life, and my book launches, would be far more dull.

And huge thanks always to Jerry Wheeler and Stacia Seaman, my editors with the most-est, as well as everyone at Bold Strokes Books who have helped me so much, especially Radclyffe, Sandy, Cindy, Ruth, and Sheri.

To all my family, and to my terrific friends who are my chosen family,
and of course my wonderful mom, Vondell.
In memory of my dad, Manford.
And to my wonderful husband, Alan,
who is always supportive, helpful, and encouraging.
Finally, to all my readers. I thank you from the bottom of my heart.

Chapter One

Late Tuesday afternoon, August 8, 1939
A room at Icon Pictures, Hollywood

"You'd shoot us in cold blood?"

"Hot blood or cold, don't matter to me. You're finished, Beaumont, in more ways than one, and so is your young friend here. This gun is loaded."

"So are you, Cabot, judging from the way you're shaking. You can't hold your revolver steady. I bet you couldn't hit either of us with that thing if I gave you three tries."

"You'd lose that bet. I'm not that drunk."

"Yeah? You smell like cheap booze mixed with formaldehyde, and you look like hell."

"Funny, Crockett. You two are quite the comedy act. I thought you were in the detective business, not vaudeville."

"Beaumont and Crockett, no case too small or too big. That's what it says on the door over there, anyway, right, Jasper?"

"That's right, Axel. Axel Beaumont and Jasper Crockett, private eyes, brave and wise. That's us."

"That *was* you. I'll bring flowers to your funeral."

"You're too kind, Cabot. Bring tulips. And put your tulips on the massive organ. I hear you like that sort of thing."

"Shut your mouth, Beaumont. And say goodbye."

"Make up your mind. It's hard to say goodbye with my mouth closed."

"And then the door to the seedy office swings open, revealing Ruth, dressed in a smart suit with a white silk blouse and a matching hat," Orland Orcott, the director, said, nodding at Eve Spellman, who was playing Ruth.

"Oh! My goodness, what's going on? What's happening? Who are you?"

"Cabot shifts his bloodshot eyes to the girl, and Beaumont takes advantage of the distraction to rush him, trying to wrestle the revolver away. He doesn't succeed. A loud bang bursts forth as the gun goes off and Ruth crumples to the floor, blood pouring from her chest, staining her lily-white blouse. Cabot stares down at the smoking gun as Jasper rushes to Ruth's side, cradling her in his strong arms," Orcott read.

"Ruth! Ruth? Oh, my God, don't die, don't leave me!"

"She stares up at him, her words barely audible," the director said, watching Eve closely.

"Jasper, I…I love you."

"Axel, call a doctor, please!"

"And then the camera pans to Cabot, still staring at the gun in his trembling hand. He lifts it close to his face and cocks it again as the camera moves in for a close-up, capturing an exquisite look of shock, puzzlement, and fear. Fade out to end credits," the director said with a wheeze as he closed the leather-bound script and removed his wire-rimmed glasses, placing them in a monogrammed case inside the breast pocket of his suitcoat. He looked like a cross between an English bulldog and a Hampshire hog dressed in an imported, tailored navy pinstripe suit.

The four actors closed their scripts also and looked over at him.

"Why does the script say I have blue eyes?" Griffin Fenwick, who was playing Jasper, asked. "We're shooting in black and white."

"It was in the book, so they kept it. And we were *supposed* to shoot in color until they slashed my budget. Anyway, that's the rewrite of the final scene," Orcott said with a burp. He took out his monogrammed handkerchief and wiped the perspiration from his high, furrowed brow before shoving it back into his outside front jacket pocket. "God, it's hot in here." He glanced over at the metal fans in two of the corners. They were doing little but blowing the warm air about as they clicked and whirred, oscillating slowly. The two large windows, which overlooked twin towering date palms, were open, but there was no breeze. The dark green curtains hung limp.

"I liked the scene better the way it was," Fenwick said, rubbing his eyes with his long, thin fingers, his elbows on the table. He had loosened his green bow tie and removed his black checked coat revealing his white dress shirt, stained and wet with sweat under the arms.

Orcott trained his beady eyes on him. "I okayed the changes, and so did the producer. This will play to the masses better."

"I'm not so sure," Eve Spellman said. "I think I agree with Griff."

Orland turned his head to stare at her. "It doesn't matter what you think, Miss Spellman, nor do I care. And I hope you can bring a little more feeling to the part of Ruth when the cameras start rolling. You're playing her as wooden as log."

"I'll work on it, Mr. Orcott," she said with a practiced smile, but her jaw was clenched.

"If you ask me, I thought she read the part rather well," said William Taylor, the older man who had been cast as Cabot. He was sitting next to Griff and looked uncomfortable.

Orcott swiveled his thick neck in William's direction now, looking him over critically. "I *didn't* ask you, Taylor, nor would I. And your voice is still too high-pitched. You need to lower it a bit and rough it up. Your character is supposed to be an alcoholic gangster raised in the streets of Chicago, not a dandy from Boston."

"Yes, sir," William said, avoiding eye contact with anyone. His voice was quiet but he looked as though he were silently seething. "I'll work on it."

"See that you do." Orcott's jowls moved up and down as he chewed on something unknown. "At least you *look* like an alcoholic gangster, anyway. What happened to you these last few years? Have you been hitting the booze? I won't stand for a drunk on the set."

"No, sir, don't you worry. I don't drink. Not much, anyway," William said softly, though his hands were trembling.

"Then what is it? You're gaunt, weathered, and haggard. You used to be a half decent looking guy. You were a leading man in the silent days."

William fidgeted in his seat, staring down at the script in front of him, feeling the smooth leather of the cover with his fingertips as he rubbed it over and over. "It's the cancer, Mr. Orcott." His voice cracked and broke.

Orland Orcott blew out his cheeks and huffed. "Jesus, cancer? I was told that was just a rumor."

"Who, uh, who told you that, sir?" William said, still staring down and looking miserable and cross.

"Never mind." Orcott tugged out his handkerchief again, blew his bulbous nose, and wheezed. "Cancer, Jesus Christ. Are you going to be able to finish this picture, Taylor? I can't have you dying on me halfway through."

William finally looked at Orcott. "Sure I'll finish it, Mr. Orcott. The doctors say I'm okay now, but it's been a rough couple of years. I'll finish it, just you wait and see."

"I'll hold you to that, believe you me. People don't usually live very long after something like cancer, you know. You die on me, and you're fired. Understand?"

"Uh, yes, sir, Mr. Orcott."

"Good." He stuffed his soiled handkerchief back in his pocket and sniffed like a bulldog. "And what the hell is that smell? It stinks like a urinal in here."

"All I can smell is sweat and your cigar smoke," Eve said.

"I'm telling you I smell urine," Orcott said.

William looked embarrassed, his gray, hollow cheeks flushing a soft pink. "I'm sorry, Mr. Orcott, that's probably me. I sometimes have some leakage issues because of my prostate, or lack of a prostate. I can't always control it."

"Geez, you're still pissing yourself?" Orcott said with a sneer. "No wonder they call you Wee Wee Taylor."

William's elfin ears turned tomato red. "I can't help it. I, uh, wear pads, sir."

"Pads? Like a diaper? God almighty. Well, don't drink anything on the days we're filming, understood?" Orcott said. "I don't want you pissing your pants in the middle of a big scene like you did on that other film."

"Yes, sir, I mean no, sir. I really am sorry."

"You're sorry, all right. I hope you don't have any bowel problems."

"No, sir, I don't. I'll do my best, Mr. Orcott," William said, sweat pouring down his thin face and neck as he shifted in his seat again.

"It's unbelievable what I have to put up with around here." Orcott's beady dark eyes panned around the table slowly. "If this picture is to be any good, I need each of you to give me one hundred percent, understood? The book this movie is based on was a best seller, so I have high hopes for this film, and for each of you."

"Speaking of the book," Griff said.

"What about it?" Orcott said, breathing heavily in Griff's direction and still wheezing.

"Well, I mean, in the book, Ruth definitely dies, but here it seems like the script just leaves it up in the air. Does she or doesn't she? And what happens to Cabot? In the book, he ends up shooting himself after killing Ruth, leaving Jasper heartbroken as Axel consoles him in his arms."

Orcott coughed, a bit of drool escaping his mouth and oozing onto his fat lower lip, which he wiped away with his coat sleeve. "Since when do you read books, Fenwick? I know you're the star of this movie, top billing and all that crap, but I call the shots. God help me, I wanted Tyrone Power for this film, but they gave me you, so listen up. Ruth dying and Cabot killing himself is too depressing. The public doesn't want that. Here it's implied she dies and he shoots himself, but it's open to interpretation."

"I think the public *does* want that original ending, Orland. As you said, the book was a bestseller," said Victor Marvel, the man playing Axel Beaumont. "No one seemed to mind the ending in the novel."

"And that book came out ten years ago, before this goddamned Depression. Now it's all 'Happy Days Are Here Again' and all that crap, even though they aren't. People want happy endings in movies because their lives are shit these days," Orcott said.

"I'm not sure me getting shot by a man who was about to kill my lover and his partner is a happy ending," Eve said.

"In the movie he's your fiancé, not your lover. It had to be changed just enough to keep the censors happy and the public satisfied. If people want to believe that she lives, Cabot goes to prison, Jasper and Ruth get married, and Axel is their best man, so be it. All live happily ever after. The end."

"Only the people that haven't read the book will ever believe or accept that ending," Griff said.

"Audiences expect films to take liberties with books. It's what we do," Orcott said, another burp escaping his thick bulldog lips. He didn't bother to excuse himself.

"Liberties?" Eve said incredulously. "The screenwriter changed the whole plot. Ruth was a much stronger character in the book. She smoked, she drank, and she's the one who tried to wrestle the gun away from Cabot when she came in, not Beaumont. She was also independent and had a career. She didn't want to marry Jasper, just sleep with him. She'd slept with Axel, too. This script makes it seem like she's virginal."

"We have to cater to the censors, you know that," Orcott said, coughing again, this time more heavily, followed by continued heavy breathing. "The PCA is tough."

"Speaking of the Production Code Administration, there's no way that line about tulips on the massive organ is going to make it to the screen, Orland," Victor said.

"I didn't write it, Marvel. If it gets cut, it gets cut, but we're shooting it that way. It's funny."

"Why can't we shoot it where Ruth is a stronger person like she is in the book?" Eve said.

Orcott frowned, the sweat on his brow beading up in the creases of his broad, high forehead. "Because audiences don't want strong female characters, Miss Spellman. They want damsels in distress, rescued by a knight on a white horse."

"In my opinion, audiences want real characters. A damsel that will knee the villain in the balls," Eve said.

"I don't recall asking for your opinion, and that's not language becoming a lady or an actress at this studio, Miss Spellman."

"But it is becoming for a man and an actor at this studio, I suppose. I heard Royce Royale say far worse in front of you the other day in the commissary, and you didn't bat an eye."

"He's a man, it's different. Besides, Rick Hosbieter wrote the screenplay for this film. If you have issues or concerns with the changes, take it up with him."

"What we need are more female screenwriters," Eve said, crossing her arms. "The book this film is based on was written by a woman, the screenplay should have been, too. Look at Margaret Mitchell and Scarlett O'Hara. Now, there's a terrific author who wrote a strong female character. The book was a best seller, and the movie is going to do gangbusters when it's released."

"And Sidney Coe Howard, *a man*, wrote the screenplay," Orcott wheezed through yellowed teeth.

"A woman could have done it better, I bet," Eve said. "Florence Ryerson wrote the screenplay for *The Wizard of Oz*, you know."

"Along with Noel Langley and Edgar Allan Woolf. Two men to one woman."

"That's because it takes two men to do the work of one woman. Someday, women will produce and direct," Eve said. "Just look at Dorothy Arzner. We need more women like her in the industry."

"What *I* need is for you to shut your mouth about what you think this industry needs, Miss Spellman, unless you want your next role to be 'woman in the crowd.' Is that understood? And I'm sick and tired of hearing about *The Wizard of Oz* and *Gone with the Wind.* MGM's churning out Oscar contenders in color left and right, and I'm stuck with crap like *The Lady Screeched* in basic black and white."

"*The Wizard of Oz* is premiering at Grauman's the fifteenth of this month, a week from today. It's supposed to be swell. I'd kind of like to go to the premiere," Griff said.

"You do, Fenwick, and you'll never work at Icon Pictures again."

"So much for supporting our fellow actors and actresses at rival studios," Eve said.

"That's enough out of you." Orcott sneezed loudly into his left hand and wiped it on the edge of the table. "Geez, this weather is bad for my allergies and my sciences."

"I think you mean your sinuses, Mr. Orcott," Eve said, adjusting her skirt under the table and coaxing an errant strand of hair behind her left ear.

Orcott leaned back in the wooden armchair, which creaked in agony. "You know what I mean, so don't try to be coy and clever by correcting me. It's not becoming. You'll never be another Bette Davis, but you could have a long, steady career in the movies *if* you behave."

"Behave and do as I'm told, is that it?" Eve said, crossing her slender arms and scowling.

"I only tell you this for your own good. If you want to discuss this further with me, you can come to my office."

"No, thanks, I've been there, remember? Almost a decade ago, just after I was signed to my first contract at Icon at the age of seventeen. And I told you no. As I recall, you didn't like that much, which is partly why this is the first decent role I've had in ten years, and *that's* only because of Victor here."

Orcott flushed, and his already small dark eyes narrowed. "Careful, Miss Spellman."

"I always try to be. Besides, there's nothing else to discuss, here or in your office. The book *was* better than this script."

"I have to agree, if you don't mind my saying so," William Taylor said, still shifting uncomfortably in his chair, his trousers damp. "I didn't read the book all the way through, but the character of Cabot seems so clichéd, don't you think? A stupid, drunk, careless gangster? I'm sure in the book he was more fleshed out." William had picked up a pencil and was jotting on a tablet next to his script.

"*You're* more fleshed out, Taylor, and you smell like it," Orcott said. "I hope you brought a change of clothes. Thank God that chair you're sitting on is made of wood. And what the hell are you writing?"

"Just some notes on how I can improve, Mr. Orcott. This role is important to me, and I want to do it the best I can."

He almost looked pleased. "Oh, well, I'm glad to hear someone is taking their part seriously. Maybe the rest of you should take notes, too."

"I don't know about that," Victor said. "I think we're all taking our roles seriously, but the book *was* better. William's character was far more complex, and so was mine. In the novel, Axel Beaumont had an affair with his young partner's girlfriend, and it was suggested the three of them slept together at one point. There's a hint of romantic love between him and Jasper, too, especially at the end."

"I'm not shooting a picture about fairies, Marvel," Orcott said. "Or any other depraved sex acts, though I'm sure you'd like that."

Victor scowled. "That was only hinted at in the book, but at least the character of Axel had depth and interest. In the script, he comes across as a two-dimensional caricature. I'm used to playing the lead, or at least a strong supporting role with some teeth to it."

"Yeah, well, you're also almost fifty years old, Victor. You're not a leading man anymore, though you've kept your looks, more or less. Your last starring role was over two years ago."

"I know that, Orland. I played police detective Phineas Hart in *Harts and Clubs*. To rave reviews, I might add. My third time playing Phineas, and in my mind, the best."

"That series ran its course, and so have you. Now you're playing a *private* dick in this film, but this time you're second fiddle, a minor supporting role. In fact, you were only cast in this picture because Griff here insisted on it. He's the star, and his name will play above yours in the credits."

"I know that, too, and I'm fine with it, honestly," Victor said, glancing across the table at Griff with a reassuring smile.

"Nothing against Griffin Fenwick," William Taylor said, looking at Orcott, "because he's doing a fine job, but wasn't Tab Rockwell originally assigned the role of Jasper Crockett?"

Orcott's muddy eyes became pinpricks, surrounded by pink, puffy, sweaty flesh. "When I couldn't get Tyrone Power for the lead, we did decide to go with Mr. Rockwell, but it was quickly agreed that he wasn't suited for this part. We're currently trying to find a different project for him. Griff's our star now, though unfortunately along with signing Griff we had to take his baggage."

"Griff's baggage?" Victor Marvel said. "Is that what you're referring to me as?"

"It's the best way to refer to you in polite company. *I* wanted Eddie Quillan for the part of Beaumont, but Griff demanded we cast you, and the producer went along with it. God damn it, I got no Tyrone, no Eddie, and no budget to speak of. How the hell am I supposed to win an Oscar? You know what kind of budget Victor Fleming has for *Gone With the Wind*? And he's got Clark Gable, for God's sake."

"I thought you didn't want to talk about *Gone With The Wind* anymore. And besides, you only wanted Quillan because you could have got him for less than you're paying me," Victor Marvel said.

"You're damned right, because there's no budget for this film, as I said. This Depression is hurting all of us."

"Some more than others," Victor said. "All the studios slashed our salaries despite our contracts, but the producers and directors barely took a hit, if at all."

"At least you're still working, Marvel, and besides, even with the salary reduction, you're earning more than Quillan, which I admit *is* one of the reasons I wanted him. But it wasn't the only one. Quillan is thirty-two. In my opinion, at forty-nine, you're too old for this role."

"Gee, thanks," Victor said.

"It's true, but we're stuck with you because Dick Sharp wouldn't let me have Mr. Power, and Tab was, well, not suited for the part of Jasper Crockett. So now Griff's the star, and Griff wanted you to play Axel Beaumont. Of course, we all know *why* he wanted you," Orcott said with a snort.

"That's not true, Mr. Orcott," Griff said. "Victor Marvel is a great actor, one of the best, at any age. You're lucky to have him. I'm lucky to have him." Griff's face flushed a soft rose. "Have him in this picture, I mean."

Orcott pointed a chubby index finger, its nail chewed and rough, in Griffin's direction. "You're a rising star, Griff. Your last three films did quite well. You'll never be a Tyrone Power or a Clark Gable, but you're a decent actor, and a nice enough looking fella. You don't need Marvel in this picture or in your life. He's a bad influence and has plateaued in his career. He's past his prime."

"I resent that, Orcott," Victor said.

He turned his thick neck to stare back at Victor, who was seated next to Eve. "I'm sure you do, Marvel, but it's the truth. Axel Beaumont is a character part, a supporting role at best. If you don't want to play those for the rest of your life, you may want to think about retiring. Take your cue from Taylor, here. He was big in the silents fifteen years ago, but now he's a has-been who pisses himself. He's not afraid to take a supporting role to pay the bills."

"Cabot's a good part, Mr. Orcott," William said. "The movie wouldn't be the same without him. It's a strong role." He'd almost filled one page of the pad with his notes.

"Which you only got because you look the part. And because of your daughter," Orcott said, coughing again, this time spewing spittle on his copy of the script.

"What do you mean? What's Lydia got to do with it?" William said, his voice quivering. He stopped writing and clutched the pencil as he stared at Orcott.

"Lydia? Is that her name? She's a pretty girl, must take after her mother. We were screen-testing Humphrey Bogart for the role of Cabot, you know. Then your daughter came to see me in my office." He glanced briefly at Eve. "And *she* didn't say no. So, now you have the part."

"I don't believe you. Besides, people used to line up to see a William Taylor picture," William said.

"Yeah, they did, a long time ago. But now you're Wee Wee Taylor. You're old, and your body is a void. Decaying and empty, like a discarded banana peel. *And* you stink."

William's eyes flashed, belying his age and general health. "My body may be bent, but it's not broken. My mind is sharp, and I *am* a good actor." The pencil snapped in two in his hand, and the pieces clattered to the tabletop.

Orcott didn't seem to notice. He shrugged his shoulders, his neck temporarily disappearing into the folds of his suit coat. "I agree. I wouldn't have allowed you on this picture if you weren't a good actor, regardless of your daughter. It's too important. But you're fifty going on seventy. Victor is a year younger than you. He's no leading man anymore either, but at least he's kept himself in shape."

"I was sick," William said.

"So I understand. Listen, I don't want unnecessary delays in filming because of you and this cancer crap," Orcott said, letting his shoulders drop back as his body shook with a slow, hacking cough.

"That's cruel, Mr. Orcott," Eve Spellman said, once Orcott's coughing had subsided.

He glared at Eve now. "Life's cruel, Miss Spellman, and the movie business is the cruelest of them all. You're a second-rate actress who is only in this film because your ersatz boyfriend, Victor, wanted you. And Victor only wanted you to keep the rumor mill at bay about him and Griffin. So Griff wanted Victor, Victor wanted you, and Wee Wee Taylor is along for the ride because of his daughter, Linda."

"Her name is Lydia," William said. "And I don't like what you're implying about her, Mr. Orcott."

"Then don't believe it. Your choice." He stared at each of them in turn. "You're all going to be working together on this movie. With me. So, do as you're told and don't make waves, understand?"

Eve seethed and gritted her teeth, her jaw clenched tighter now, but she nodded. "I understand perfectly," Eve said, "but I'm *not* a second-rate actress."

"Says you. You're twenty-seven, if your studio bio is to be believed. Soon to be twenty-eight, and thirty in a couple of years. You can't act all that well, you can't sing, and you can't dance. Your only real attributes are your face and your figure. But that's enough to sell tickets as long as you still got them. I figure you have another five good years in you if you work at it and take care of yourself. You blame me for not getting better parts, but it's you who's at fault, Miss Spellman, or your lack of real talent and your smart mouth, at any rate."

"Mr. Orcott, that's uncalled for," Griffin said.

"No, it's very called for, Griff. I don't like troublemakers, I like obedient, well-behaved actors and actresses who know their places. I'm relying on you to carry this picture, Fenwick, and I'm going to see that you do if it kills me. All Taylor has to do is keep himself dry and work on his voice, all Victor has to do is remember his lines, and all Eve has to do is look pretty, watch her mouth, and behave."

"Why you—" Eve said.

"Careful, Miss Spellman."

"Or what, Mr. Orcott? Don't forget, I have a seven-year contract," Eve said. "We all do."

"And every six months we have the right to release you from that contract if your latest picture doesn't perform well. Plus, if you choose to turn down a role assigned to you, such as *woman in the crowd* in an upcoming film, Icon Pictures can cut off your salary and add time to your contract," Orcott said with a wave of his thick wrist.

"So, you have us all over a barrel," Eve said.

Orcott smiled thinly. "That's one way of putting it. You can be replaced on this picture, Miss Spellman. And if Victor doesn't like it, so can he." He turned and stared over at Griff. "And if Griff doesn't like that, I'm fine with starting from scratch."

"The studio head, Mr. Rainier, wouldn't stand for that. Besides, Eve's a fine actress," Victor said. "And so are William and Griff. Name-calling and threats are unnecessary."

"Mr. Orcott," Eve said, "I know Griff and Victor, and I'm getting to know Mr. Taylor. They are all professional, and I do my best, I really do. Perhaps I still have some learning to do, but I'm trying."

"You're very trying. You've made countless films for the studio ever since Victor discovered you in that seedy burlesque hall. They may not have been the roles you wanted, but they're the ones you were suited for, whether you believe it or not. You've made a fine living doing it, and you can continue to do so. But you can't go shooting off your mouth or spouting your hare-brained opinions."

He closed his beady eyes briefly and took in a breath, letting it out through his large, hairy nostrils. "Anyway, it's late, I'm tired, and we start shooting this mess next Monday morning. In the meantime, you each have a lot of lines to memorize if you haven't already. Our first shoot will be the garden scene. You're all in that except for Taylor, so be prepared."

"Sure," Griff said. "We'll be ready."

"Good. Makeup and wardrobe call is at five a.m. sharp. And don't forget, I expect to see you all at my house this Saturday night for my wife's thirtieth birthday party. It's black tie, of course. Gifts are optional but strongly encouraged. The festivities begin at seven sharp. Oh, and don't mention I told you it's her thirtieth if you know what's good for you." He put both his pale white hands on the table, hoisted himself up with a grunt, took out a cigar, lit it, sneezed again, and walked out of the room on his short, thick bowlegs, the bound leather script—spackled with dried spittle—tucked under his arm.

When the door had closed behind him, the other four looked at each other.

"Well, that was fun," Eve said.

"Tons," Victor said. "Nothing like being made to feel like a fool since I'm apparently only on this picture because of you, Griff. Baggage my ass."

"And I'm only in it because he couldn't get Tyrone Power, and

Tab Rockwell was not right for the role, it seems," Griff said. "When I was assigned to this picture, I told Mr. Orcott I wanted you in the movie, too, Vic, because I know you're an excellent actor. And because I owed it to you."

"You told Orcott you owed it to me?" Victor Marvel said, raising a perfectly shaped black brow.

"Well, yeah, but just because I had to say *something* when he asked me why I insisted on you getting the role of Axel Beaumont. You really are great, Vic, you know that. And you'll be terrific in this film, I can feel it."

"You will be, Victor, and at least Orcott doesn't think you're a second-rate actress who can't act, sing, or dance," Eve said.

"And he didn't tell any of you that you stink, literally," William said, his skin, no longer tomato red, gray and tight against his narrow face.

"He's a blowhard," Eve said.

"He's a wet sock and an ass," William said, "if you'll pardon my language, Miss Spellman. And I don't believe what he implied about my daughter, Lydia. She'd never do anything with the likes of him to help me get a part or for any other reason. He only said that to upset me."

"He makes me gag," Griff said. "And that's saying something because my gag reflex is nonexistent."

Victor stifled a laugh. "He does like to hurt and humiliate people. It's how he controls them. But he's not stupid, either."

"No, that's true, he's not," Griff said.

"You're right about that," William said. "He knows about you and Victor, I mean."

"So it would seem," Victor said.

"I've heard the rumors about you fellas, too," William said. "Personally, I don't care what you two do in private, but Orcott does, and I doubt he's thrilled with having you both in this film. I'm sure he's willing to overlook it as long as it doesn't affect the movie, but when the filming is finished, well, I wouldn't trust him."

"I never have," Victor said. "So, if he knows, he knows. There aren't many secrets in Hollywood."

"Not for long anyway, it seems. I guess we'd better be more careful, Vic. If something like this gets out, I'll be ruined. My career will be over." Griff's face looked slightly pale as he got to his feet and put his suit coat back on.

"Orcott will do what he can to protect you, Griff, whether he wants to or not. You're a hot commodity at Icon Pictures, a rising star, and thus a moneymaker. Me on the other hand, well, I'm disposable."

"Not to me, you're not. And I won't let him destroy you or your career if I can help it," Griff said. "He was right about one thing, though. It's hot as hell in here. I need to get some water, if you will all excuse me."

"Sure, see you in a bit," Victor said with a soft smile. "And don't worry, it will be okay."

"Yeah," Griff said, but he didn't sound convinced.

The three of them watched as Griff went out the glass-paneled door into the hall.

"Poor kid," William said, shifting again.

"Don't you, uh, need to use the washroom, too, Mr. Taylor?" Eve said delicately.

"I will on my way out. I wear pads, you see, under my trousers."

"Yes, you mentioned that, William," Victor said.

"They don't always do the best job, but they help. The smell isn't that bad, is it?"

"No, William, I never noticed an odor," Victor said. "Not much, anyway."

"I didn't either," Eve said. "Honestly, Mr. Orcott's cigar overpowered almost everything else."

"Bringing up the urine smell was Orcott's way of keeping you subservient and obedient, William. Embarrassment and humiliation. I'm sorry about the way he treated and spoke to you."

"Thanks, Vic, I appreciate that, but he wasn't exactly cordial to any of us. Even to Griff."

"I know," Eve said. "Poor Griff."

William nodded, his thin, wispy hair plastered to his skull with Brylcreem. "I was like Griff long ago, you know, Miss Spellman. I was young, talented, and ambitious, and a leading man in a couple of pictures. I was never as big a name as Victor here, but I did okay."

"We both did okay, William," Victor said.

"Sure, but you were always more successful and better looking, and you still are. That dark, wavy hair with just a touch of gray, those black, smoldering eyes, that olive skin, your Roman nose and cleft chin. You're the stuff movie stars are made of, all five-eleven of you. I remember your fan mail used to come in huge canvas bags, every day, from all over."

"You got your share of fan mail," Victor said.

"True, but not nearly as much as you did. I didn't mind, really, because I was doing what I loved and making good money." He looked back at Eve. "Anyway, when the talkies came along in 1927, Vic and I both transitioned okay. A lot of actors weren't so lucky."

"That's right," Vic said. "Too many didn't have the voice to match their physical appearance. Nasal, thick accents, high pitched, you name it. Some people went from top box office draw to unemployment virtually overnight."

"Yeah, some big names," William said. "I guess you and I were lucky. I was worried about my vocal abilities, but it worked out okay."

"Your voice is excellent, William, despite what Orcott says."

"Thank you, but I do still have a trace of my Boston accent now and then, despite how hard the studio voice coaches worked to eradicate it, and it *can* sometimes be high-pitched. Anyway, when the talkies came along, I was thirty-eight and still getting decent parts. But then, ten years later when I was forty-eight, I got sick with cancer. My prostate, you know. They say they caught it early, luckily for me. I had my prostate taken out surgically, but there were complications. I told people I was off work because of bronchitis since cancer is taboo in this business. But then rumors started about my incontinence problem after I returned. I couldn't drink any liquid for something like twenty-four hours before a shoot. I got dehydrated and passed out under the hot lights one day when I was making *Clay Pot*."

"I remember hearing about that," Victor said.

"You weren't the only one," William said. "Rumors started that I was dying from all kinds of things because I'd lost so much weight and had fainted. People whispered about my bladder problem, and they pointed fingers when I wet myself in the commissary one day. When I had an accident on the set shortly after that, I was replaced in the film, and then Icon loaned me out to other studios for bit parts as punishment. I guess I'm thankful they didn't cancel my contract altogether, but still, it was difficult and humiliating. This is my first decent role in two years."

"I'm sorry, William," Victor said. "I can't imagine how frightening and awful it must have been for you. You never told me the whole truth."

"I'm sorry about not confiding in you, but by then we'd drifted apart. You and I were moving in different circles."

"It wouldn't have mattered to me, you know that."

"I do know that. You're a good man, a rare breed, especially in this town. But I was scared stiff back then. You know, my doctors said I'd be lucky to live three years after the surgery, but it's been two years now, and I'm out to prove them wrong."

"You will prove them wrong, Mr. Taylor," Eve said, reaching out a hand to him across the table.

"Damned right you will," Victor said.

"Thanks, both of you. I don't care if you're a homosexual, Victor, I don't. It's none of my business. But I do worry about Griff, and you should, too. I know firsthand what rumors and gossip can do to someone."

"Yeah, I suppose you do, William," Victor Marvel said softly.

"I'm so sorry, Mr. Taylor, about everything you've been through, and how you've been treated," Eve said, and then she swiveled to stare at Victor. "It's your fault, you know."

Victor recoiled in surprise. "What's that supposed to mean? What's my fault?"

"This mess with Griff. I mean, you've been under contract here for what, almost twenty years? You told me yourself that in the early years you played the part in real life of a happy-go-lucky bachelor, but that only lasted so long, of course. Once you hit forty, the studio got worried and nervous. People were talking, gossiping, and pointing fingers, just like they did to Mr. Taylor, here, only for different reasons. Old Mr. Rainier himself called you into his office at the studio and gave you the ultimatum to get married or get out."

"Yeah, so what?"

"So, you chose to get married, finally, at the ripe old age of forty-three. To Barbara Dunne, a studio secretary. But that only fooled the ticket-buying public, Vic. Almost everyone on the lot knew the truth, and they still know it, isn't that right?"

William shifted uncomfortably. "Well, uh, er, yes, to some degree. Rainier did the same thing to Victor here that Louis B. Mayer did to Billy Haines, only Haines refused to play the game and quit rather than enter into a sham marriage."

"But Billy was in love with Jimmy Shields," Marvel said. "I was all alone. I had no reason not to go along with it."

"And Barbara was agreeable, so no harm was done," Eve said. "The marriage ended amicably after fourteen months. Then, after a while, along came Griff, what, almost three years ago now? You were forty-seven, I believe, and he was twenty-seven, fresh-faced, clean-cut, handsome, eager, and talented. He met you, you took him under your wing, got him his first big break, and introduced him to the right people. His career took off, soaring to unforeseen heights, and it's still on the ascent. But there's more than just a mentor/mentee relationship between the two of you. By default, Griff is now suspected of being a homosexual, too, at least at the studio. After all, you two practically live together. You're inseparable."

"We're discreet."

Eve laughed. "Like a pink elephant wearing sunglasses and a derby. Unfortunately, everything I said is true, and you know it. Our arrangement only goes so far. Orcott can see through it, and it may only be a matter of time before the public does, too."

"Maybe he can," Victor said, "but the public hasn't so far, and neither have the movie magazine reporters and gossip columnists. As far as they're all concerned, Griff's just a friend and you're my girlfriend."

"And in return for my playing the role of your sweetheart, which so far I've done first-rate, I must say, you've promised to get me decent parts in good pictures."

"That's our agreement, yes. Though if I am to believe what Orcott says, my influence around here has waned."

"Well, you got me a part in this film, at least. If *The Lady Screeched* is a big enough hit, maybe my career will finally take off, Orcott be damned."

"You're going to be great," Victor said.

"I agree," William Taylor said. "I have confidence in you and your abilities, Miss Spellman."

"Thank you, Mr. Taylor, and call me Eve, please."

"I will, and please call me William."

"Thank you, William." She turned to look at Victor again. "Regardless of what happens, I'll never forget that you got me my first big break in this film. I owe you. I'll always owe you. You saved me from burlesque and from Orcott's clutches."

Victor took her hand in his. "Eve, love of my life, you don't owe me anything, and neither does Griff. We all have our secrets."

"He's right," William said. "And we all have to keep each other's."

"Yes," Victor said. "It's a fine arrangement."

"Okay, but what happens if things start to go places with you and

Griff?" Eve said. "I'm not going to move in with you two just to keep up appearances."

Victor laughed. "He's nearly thirty and I'm almost fifty. He'll tire of me soon enough and shift to someone else, don't worry."

Eve shook her head, her dark curls dancing. "I'm not so sure, he's pretty smitten. You know, that man from the *Hollywood Reporter* referred to us as a love triangle. According to him, you love me, I love you, Griff loves me, and I'm interested in Griff."

Victor snorted. "They're always making up some story or another in order to sell their rags."

"My mother believed it when she read it," Eve said. "After all, I'm twenty-seven, much closer to Griff's age than to yours."

"Your mother also believes I'm a heterosexual in love with you. And so does the general public. That's the way it needs to stay."

"That's the way what needs to stay?" Griff said, swinging back through the door. He had retied his bow tie and wiped his face with cool water, but he still looked hot and tired.

"The way it is. Or the way the public thinks it is, that is. Between the three of us," Victor said.

"Oh, I see. I think." Rather than sit back down at the table, he arched his back and leaned against the doorframe.

"Don't think on it too much."

"I never do. Are we about done? I feel like a limp biscuit, and I'm beat."

"Well, you look great. Handsome as ever," Victor said.

"Thanks, Vic, I wish I felt that way. Ugh, I'm not looking forward to Monday."

"The day we start shooting? Why?" Eve said.

"I'm nervous about the garden scene."

"Whatever for?" William said. "I'm not in it, but it seems pretty straightforward from what I've read."

"It is," Griff said, "But Vic and Eve here are fully dressed, and my character is walking around with his shirt off, supposedly because he's working in the garden. Did you notice in the script there are three scenes where Jasper appears shirtless in the movie, including the garden scene? Not to mention the swimming pool set where I'm in nothing but a bathing suit." Griffin rolled his eyes and grimaced. "Old man Orcott told me he won't shoot those scenes in private. The whole crew has to be there, gaping at me."

"You look great shirtless, Griff, *and* in a bathing suit. And by the way, 'old man Orcott' is only two years older than I am, I'll have you know," Victor Marvel said.

"Oh, uh, sorry, Vic," Griff said. "It's just that you are in such better shape, and much more attractive. You seem years younger than him."

"Nice save," Eve said, winking.

"You do look a lot younger than him, Victor," William said. "Orcott makes fun of my appearance and tells me I look old, but he looks like he's in his mid to late sixties."

"Thanks," Victor said. "And don't worry about the shirtless scenes or the swimsuit one, Griff. Besides, Eve's in that swimming pool shot with you, *and* she has that solo bathtub scene, don't forget. Of course, she's used to taking off her clothes in front of people from her burlesque days."

She jabbed Vic hard in the ribs. "Very funny, wise guy."

"Ouch! Sorry," Victor said, grinning. "And you'll both be fine."

"I hope so. I'm going to have to do a bunch of sit-ups between now and Monday. I don't remember any of those shirtless or swimwear scenes in the book," Griff said.

"They weren't in the book," Victor said. "Rick Hosbieter added them to the screenplay."

"Because handsome shirtless men and pretty girls in bathing suits and bathtubs sell tickets," William said.

"I suppose," Griff said, "but it still makes me uncomfortable."

"It will all work out," William said, glancing at his watch. "You'll be swell. We'll all be swell. Anyway, I'd better be getting home. I want to speak with my daughter when she gets back from work." He got slowly to his feet, holding on to the table for support with thin, veined hands, his breath shallow. He picked up his script and the notepad and held them tightly to his chest.

"Can we help you out to your car, Mr. Taylor?" Griff said.

William shook his head adamantly, his wispy gray hair still clinging to his scalp, unmoving. "No, thank you, I'm okay. I'm stronger than I look, believe me. I just get tired easily. It's been a long day, and Orland Orcott is frankly exhausting. I'll see you all Saturday at his house for the party. Not that I'm all that thrilled about going, but I am the obedient servant, apparently."

"As are we all, it seems," Eve said.

"Speaking of the party, what are we supposed to give Mrs. Orcott for her birthday?" Griff said. "I mean, he said gifts aren't required but strongly encouraged."

"Meaning they aren't optional," William said. "I have no idea what to get. She has everything, I'm sure."

"A new husband would be most appreciated, no doubt," Victor said.

"But hard to wrap," Eve said with a wicked grin. "How about a cyanide tablet she can drop into his coffee?"

"I'll provide the coffee," William said.

"Funny, but I'm serious, folks. I need some suggestions," Griff said.

"Okay, then I'd suggest you get her perfume, top shelf. Eve and I will get her flowers and a box of premium candy," Victor said.

"I suppose I can buy her a book of poetry. I'm told she likes that sort of thing," William said. "Or maybe I'll write her an original poem." He glanced at the pad he'd picked up. "Something like, 'My husband is a nasty pig. / He's insulting and quite rude. / His stomach's really rather big, / and he's full of attitude. / He's boastful and not funny, / he's arrogant and rude. / But I still call him honey / though he's distasteful and quite crude. / Why, you ask, do I love him so / when he has water in his tank? / It's hard sometimes, if you must know, / but he has money in the bank.' "

Victor erupted in a laugh as Eve and Griff joined in. "Oh my, William, did you just think of that?"

"I might have been jotting down a few lines while Orcott was blathering away earlier," William said, grinning, his pale thin lips spread wide. "When I told him I was taking notes on how to improve. And on that note, I'll say goodbye. Always leave them laughing."

CHAPTER TWO

Saturday evening, August 12, 1939
Eve's bungalow

Victor Marvel, dressed in a midnight black double-breasted tuxedo, pulled up to Eve Spellman's Spanish-style bungalow just after seven thirty and parked his 1938 cherry red Cadillac in front, careful not to brush the whitewall tires against the curb. He raised the ragtop and then strode across the walk to the brick stoop, where he rang the bell.

"Good evening, Victor," Eve said, swinging open the hammered wooden door. She was backlit by the soft glow of the living room lights behind her, and she positively shimmered.

"Good evening. Don't you look lovely, Miss Spellman?"

"Why thank you, kind sir. You're quite dashing yourself."

He bowed. "I thank you, milady. Sorry I'm a bit late, but I stopped to buy a dozen red roses and a box of premium chocolates to give to Mrs. Orcott for her birthday. They're in the back seat. I put both our names on the cards."

"Oh, good, thanks for doing that."

"You're welcome. Who knew finding roses and chocolates at this time of night would be so challenging?"

"That's what you get for waiting until the last moment," Eve said.

"I wanted the flowers to be fresh, that's all."

"Victor, you bought the same flowers now that were for sale earlier in the day, but it doesn't matter. Come in for a minute, I'm almost set," she said, standing aside as he entered.

"Thanks, and what do you mean, almost set? You're still not ready? You look perfect."

"Sweet talker," Eve said, closing the door. "I won't be much longer. Have a seat and make yourself comfortable."

"The party's already started, you know," Victor said, settling into an armchair.

"I *do* know, but I couldn't decide what to do with my hair, up or down. I went round and round with it, trying it every which way before I got dressed. Consider yourself lucky you don't have to deal with such things."

Victor laughed. "I consider myself lucky I still have a full head of hair."

"You have beautiful hair," Eve said. "Lightly touched with silver. So distinguished."

"Just came naturally. I'm glad you decided to wear yours down, gently kissing your soft, pink shoulders."

"Thank you for that. Yes, I finally chose a romantic wave and curls. And at least *something* will be kissing my shoulders tonight," she said, raising a painted-on eyebrow in his direction.

"Oh, I might nibble on them while we're dancing, just to keep everyone guessing, of course. Where did you get that dress? It's gorgeous."

She was wearing a gold off-the-shoulder sheath, accented with a wide belt and black brocade. "It ought to be, it cost me over a week's salary, and I'll probably never wear it again. Unlike you and that tuxedo."

"True. I've worn this suit at least six times so far since I bought it, including to last year's Academy Awards. No one ever notices."

"You're lucky. *Everyone* notices what a woman wears. I sometimes feel a bit funny about dressing up for the awards and for parties, though, while the country is still going through this Depression." She had opened the closet and was checking herself over in the full-length mirror attached to the inside of the door.

"I know what you mean. It does seem a bit gauche to display wealth with so much of the country unemployed," Victor said.

"Exactly. Like most of us, I don't come from a rich family. We weren't poor, but we were far from wealthy."

"I don't come from rich either, far from it. My family was just a step up from poverty. We learned early on what a bill collector was, and my mother was adept at sweet-talking them with one of her homemade pies until payday."

"That had to be difficult," Eve said. She took off her black heels and put on a pair of gold ones with a strap.

"I left my family in Milwaukee at a young age and never looked back."

"And I left home at seventeen, as you know."

"To star in a burlesque show," Victor said.

"That was just temporary."

"I know, I'm only teasing."

"Being in a burlesque show at the tender age of seventeen was something I'd never imagined doing as a child. But I saw it as a stepping stone to a movie career."

"We both did what we had to do," Victor said. "Times were tough financially when I was a kid, but nothing compared to the Depression these last nine years. I can't even imagine a big family trying to make it nowadays."

"I know, that's what I mean about wearing fancy gowns and tuxedos and going to big parties. But my mother told me she likes to see movie stars dressed up and having fun at swell affairs. It's a form of escaping reality for her, like going to the movies."

"Movies with happy endings, like Orcott said."

"Happy endings and beautiful people in gorgeous clothes, singing and dancing without a care in the world. If only life were more like a Hollywood film."

"Indeed," Victor said. "Even Mr. Rainier, the head of the studio, decreed we should put on a show everywhere we go. It's even written into our contracts to be well dressed, well groomed, and well behaved in public at all times, so like it or not, we do."

"Our lives are one big performance." She glanced out the front window. "What's it like outside, by the way? Will I need a wrap? I don't have anything that goes with this dress, unfortunately, and I couldn't afford to buy anything else, but I could make do with a black shawl if necessary."

"You should be fine without it, it's a beautiful night. The skies are clear, there's a lovely moon, the stars are twinkling, and the temperature is ideal."

"Mr. Orcott probably demanded it of Mother Nature," Eve said, laughing gaily.

"I have no doubt. After that torrential rainstorm this morning, he probably gave her a good talking-to."

"And when he talks, everyone listens, including Mother Nature. Who is Griff bringing tonight, by the way? He never mentioned it," Eve said, changing back into the black heels and checking her reflection yet again.

"Sheila Burton, an actress at the studio."

"Oh," she said, looking at him briefly over her pale, pink shoulder.

"What?"

"Nothing," Eve said, turning back to the mirror again.

"That 'oh' said a mouthful. You know her, I take it."

"We've met a few times, of course."

"And you don't care for her."

Satisfied with her appearance for the moment, she turned to him. "Sheila just seems an odd choice for Griff, that's all. But she is pretty."

"She's a knockout. I've met her a few times. Hourglass figure, ginger tresses, blue eyes, long lashes, and skin that's almost like ivory piano keys, smooth and soft."

"And a lot of men's fingers have played those keys, I'm sure. She's all right I guess, if you like that sort of thing," Eve said.

"Griff doesn't, nor do I, obviously, but he and I can't be seen arriving together, and Sheila was available."

"She doesn't know, I hope. Griff hasn't told her, has he?"

"Of course not. We're trying to be discreet, remember? Far too many people know already."

"Still, she may have heard the rumors, though I doubt she'd understand. She's a bit dense," Eve said.

"Is she?"

"Are you kidding? She's like the San Francisco fog in the morning. Oh well, it's just for one night, but why Sheila? He could have asked at least a dozen other starlets at the studio. Any one of them would have been dying to go with him tonight."

Victor shrugged his broad shoulders. "Oh, you know Griff. By the time he got around to thinking about a lady to escort, most of them already had dates. I think just about the entire studio has been invited. Besides, *she* actually approached him."

"Ballsy of her, but not entirely surprising. I heard the man she was seeing broke up with her, and of course, she just had to attend tonight, being the rising starlet she thinks she is. See and be seen and all that. She's only been under contract a year or two, I think."

"Sure, being seen at Orcott's party is a smart move, career-wise.

For a new kid on the block, I believe she's already been in a couple of Orcott's pictures."

"Yes, minor roles, but speaking parts, at least," Eve said. "I saw one, and I wasn't impressed. Mr. Orcott criticizes my acting abilities, but she's dreadful. I can't imagine how she keeps getting cast."

"I have an idea or two, but I'm not one to gossip."

"You think she was one of his projects?" Eve said.

"I'd say it's likely."

Eve shook her head. "It doesn't surprise me. I just don't understand him, though. His wife is a smart woman and very pretty. Why does he feel the need to fool around with young actresses?"

"Mrs. Orcott is turning thirty. He married the first Mrs. Orcott when she was just eighteen and pregnant with their son. He divorced her when she was thirty-five and he was forty-five. He likes them young."

"Well, I think it's disgusting. He uses his power and influence to bed young women that would otherwise most likely have nothing to do with him. He looks like an old bulldog and smells worse."

"I agree, but that's the way he operates. His time will come, I'm sure. And speaking of time," Victor said, glancing at his Rolex, "it's after eight o'clock."

"Okay, I guess I'm all set," Eve said, picking up her black beaded clutch and closing the closet door.

"Fine, let's go then, Miss Spellman. You look gorgeous."

CHAPTER THREE

Saturday evening, August 12, 1939
The Orcott mansion

Eve turned off the lights in the living room, locked the door, and took Victor's arm as they walked to his car, Victor opening the door for her before going around and climbing behind the wheel.

"Where exactly does Mr. Orcott live, anyway?" Eve said, settling into the leather seat of the lush V16 Cadillac convertible coupe. "I've never been to his house."

"He lives in Bel Air, of course, on St. Cloud Road, about twenty miles from here. Not too far."

"But a whole different world away from my quiet little street."

"In more ways than one," Victor said as he drove away from the curb.

"I'm glad you have the top up," Eve said. "Thank you."

"You're welcome. I understand about your hair and all."

"You're a dear. I'm sorry, by the way," Eve said. "About how Mr. Orcott spoke to you the other day during the table read."

"Thanks, but he spoke to all of us pretty horribly."

"He did. Including Griff, as William pointed out."

"Yeah, and Griff didn't deserve it. I mean, none of us did, of course, but especially not him. He's a terrific actor and very handsome. In my opinion, Tyrone Power's got nothing on Griffin Fenwick."

"But you wouldn't kick Tyrone out of bed," Eve said with a sly smile.

Victor chuckled as he turned a corner and accelerated. "Mr. Power's never asked, so I've never been given the opportunity. Anyway, Griff's a rising star, while mine's on the descent."

"Are you bitter about that?"

"Me? No, not really. I had my time in the spotlight. I care for Griff a great deal, and I'm proud I had something to do with his start in this crazy business. I'm happy to be his mentor, and even happier to be his lover, albeit a clandestine one."

"He cares for you a great deal, too, you know. As do I, in a sisterly way, of course."

Victor turned his head briefly to give her a grin. "Thanks, Sis, and I care for you. You've been a terrific friend and confidant. I'm a lucky guy in many ways."

"I think some of that luck was self-made, Mr. Marvel. You worked hard to get where you are."

"So did you."

"I'm still working hard. Sometimes I wonder if it's all worth it. Ten years in this business and I'm still an unknown, more or less."

"That will change, I can feel it."

"I hope so. By the way, you said before you were just a kid from Milwaukee when you left home. That had to be difficult."

"Well, not exactly a kid, but I was pretty young. I was born Victor Marvellis. My father was a stern man who worked his whole life in the tanneries and had two boys and four girls. I was the youngest of the boys. I ran away to Chicago at the age of sixteen."

"What did your folks say about that?"

"I think they were happy I was out of the house so they didn't have to feed and clothe me anymore, especially since my four sisters were still at home. Oh, I know my parents loved me, but they always had a hard time making ends meet. So, once I got settled in Chicago, I got a job in a factory making thirteen dollars a week, and I sent a few bucks home to the family once a month."

"Thirteen dollars a week was pretty good money back then, wasn't it?"

"Yeah, more than I'd ever seen. But it was six days a week, ten hours a day of back-breaking, exhausting work. The only good thing about that job is that it built up my body, which paid off later on. When I'd saved enough dough, I went to New York and got a place in Greenwich Village at the tender age of twenty. I worked a variety of odd jobs before becoming a model, thanks in part to an older man I'd met who had taken me under his wing, Mr. Henry P. Shufflebottom."

"He took you under his wing?"

"That's right, and you know exactly what I mean by that. I was appreciative, believe me. *Very* appreciative. Anyway, not long after that, I was discovered by a talent scout for Icon Pictures and signed to a forty-dollar-a-week contract in 1920 at the age of twenty-nine. I celebrated my thirtieth birthday that year on the set of my first picture. The rest, as they say, is history."

"And then you discovered me nine years later in 1929 in that burlesque hall, where I was dancing as Martha Willowby, the willowy 'take it off' showgirl."

"Yes, that's right, I'll never forget it. I stopped into Bisby's Burlesque to do research for my role in *Dancing the Night Away*, and there you were. I knew right then you had that something extra."

"And you got me a screen test and told everyone I was eighteen."

"You were only a few weeks shy at that point. I could tell you had star quality, so it was worth a little white lie."

"Thanks, Victor. Now if we could just convince Orcott of that."

"Don't worry about him, Eve. He's a big director, but there are others. You're underutilized at Icon. I'm going to see what I can do about getting you assigned to a film at MGM. I know a guy."

"Gee, Vic, that would be swell, but my contract…"

"It can be arranged. The studio can loan you out. It happens all the time. I'm thinking of pursuing a few films there myself since I no longer seem to be appreciated at Icon."

"You and I are in the same boat."

"So we sail it over to MGM. Problem solved."

"If we don't sink first," Eve said.

"We won't. There's a gas station, I'd better fill up and have them check the radiator."

"Okay, and I need to use the ladies' room. Want some music?"

"Sure." Victor turned the radio to station KFI, and soon the soothing sounds of Glenn Miller and his Orchestra came warbling out of the cloth-covered speaker.

After leaving the gas station they drove along quietly the rest of the way, Eve sometimes singing aloud to one of the popular tunes. Victor pulled up to the ornate gates of the Orcott estate about forty-five minutes later. "We made good time, considering," he said, turning off the radio. "Here we are."

"Still, we're terribly late," Eve said. "It's after nine o'clock."

"I'll take all the blame," Victor said, swinging his Cadillac through the gates and proceeding up the drive.

"My knight on a white horse? Thanks, but I can take the blame for myself. Mr. Orcott doesn't scare me. Much."

"I feel the same, actually. And there's the house."

"My, it's huge," Eve said as she stared out the car window, her lips slightly parted, at the off-white stone house with the red tile roof, imposing façade, and regal symmetry. Ornamental wrought iron balconies framed each second-story window. A larger, curved one was set above the carved limestone entrance.

"Yes, old Orcott does pretty well for himself. No one needs a house like this, though."

"It's a statement to the masses of his wealth and power."

"Both of which he has in vast quantities. Wait till you see the inside."

"I can just imagine," Eve said.

"I wonder if you can. Prepare to be suitably impressed," Victor said. "See if you can reach the flowers and chocolates in the back seat, will you?"

Eve twisted around and took them in her arms. "Okay, got them."

"Great, thanks." He slowed his speed more as they approached the entrance on the circular drive, coming to a stop just outside the massive, carved wooden front doors, where a handsome young man in a short white jacket was waiting on the curb. Victor nodded to him as he climbed out and went around to help Eve, who was holding the roses and chocolates.

"Good evening, Mr. Marvel," the young man said with a familiar tone. "It's nice to see you again."

"Uh, thank you," Victor said.

"It's Lukas, sir. Lukas Gamble."

"Ah, yes, of course."

"Let me know when you're ready to leave, and I'll bring your car around personally."

"Fine, Lukas, the keys are in the ignition. Take good care of her." He gave Lukas a quarter, and Lukas smiled at him appreciatively.

"Thank you, Mr. Marvel, I will. It really is nice to see you again."

"Yes, Lukas, likewise." He turned to Eve as Lukas climbed behind the wheel of the Caddy. "All set, Eve?"

She handed the flowers and chocolates to Victor, smoothed out the gold silk of her gown, and took his arm. "Yes, all set."

As they climbed the stone steps to the entrance, where an older uniformed man was waiting, Eve whispered in Victor's ear. "Lukas Gamble?"

Victor shrugged almost imperceptibly. "He's a young man I first met a few years ago, before Griff. I got him a screen test, but nothing ever came of it."

"Nothing ever came of the screen test, or something else?"

"A little of both. This town is full of Lukases. Young, hopeful, and eager."

"Nice of you to help them out," Eve said dryly.

"I do what I can. Or I did, anyway."

"I'm sure," Eve said as they reached the top step and the attendant swung open the doors with a nod and a touch of his cap.

They stepped into the Spanish-tiled entry hall, which soared two stories high. A sweeping, curved staircase rose from the left and up to a balcony on the right. Eve took in as much as she could without gaping and staring.

"Good evening," said yet another white-jacketed young man, this one without a cap. Just behind him stood a well-groomed, middle-aged woman in a maid's uniform.

"Good evening," Victor said. "Victor Marvel and Miss Eve Spellman."

"Welcome, sir, miss." The young man motioned to the woman behind him. "Shirley will take the chocolates and the flowers and put them in water."

"I don't think the chocolates would do well in water," Victor said, chuckling at his own joke as Eve rolled her eyes.

The young man raised his eyebrows ever so slightly, but his expression never changed. "Indeed not, sir. Is there a card?"

"Er, yes, there's a card attached to each," Victor said, handing over the items.

"Very good," he said as Shirley moved off down a side hall with the flowers and candy. "A cold buffet is in the dining room, and a bar in the reception room. Champagne and hors d'oeuvres are also being passed, of course. Music and dancing are in the grand salon, just through the double doors under the stairs. The ladies' lavatory is across from the dining room and the gentlemen's is off the reception room."

"Thanks," Victor said. "I imagine you've given that speech more than a few times tonight."

"Just doing my job, sir. I see you don't have any outer garments or hats to check, but some of the ladies are leaving their handbags in the ladies' lavatory with the attendant."

"Thank you," Eve said, "But I just have this small clutch. I'll keep it with me."

"As you wish, miss. Please let me know if there's anything I may assist either of you with. Would you like to be announced?"

"No, thank you, we'll just slip in quietly," Victor said. "Where are our hosts?"

"Mr. and Mrs. Orcott are in the grand salon, I imagine, sir, though I'm not entirely sure. Most, if not all, of the other guests have already arrived."

"Right, I know we're a trifle late. Well, thanks again." He looked down at Eve. "Shall we, then?"

She smiled up at him. "We shall."

Arm in arm, they strode toward the sound of a Viennese waltz emanating from beyond the beautiful double doors, which yet another attractive young man in a white jacket opened. As they stepped inside the large, elegantly appointed room, Eve glanced about, taking it all in as discreetly as she could. Beautifully dressed people of all shapes and sizes were everywhere, a shining sea of men and women, the former in black tuxedos, and the latter resplendent in long, beautiful gowns of every possible color and style.

"Looks like all of the upper class as well as most of the movers and shakers of the movie industry are here tonight," Eve said.

"Yes, along with the studio's contract players, actors, and actresses scattered here and there," Victor said. "They're here out of obligation, of course, like we are, playing the part of an invited guest but knowing their job is to make small talk with the rich and powerful, who enjoy mingling in person with the images they've seen on the silver screen."

"It's quite a sight," Eve said. Cigar and cigarette smoke collided with the various aromas of different perfumes and aftershaves, assaulting Victor and Eve's nostrils. White-jacketed waiters with trays of champagne glasses and beautifully arranged hors d'oeuvres swam expertly through the crowd. The center dance floor was overflowing, and everyone seemed to be chatting and laughing at once, sounding like a large swarm of bees buzzing to a string quartet.

"My, I had no idea Mr. Orcott did so well, Victor. This house is amazing, and this party is quite extravagant."

"I'm told Mr. Capra earned over two hundred thousand dollars last year. Orland's no match for Frank Capra, but I'm sure he took home at least half that."

"Impressive. I'll have to ask for a raise. My salary last year was somewhere in the neighborhood of two thousand dollars."

"Still, that's nothing to sneeze at, considering the average American makes only around eight to nine hundred dollars, and a lot of people aren't working at all right now."

"You're right. I do consider myself lucky, but I wonder if Mr. Orcott does. Oh, look, there's William," Eve said, nodding toward William Taylor, dressed in an old tuxedo that once fit him like a glove but now hung rather loosely off his slender frame. "And who's that pretty girl with him?"

Victor followed Eve's gaze toward the doors to the dining room, where William was standing, drink in hand, next to a pretty young woman in a soft blue floor-length gown. "That's his daughter, Lydia. I've met her a couple of times at the studio. She moved in with William when he got sick and never left. She's his companion and his caregiver. She's devoted to him, an only child."

"What happened to Mrs. Taylor?"

"She died of tuberculosis when Lydia was just a child."

"How sad, and now her father isn't well."

"William's stronger than he looks, I think. The doctors originally didn't think he'd live more than a few years."

"I remember him mentioning that the other day. I'm glad he's feeling better and he's back to work."

"Me too. That's thanks in large part to his daughter, I think," Victor said.

"I should like to meet Lydia," Eve said.

"I'll introduce you later."

"All right, thanks."

"There you two are," Orcott said in a booming voice as he approached them on his thick bowlegs, a whiskey in one hand and a cigar in the other. "Where have you been?"

"My fault, Mr. Orcott," Eve said. "I had a bit of trouble with my dress and my hair, and I kept Victor waiting."

He looked her up and down, huffing and puffing, smoke floating about his head like a crown. "Well, you look pretty as a picture, so I suppose it was worth the wait."

"Thank you, sir," she said with her practiced smile.

"You'll have to save me a dance, of course. I do a mean rumba, if I do say so myself," Orcott said, his voice raspy.

"Certainly, it would be my pleasure."

"Good. And be sure you two dance together. I want people to see you, Victor, in the arms of a beautiful young lady, understand?" he punctuated his words with a thrust of his cigar toward Victor's face.

"Of course, Orland, I'd be delighted."

"I doubt it, but do it anyway." He pointed his cigar at Eve now. "And Eve, dance with anyone and everyone else who asks you. As for you, Victor, dance with some of the ladies. You're both here for a reason, don't forget."

"Whatever you say, boss," Victor said.

"That's what I like to hear. You may be washed up, Marvel, but people still remember you and they want to meet you, and everyone likes a pretty girl."

"Eve is lovely," Victor said, "but she's also an intelligent, talented woman."

"Yeah, sure," he said, sticking the cigar back in his mouth and clamping down on it with yellow teeth. "Oh, and be certain to find Marjorie, too, and wish her a happy birthday. She's here someplace."

"Of course," Eve said.

"Fine, fine. Dance with the birthday girl, too, Victor. Marjorie will like that."

"I would be happy to."

"Good. I'm going to go tell that bandleader to play a rumba or two later on for you and me, Miss Spellman. Excuse me. Go enjoy yourselves." He didn't wait for a reply but ambled off through the crowd, still huffing and puffing in between gulps of his drink.

"My, he certainly is something, isn't he?" Eve said.

"Simply divine. He's actually in a good mood for once."

"How can you tell?"

"Good point. I'm going to the bar in the reception room for a stiff drink to get me through this night. Want anything?"

"No, thank you. I'll take a champagne the next time a waiter passes by. I think I see Mrs. Orcott over there by the doors to the terrace."

"Yup, that's her all right," Victor said.

"She looks like she's in a good mood, too. She's positively glowing."

"She should be. This party had to cost a couple of thousand dollars, and it's all for her."

"A party that costs as much as I make in a year. Lovely. I suppose I should go say hello."

"Good idea. Tell her I'll stop over in a bit after I get a drink or two. I have my priorities straight."

"All right. Save me a dance later," Eve said.

"I will," Victor said with a wink of an eye. "I was ordered to, remember? That is, if I have time after dancing with Mrs. Orcott and all the other ladies." He moved off through the finely attired partygoers toward the double doors to the reception room.

Eve, her black beaded clutch bag tucked under her arm, snagged a glass of bubbly and made her approach as soon as the couple Mrs. Orcott had been speaking to stepped away.

"Happy birthday, Mrs. Orcott," Eve said.

Marjorie Orcott smiled thinly at her. "Thank you. You look familiar. Who are you again?"

"Eve Spellman. I'm an actress at the studio. We met a few months ago."

"Oh, yes, of course, how silly of me. Don't you look lovely, Miss Spellman?"

"Why thank you, as do you. That gown is stunning."

"You are too kind. Are you enjoying yourself?"

"Oh, yes, very much so. Everything is so, so lovely. Your home is beautiful."

"Thank you. I'm glad you're having a nice time. I remember you now. I understand you've been assigned to my husband's new picture, *The Lady Screams*."

"It's *The Lady Screeched*, but yes, I'm playing the leading lady, Ruth Bennett."

"Congratulations. And who's your escort this evening?"

"Victor Marvel. He went to get a drink at the bar. He said he'd be over soon to say hello."

"Ah, yes, Victor. I heard you two were linked romantically."

"Yes, that's right. We've been seeing a lot of each other lately."

"Oh, he is a handsome man, isn't he? But isn't he old enough to be your father? And then some?"

"Victor is young at heart, and a marvelous gentleman. And Mr. Orcott is quite a bit older than you, too, if I may say so."

"Touché, Miss Spellman. You're quite correct. Victor's a bit more attractive than Orland, though."

"Oh, um, I'm sure Mr. Orcott has some fine qualities."

"Well, if you figure out what they are, do let me know."

"I beg your pardon?"

"Just a little joke, Miss Spellman. I understand Mr. Marvel's also in the new movie, isn't he?"

"Yes, that's right, along with Griffin Fenwick."

"So I've heard. Griffin's the star of the picture, of course. He replaced Albert, though I'm still not quite sure why he was taken off the film."

"Albert?"

"My stepson, Orland's son from his previous marriage."

"Oh, but I thought Tab Rockwell was promised the role originally."

Mrs. Orcott smiled, her diamond earrings shimmering in the light from the chandeliers overhead. "Albert *is* Tab Rockwell. He changed his name last year at the studio's suggestion. I keep forgetting to call him Tab."

"I wasn't aware of the name change, but it makes sense. My birth name is Martha Willowby."

"Hmm, Martha Willowby's not a bad name, but Eve Spellman does sound more intriguing."

"Thank you. I didn't have much to do with it, though. The studio assigned it to me, and that was that."

"As they often do."

"Yes, I suppose they know best, or think they do. So, what happened with Tab and the picture?"

"As I said, I'm not really sure. He was all set to play the lead when he had some sort of an argument with his father. Neither one of them will tell me what it was about. Now Mr. Fenwick has taken over the role, and I'm sure he'll do a fine job. Anyway, I look forward to seeing the film when it's finished."

"I hope you'll enjoy it, Mrs. Orcott."

"No doubt I will. I liked the book very much, as I recall. By the way, speaking of Mr. Fenwick, he's here this evening, as I'm sure you know. I spoke with him earlier."

"I knew he was coming, but I haven't yet run into him. Victor and I only just arrived a short time ago."

"Did you also know that Griffin's here with Sheila Burton tonight?" Mrs. Orcott said, pursing her full, pink lips.

"Yes, I was told he was bringing her."

"Were you? My husband never mentioned it."

"He probably wasn't aware, Mrs. Orcott. Victor told me. Griff and Sheila aren't dating or anything, he's just her escort for the evening."

"I'm glad to hear they're not dating. Sheila's stupid, witless, and vain. Surely you've noticed."

"I, uh, don't know her that well."

"I, unfortunately, do, and more unfortunately, my husband knows her better."

"I see."

"Everyone in Hollywood sees, no doubt. And speaking of Miss Burton, I hear Mr. Fenwick has become quite close with Victor Marvel."

"Yes, they're friends. Griff looks up to Marvel as a mentor and father figure."

"A father figure who is fifty years old and unmarried."

"*Almost* fifty, and he was married. They divorced."

Mrs. Orcott clucked her tongue. "Oh, Miss Spellman. That was a studio-arranged partnership, nothing more. My husband told me they never officially lived together. It ended after only a year or so."

"I don't know anything about that."

Mrs. Orcott eyed her shrewdly. "I think you do. You look like a clever girl."

"I like to think I am. But what does any of that have to do with Sheila or with Griffin and Victor being friends?"

"Victor is old enough for it to not matter, of course. His career is just about finished. But Griff should be careful. Personally, I couldn't care less, but it bothers Orland a great deal, and it would upset a great many others, too, if it became known."

"I'm sure I don't know what you're talking about, Mrs. Orcott."

"And I'm sure you do. If I were you, I'd keep both Griffin and Victor away from Sheila Burton. She's a terrible gossip and can't be trusted. If she knew the truth, she wouldn't hesitate to tell the world."

"Thanks for the advice," Eve said.

"You're welcome. This town thrives on gossip, you know."

"I do know, believe me. That's why I mind my own business, and I keep my mouth shut, Mrs. Orcott."

"Do you? That's rare in this town. I don't think Sheila's lips have ever met, much less been shut."

"Hey there," a redhead with an hourglass figure said, sidling up to the two of them, martini in one hand and a cigarette in the other. "Did someone mention my name?"

"The word used was 'shut,'" Mrs. Orcott said sweetly as she gazed at the overly made-up redhead, "but I suppose that's close enough for you. Just substitute an 'L' for an 'H.'"

"What does that mean?" Sheila said. "What 'L' and what 'H'?"

"Just letters of the alphabet," Mrs. Orcott said. "Forget it."

Sheila shrugged her pale pink shoulders, her blue strapless gown rising up and down. "I already have." She looked at Eve. "Hello, Eve. I heard Victor was bringing you tonight."

"Good evening, Sheila. You look lovely."

Sheila eyed Eve up and down. "Thanks. So, what were you two talking about?"

"Nothing that concerns you, Sheila," Marjorie said.

"I heard you mention my name, and I don't like people talking about me behind my back, you know. If you have something to say, you can say it to my face."

"And such a lovely face it is," Marjorie said. "It's a wonder what they can do with makeup nowadays, isn't it?"

"I wouldn't know, I use very little," Sheila said coolly. "Just some powder and lipstick."

"And your nose seems smaller than the last time I saw you, I think."

"Thank you, but my nose is the same as it's always been, Mrs. Orcott. A cute little button nose, as Mr. Orcott liked to call it."

"Did he?" Marjorie said, smiling. "Wasn't that sweet of him? He tells me you've been cast in the new Gary Cooper film. The one William Wyler's directing."

"That's right."

"And naturally you got the part because of your charming *ass*ets," Mrs. Orcott said.

"They were looking for a certain type, and I fit the bill," Sheila said, taking a sip of her martini and leaving bright red lipstick prints on the rim.

"I thought the casting director was Roger, not Bill."

"My, Mrs. Orcott, aren't you quick-witted? And at your age. I hear this is your thirtieth."

"Careful, dear," Marjorie said, narrowing her eyes. "My husband and I are close friends with the director, Mr. Wyler. The picture hasn't started shooting yet. It's not too late to recast, I'm sure."

Sheila's face never changed, but her tone sharpened considerably. "There's a real reason I got that part, and I'm sure you know it."

She smiled through gritted teeth. “Unfortunately, I do know it.”

“What’s the real reason?” Eve said.

Sheila looked at Eve. “Orland and I, I mean Mr. Orcott, are friends. Close friends.”

“Is that what you call it, Sheila? You have so *many* male friends in this town, I’m sure.”

“Not like Orland,” Sheila said.

“But he ended his friendship, as you call it, with you.”

“He did. I was pretty upset about it, as you can imagine.”

“I’m sure. Still, as a parting gift, he got you the role in Mr. Wyler’s new film.”

“Yeah. That was what he promised me. Though it kind of stinks,” she said, taking a long drag on her lipstick-stained cigarette.

“How is that, Miss Burton?” Marjorie said.

“Well, when he wanted to stop being my friend six months ago, he told me he’d get me a role in the new Gary Cooper western.”

“Which he did,” Eve said.

“Yeah, but what he didn’t tell me is that it was a bit part. It’s barely more than a walk-on. Mr. Cooper and me don’t have any scenes together, either. I probably won’t get to meet him.”

“Oh, that is a pity, dear,” Marjorie said. “Mr. Wyler should know you’re not suited for a walk-on. You’re much better on your back than your feet.”

Sheila looked slightly confused. “I don’t think I ever played a role on my back. There was a part I tried out for where I was to play a beautiful woman in a coma in a hospital bed, but I didn’t get it.”

“What a pity. That would have been a terrific role for you, I’m sure.”

“Aw, that’s sweet of you, considering,” Sheila said. “No hard feelings, of course.”

“None where you’re concerned. I’m rather surprised to see you here tonight, Sheila. Does Orland know?”

“Yeah, I saw him. He didn’t look too happy about it. I’m here with Griffin Fenwick, though, so there’s nothing he can do. Besides, why shouldn’t I be here? I’m still under contract at Icon, and there’s a lot of influential people at this party that might want to get to know me.”

“I doubt it. Girls like you are a dime a dozen in this town. You come to Hollywood from Nowhere, USA, hoping to make it big in pictures. Only you find out it’s harder than it looks, and this town is tough. So, you get friendly with older men who can give you a hand. But that only lasts until the next girl from Nowhere shows up, younger and prettier, and then you're cast aside."

Shelia looked slightly annoyed, though it was hard for Eve to tell. "Orland's fifty-two and you're thirty, so I wouldn't talk."

"I didn't marry my husband for his money or his position. I was born in Pasadena, and my father is the head of First Pasadena Bank. I have never had any desire to be on the screen."

"You're a lovely woman, Mrs. Orcott," Eve said. "I'm sure you would have done well in pictures if you'd wanted it."

Marjorie looked at Eve again. "Thank you, Miss Spellman, that's kind of you, but I have never had any wish to be gaped at by strangers. As you two should know better than anyone, it's not as easy as people think being an actress. People criticize your face, your voice, your body, everything. You're either too young or too old. They adore you or they hate you, and they don't even know you."

"Isn't that the truth?" Eve said.

"I don't care if people want to gape at me. I kinda like it," Sheila said, taking another sip of her drink and another puff on her cigarette, which was almost out.

"I'm sure you do, Sheila," Mrs. Orcott said. "Especially men like my husband. Orland and I have been married for almost six years, you know. I was twenty-four when we first met, he was forty-six. A lot has happened since then, and a great many pretty girls have come and gone. But he has promised me there will be no more. He's finished with all that. So no, no hard feelings, Sheila, I wish you luck. You're going to need it."

"Thanks ever so, and so are you."

"What's that supposed to mean?" Marjorie said.

"Surely you don't really believe he's given up pretty young women to only be with you, Mrs. Orcott?"

"Sheila," Eve said in a warning tone, glancing between Sheila and Marjorie.

"What? Mrs. Orcott said herself that it only lasts until the next girl shows up, younger and prettier, and then they toss you aside. That's what Orland did to me when that bitch Charlotte Masters came along, and that's why I wish you luck, Mrs. Orcott," Sheila said. "Orland and Charlotte have been together for the last six months. She's only twenty, though personally, I don't think she's prettier than I am."

"My husband is a friendly fellow, but as I said before, he promised me that you were the last," she said with a dangerous tone. "And I believed him. Are you sure you're not mistaken about him and Miss Masters?"

"I'm sure, trust me."

"But Charlotte's here tonight with Tab," Marjorie said. "I spoke with them both earlier."

"Yeah, but only because Orland asked him to bring her so you wouldn't find out. Tab's your stepson, ain't he?"

"He is."

"That's funny having a stepson who's only six years younger than you are," Sheila said.

"Hilarious. And now that you mention it, I've noticed my husband *has* danced with Charlotte several times already this evening while Tab's been drinking in the bar."

"I'm sure Mr. Orcott's just being friendly," Eve said.

"It sounds like he's being very friendly," Marjorie said, scowling. "Hmm, Miss Masters was screen-tested a few months ago, I believe, when *The Lady Screeched* was in pre-production. You, Miss Spellman, were already assigned to the part of Ruth Bennett."

"That sounds about right," Eve said. "I signed on in March of this year."

"Yeah, after Orland gave me the brush-off," Sheila said, pouting her full, pink lips.

"And then, just recently, Orland got Miss Masters a part in *Over the Sea*, the studio's biggest budget picture yet. They've signed Lionel Barrymore and Charles Laughton so far. And Miss Masters is playing the female supporting role. He told me it was actually the producer's decision, but I wonder. Quite curious, as she's an unknown and this will be her first film."

"Wait a minute," Sheila said, "Orland got Charlotte a female supporting role? The bastard."

"Language, Miss Burton."

"What language? It's English, ain't it?"

"Barely," Eve said.

"Anyway, Charlotte gets a major role in a big movie, and I'm stuck with a bit part, barely more than a walk-on. I think it stinks."

"So you've so eloquently said before, Sheila. Excuse me, ladies, but I think I'll go have a chat with my husband, if I can pry him away from Miss Masters." Mrs. Orcott swept away, the taffeta of her pale yellow gown swishing back and forth as she walked.

"Honestly, Sheila," Eve said when Mrs. Orcott was out of range. "You do like to stir up trouble."

"What did I do?"

"All that talk of Mr. Orcott and his so-called friends, including you."

"Well, I can't help it. Orland and I *were* friends, and friendly, if you catch my drift, until Charlotte came along."

"You made that painfully obvious. So, it's true? Mr. Orcott is having an affair with Charlotte Masters?"

"I wouldn't call it an affair, but yeah, it's true. Charlotte admitted it when I confronted her. He dumped me to chase her. And he caught her by getting her that part in *Over the Sea*, the louse. That role should have been mine."

"Is Tab aware of the relationship between his father and Charlotte?"

"Sure he is. Like I said, Tab told me he's only escorting her as a favor to his old man. I mean, obviously Orland couldn't bring her himself to his wife's birthday party, but he wanted her here. His wife's going to kill him now that she knows."

"And you're delighted by that, aren't you, Sheila?"

"Why shouldn't I be? It's all true. Take my word for it, I know. Orland's a rat. He promised me the moon, and all I got was dirt. And don't act all high and mighty and superior. I'm sure you had your turn with Orland when you were younger."

"Actually, I didn't. Oh, he called me into his office and chased me around his desk, but I said no. Lucky for me, Victor saw to it that I got a few roles."

"And Orland saw to it that they were only bit parts."

"Mr. Orcott hasn't exactly helped my career, it's true. But I refuse to play his game."

"Maybe you're the smart one, after all. Look where it got me. I still can't believe he gave Charlotte Masters that big role."

"Maybe she screen-tested well for it."

"Ha, sure she did, in his bed. I feel sorry for her, you know. She'll find out what he's really like."

"I feel sorry for Mrs. Orcott," Eve said.

"Yeah, well, it's not my fault she found out. I mean, it is my fault,

I guess, but I'm sure she wanted to know the truth about her rotten husband."

"Well, maybe so, but I wouldn't go shooting my mouth off about it. Mr. Orcott will be furious when he finds out you blew the whistle on him."

"Aww, who cares?" Sheila said. "He's through with me, and I'm through with him. It's about time he gets what he deserves."

"Unfortunately, I can't argue with that," Eve said.

"Besides, I've got my sights set on Cooper Aldridge over at Universal. Rumor has it he's going to be directing a huge motion picture next year and is looking for an actress just like me."

"I pity Mr. Aldridge. By the way, where's Griff?"

Sheila shrugged her shoulders once more. "I don't know. I used the powder room, and when I came back out, he was gone. He's probably by the bar. He and I are just friends anyway. He told me tonight he's in love with someone else."

"He did?" Eve said, slightly alarmed.

"Yeah, some dame named Vivian or Victoria or something. She's in England or Canada, one of those overseas states where they don't speak a foreign language."

"Oh, I see. A long-distance romance."

"Yeah, I doubt it will last, though, they never do." Sheila glanced over Eve's shoulder, her expression changing once more. "I see the famous Agatha Mudd is still lurking about."

"The gossip columnist?" Eve said, turning to look.

"How many Agatha Mudds do you know, Eve? Of course, the gossip columnist. Ace reporter for *Star Shine Movie Magazine* and columnist for the *L.A. Times* Sunday edition. Hedda Hopper and Luella Parsons have nothing on her."

"I didn't know she'd be here."

"She's covering the party, of course."

"I must admit she scares me a little," Eve said.

"You're afraid of her?" Sheila said with a laugh. "Are you a scared little mouse afraid of a big old cat like Agatha?"

"She's made and destroyed a few careers with her pen," Eve said.

"Yeah, well, she don't bother me. Nonetheless, I think I'll go find Griff in case she's got a photographer with her."

"Fine, and I'll track down Victor. Nice chatting, Sheila."

"Mutual, I'm sure."

Eve finished her champagne and deposited the empty glass on a side table before making her way around the perimeter of the room toward the reception room and bar. Victor was still there, talking with Griff and another man she recognized as Tab Rockwell.

"Eve, there you are. Did you find Mrs. Orcott?" Victor said as she approached them.

"I did, I'll tell you all about our conversation later."

"Okay. Oh, by the way, Mr. Rockwell, this is Miss Eve Spellman."

"How do you do, Miss Spellman?" Tab said. "I've heard of you."

"How do you do, Mr. Rockwell?" she said with a practiced smile. "I've seen a few of your pictures."

"Thank you. I was just congratulating Griff here on getting the part I was supposed to have in *The Lady Screeched*. But I'm not bitter. Griff's a competent enough actor, and I'm sure he'll do swell."

"He's a fine actor," Eve said.

"Thank you, Eve," Griff said.

"That's debatable, of course," Tab said. "No offense, but I could have played Jasper Crockett better. Unfortunately, my father and I had a parting of the ways, so he went with his second choice. Or were you his third, Griff? I heard a rumor about Tyrone Power…"

"I'm sorry to hear that, Mr. Rockwell," Eve said. "I mean about your father and you."

"Thanks, but he's an ignorant blowhard. I'm only here tonight to appease him."

"To get back in his good graces?" Griff said.

Tab cocked his head. "More or less. Because of our argument, he's threatened to disinherit me and ban me from the studio."

"That must have been some argument," Victor said.

"Eh, he'll get it over it eventually."

"Sheila told me you're escorting Charlotte Masters this evening as a favor to him."

"Sheila's got a big mouth, but yeah, that's right. He couldn't find anyone else to ask that he trusted not to make a pass at her."

"Make a pass at her?" Griff said. "Why would your father care about that?"

"Because Charlotte is his new mistress. In return for escorting her here tonight, he promised to reconsider his earlier threats."

"I'm sure he'll come around, Tab," Victor said. "You're his only child."

Tab snorted. "I am, lucky me. But I'm sure you know Orland Orcott well enough to know that he's stubborn and obstinate, Victor. Oh well, it doesn't matter if he does or doesn't. My agent, Nora Dinsdale, is trying to arrange for a screen test for me at MGM."

"You'll be fine," Griff said, patting him on the back.

"Of course I will. I'm Tab Rockwell. I'll show my father, and I'll have the last laugh."

"He who laughs last laughs best, as they say," Victor said.

"I'll be laughing all the way to the Academy Awards one of these years."

"You're ambitious if nothing else, Mr. Rockwell," Eve said.

"Ambition is important," Griff said.

"To a degree," Eve said. "Oh, by the way, Sheila's looking for you, Griff."

"Is she?" Griff said.

"Lucky you," Tab said. "I thought she'd be off somewhere scratching Charlotte Masters's eyes out."

"Why would she do that?" Victor said.

"Petty jealousy," Tab said, rolling his blue eyes and shaking his head, though his coifed brunette hair never stirred. "She was my father's former mistress. Two cats fighting over a rat."

"Where is she?" Griff said.

"She and I were talking with Mrs. Orcott by the terrace doors."

"Oh, the birthday girl," Tab said. "My dear stepmother."

"Yes, well, the three of us were chatting and then your stepmother stepped away," Eve said. "Then we saw, or Sheila saw, Agatha Mudd. After that, Sheila said she was going to come look for you, Griff."

"Agatha Mudd is here?" Victor said. He sighed and finished his drink, setting the empty on the bar. "I should have known. I suppose we should dance, Eve."

"I'd be delighted," Eve said.

"And I suppose I should find Sheila before she makes an ass of herself and says something stupid to Agatha," Griff said. "Fortunately, Mrs. Mudd seems to like me. For now."

"Yes, well, excuse us, gentlemen," Victor said. "I owe this lovely lady a dance." Eve took his arm, and they returned to the grand salon where the quartet was playing a slow two-step.

"All right, dance with me," Eve said as they approached the dance floor, "and make sure Mrs. Mudd and Mr. Orcott can see. Whisper in my ear and nibble on my shoulders if you like."

Together they stepped onto the parquet dance floor and began to dance amongst the other couples.

"Where is she, exactly?" Victor said, glancing about casually. "Mrs. Mudd, I mean."

"I'm not sure. She's wearing an organdy dress and a matching hat. She has large, black-rimmed glasses."

"She's known for those glasses. Even if we don't see her, she probably sees us. She's vicious if you aren't one of her friends."

"I've heard," Eve said. "Are you one of her friends?"

"So far we've gotten along, but even then, I try to be careful. Her modus operandi is to sidle up to you sweetly and make it seem like she wants to do a human interest story on you. But what she really wants is to pump you for information and see if she can trip you up, either about yourself or about those you know."

"It's hard to believe. She looks harmless, like my Aunt Betty back in Tulsa."

"She's nothing like your Aunt Betty, I'm sure. Word is, Agatha was once an aspiring movie actress, but she became pregnant and was forced to quit. That was fifteen years ago."

"She had to quit just because she had a baby?"

"She was unmarried, Eve, and a certain someone told me she still is, though she claims to be a widow. One of the movie star rags got hold of the story back then, and she was pretty much finished."

"So now she does to others what someone once did to her. How sad."

"Agreed. Just watch your back. And your front and both sides."

"I will," Eve said, resting her head on his shoulder. "Who was the father?"

"It was never disclosed, and she never said. Someone big in the business. I believe she was in her mid to late twenties at the time."

"Heavens, she looks much older than her early forties."

"Don't tell her that."

"I wasn't planning to. So, did she have the baby?" Eve said, lifting her head up again to look at Victor lovingly in the eyes, their noses almost touching.

"Yes, a little girl, fifteen now, of course. I forget her name. She's in an institution, not right mentally, I guess."

"You seem to know an awful lot about this gossip woman."

"Oh, Agatha's all right. She's good at her job. But what is it they say? If you know the enemy and know yourself, you need not fear."

"'If you know the enemy and know yourself, you need not fear the result of a hundred battles. If you know yourself but not the enemy, for every victory gained you will also suffer a defeat. If you know neither the enemy nor yourself, you will succumb in every battle.' It's from Sun Tzu's *The Art of War*."

Victor raised his eyebrows in surprise. "Well, look at you, Eve Spellman. I'm impressed."

"I'm not just a pretty face with big boobs and a nice behind."

"I never thought otherwise."

"Thank you. I was class valedictorian of Central High, I'll have you know, and my mother is the librarian at Tulsa's main library, while my father is an English teacher. I was also on the debate team and in the drama club, where we studied Shakespeare ad nauseam."

"How about that? It sounds like you had a very wholesome upbringing."

"I did. I was prom queen my senior year."

"So how did you end up at Bisby's Burlesque in West Hollywood at the age of seventeen?"

"After I graduated, my parents wanted me to go on to college and become a teacher and then get married and give them lots of grandchildren."

"Sounds dreadful."

"Right, and I'd had enough of school and enough of Tulsa. I always loved going to the movies and I wanted to be in them, like a lot of young women. My former high school drama coach knew an agent out here, and he set me up with an interview against my parents' objections."

"I can imagine they weren't happy," Victor said.

"My father was furious. But with the money I'd saved up, I bought a ticket for a bus ride to Hollywood, got a room at a boarding house, and met my teacher's friend, George Mathers. He's the one that got me the job at Bisby's, just as a stepping stone, in his words. Then, a short while later, you came along and got me a screen test at Icon."

"So, I was your knight on a white horse?"

"Maybe, but I would have saved myself in time if you hadn't, I'm sure."

"Of that, I have no doubt, Miss Spellman."

"Thanks again. So, what were you three talking about in the bar?"

"Oh, mostly about Tab Rockwell, or at least Tab was. He's twenty-four and full of himself. Entitled, arrogant, and damned attractive."

"I noticed."

"Hard not to. He's also not a very good actor, and he doesn't have much interest in becoming better."

"Because he probably thinks he's a great actor," Eve said.

"My, you are very perceptive."

"First impressions. And with a father like Orland Orcott, he probably doesn't need to improve. Or didn't, anyway."

"You're right, Orland's gotten him a few roles in his films. No lead characters or starring parts, but speaking roles. The reviews weren't very kind. Still, Orland continued to get him cast. Nepotism at its finest. The role of Jasper Crockett in *The Lady Screeched* was to be his first starring role."

"And then they had that big disagreement. What was it all about?" Eve said.

"I don't know for sure. Tab was rather vague." He paused to nibble her earlobe, which caused Eve to giggle.

"That tickles, Victor," she said, running her free hand up his spine to caress the back of his head.

"Sorry. Anyway, I suspect it all has something to do with the fact that Tab plays for our team, and Orland found out."

"You mean Tab's a homosexual?" Eve said, almost shocked.

"Shh, and yes, that's the team I was referring to. Griff told me about it. The two of them met in the steam bath at the Hollywood Athletic Club a few years ago. Tab's been seen lately with a young man named Tony Bolt, a fitness model and aspiring actor himself."

"So, Mr. Orcott found out and fired his own son from the picture?"

"That's my theory."

"And he threatened to disinherit him and make sure he never works at the studio again," Eve said.

"Sadly, that's not surprising."

"But now that Tab agreed to escort Miss Masters tonight, his father plans to reconsider."

"Supposedly. Since Tab's a homosexual, Orland felt he could trust him not to make a pass at her, as Tab said. I wouldn't trust Orland Orcott, though."

"Agreed," Eve said. The song ended, and the two of them stepped off the dance floor arm in arm as another tune started up.

"I could use some fresh air. Would you like to join me on the terrace?" Victor said.

"Certainly. It is rather stuffy in here," Eve said. "But you still haven't danced with Mrs. Orcott, or anyone else."

"Neither have you," Victor said.

"I doubt Mrs. Orcott leads."

"Funny girl, you know what I meant."

"Sorry. Anyway, no one's asked me, not that I'm complaining. Mr. Orcott won't like it, though."

"We'll both make a point of being more social when we get back inside."

"Okay." The two of them strolled out one of the two sets of French doors onto the flagstone terrace, which led to an expanse of lawn and an in-ground pool. Beyond the pool, Victor recalled, were tennis courts, though they weren't visible in the dark.

"Good evening," William said, his daughter on his arm, as he approached Victor and Eve.

"Hello, William, it's nice to see you," Eve said, turning to him.

"Likewise, I'm sure. Getting some air or escaping the crowds?"

"Both," Victor said.

"Same with us," William said. "May I present my daughter, Lydia Taylor? Lydia, this is Mr. Marvel and Miss Spellman."

"Yes, I've had the pleasure," Victor said. "How do you do, Miss Taylor?"

"Oh, that's right," William said, "I forgot you two had met before."

"Yes, we've met a couple of times, though it's been a while. Do you also know Miss Spellman, Miss Taylor?" Victor said.

"No, I'm afraid I haven't yet had the pleasure," Lydia said. "How do you do? That's a lovely gown."

"Thank you, Miss Taylor, as is yours."

"Thank you, it was my mother's. I had it altered. And please call me Lydia, both of you."

"All right, Lydia, thank you," Eve said. "And please call me Eve. Are you two enjoying yourselves?"

"We're making the best of it," William said with a soft sigh. "Mr. Orcott is drunk. He introduced me to someone as Wee Wee Willie a short while ago. He thought it was hilarious."

"Oh dear," Eve said, looking horrified.

Lydia glanced about and lowered her voice. "I despise that man. He's triple-A all the way."

"Triple-A?" Victor said.

"Yes, arrogant, annoying, and an ass."

"Ah, yes, a common consensus," Victor said.

"He's telling people my father only got the part in *The Lady Screeched* because of me, implying I did something unseemly with him. I can assure you all I did was pay him a visit in his office to plead my father's case. I told him Dad really was the best choice to play the thug in the film. Did Orcott make a pass at me? Of course he did, the swine. I politely declined, though I wanted to slap him, and I thought after that he would never give Dad the role, so I was quite pleasantly surprised when he did. I'm sure he realized my father fit the part perfectly, though he's been sullying my reputation ever since."

"I'm tempted to quit," William said. "To walk off the picture, but Lydia's been telling me not to."

"I wouldn't give that man the satisfaction of you quitting. Besides, it's a good part for you, we need the money desperately, and you'll be great in it. He will get what's coming to him, believe me."

William appeared agitated. "He *will* get what's coming to him. Come on, Lydia, I think we both could use a drink. Won't you excuse us?"

"Of course," Victor said.

"A pleasure meeting you, Lydia," Eve said.

"Likewise, Miss Spellman, Eve, I mean. I hope we have a chance to chat more later," Lydia said as she took her father's arm and they moved off and back into the house.

"I can't believe Orcott would humiliate William like that," Victor said. "Well, actually I can believe it, but it infuriates me."

"I know what you mean. And to treat Lydia like that is disgusting."

"I agree. He's a vile human being," Victor said.

"I don't know how Mrs. Orcott can stand him. Though after tonight, that may change."

"Oh?"

"Yes, Sheila Burton shot her mouth off to Mrs. Orcott about Orland and Charlotte."

"Good grief."

"I know. I think she did it deliberately to get back at Mr. Orcott. And oh brother, don't look now, but here comes Agatha Mudd," Eve said.

Victor wrapped his arm about Eve's waist and kissed her gently in the moonlight.

"Oh, look at you two lovebirds," Agatha said as she sidled up to them, beaming.

"Agatha, hello, don't you look lovely?" Victor said, smiling down at her, his arm still about Eve's waist.

"Do I? Thank you, but where have you been all evening? Have you been avoiding me, you naughty boy?"

"Not at all, Agatha. Miss Spellman and I arrived late, that's all. Have you two met, by the way?"

She looked at Eve appraisingly. "Not officially, no, but I know all about you, and about the two of you." She tittered into her hand and then smiled broadly. "How do you do, Miss Spellman?"

"How do you do, Mrs. Mudd? That truly is a beautiful dress. The color suits you."

"Thank you. I've nothing on you, though, your gown is divine. Madame Vionnet?"

"No, Chanel, Coco Chanel."

Victor could see Agatha making a mental note. "Oh, of course. Well, it's just beautiful, as are you, Miss Spellman. You and Victor here make a charming couple. I noticed you two dancing earlier. Quite the show."

"I'm not exactly sure what she sees in an old fellow like me," Victor said, smiling, "but I'm glad she does."

"Oh, Victor, don't be so modest," Agatha said. "You're handsome, wealthy, successful, and talented. You've many fans and admirers."

"That's kind of you, Agatha."

"You know it's all true," Agatha said. "So, you two are in Orland's new picture together, along with that devastatingly gorgeous young Griffin Fenwick."

"That's right," Eve said. "I consider myself lucky to be among such esteemed talent, including my boyfriend here, and William Taylor, of course. Mr. Taylor has the part of the heavy in the film, and he's going to be brilliant."

Agatha nodded thoughtfully. "Yes, I'd heard William Taylor was in it. I shall have to talk to him."

"He'd be happy to speak with you, I'm sure," Victor said.

"Hmm, yes, though I'm not sure I'll be able to tonight. It's getting late, and people are already dispersing, and I still want to speak with Griffin."

"All right," Victor said. "But I'm sure William would be delighted to chat any time. He could use some good publicity."

"Hmm. Mr. Taylor hasn't made a movie in several years, has he?" Agatha said.

"It's only been a year or two. He took some personal time away, family trouble," Victor said. "But that's all resolved now. As Eve said, he'll be swell in this film."

"That remains to be seen. I saw him earlier this evening with a pretty young lady I'm told is his daughter. I nearly didn't recognize him. He's lost weight, and he looks older than his years, rather unwell."

"The part he's playing in the new film calls for him to appear gaunt and old," Eve said. "Mr. Taylor believes in getting into character as much as possible."

"How fascinating. Well, as I said, I shall have to corner him for a chat sometime soon, and his lovely daughter, too. Orland tells me she was instrumental in Mr. Taylor getting the part. He said she was very persuasive," Agatha said with a wink and another titter.

"I'm familiar with what Mr. Orcott is implying, Mrs. Mudd, but I don't believe it," Eve said. "Mr. Taylor's daughter told us herself that she only went to his office to speak with him and plead the case that her father was right for the role."

"I agree with Eve," Victor said. "Oh, I've no doubt Orland tried to seduce her, possibly even make it a condition of her father getting the role, but I don't believe she went down that path."

"Don't be so quick to defend your friend and his daughter, Victor. I don't know Miss Taylor, of course, but I know many like her, though usually they're on the couch to better their own careers, not the careers of their fathers. Naturally, she'd deny it. She's not going to admit it. Something like that would ruin her reputation and crush her father."

"It most certainly would," Victor said. "And I think Orland is lying."

"You may be right, Victor," Agatha said, "but I'm willing to bet Mr. Taylor believes it's true. I saw him watching Orland tonight with something akin to quiet rage in his sunken eyes. I'm sure Miss Taylor's also none too pleased Orland's been shooting his mouth off about her, true or not. Orland is a braggart and a fool who thinks nothing of hurting someone else in order to make himself look good. Unfortunately, because he's in a position of power, people believe whatever he spews."

"You sound as if you're speaking from personal experience, Agatha," Victor said.

She frowned, and a worried look came over her face. "Oh dear, do I? I'm afraid I've had too much champagne. Well, Orland and I go back many years in this industry, you know, more than I care to admit. I went from an aspiring actress to a gossip columnist, and he's continued to be successful in his career. No one's taken him down. *Yet*."

"I don't think anyone dares," Eve said.

"Maybe not, or maybe they're just waiting for the right opportunity." Her expression changed instantly again and she beamed once more. "Now then, I simply must say hello to Griffin before the night is over, and it's nearly over now. Where is the dear boy? I heard he's here with Sheila Burton."

"Your sources are ever accurate, Agatha," Victor said.

Agatha shook her head and clucked her tongue. "I definitely need to have a word with him in private. Sheila Burton is a parasite. You're his mentor, Victor, or so he's told me in the past. How could you allow him to go out with the likes of her?"

"Griff's a grown man, Agatha. Besides, he's just her escort for the evening. I don't think they're serious."

"I should hope not. You know, of course, that Sheila was friendly with Orland up until just a few months ago. Frankly, given that, I was surprised to see her here at all. As were Orland and Marjorie, no doubt. Honestly, what was Griff thinking bringing her here?"

"I don't think Griff realized the history between Shelia and Mr. Orcott when he asked her," Victor said. "I wasn't aware of it, either."

"I'm sure not, but she certainly knew, and she shouldn't have accepted the invitation from him. What is she hoping to accomplish?" Agatha said.

"Maybe just to show Mr. Orcott she's found another companion," Eve said. "And it's my understanding she actually asked him."

"Did she? How interesting. She asked Griffin Fenwick to escort her to this party? The star of Orland's new picture? Not a wise move. It's sure to cause problems. But I suppose Sheila couldn't care less."

"I'm sure not," Victor said. "And I certainly hope Orcott wouldn't hold that against Griff."

"I wouldn't put anything past him. He fired his own son from the film. Of course, Tab only got the part because he *is* his father's son. My sources tell me the two of them had quite the argument, which led to Tab's dismissal."

"I wouldn't know," Victor said. "Tab's here tonight, though."

"Yes, and with a lovely young woman named Charlotte Masters. I've already spoken to both of them. Charlotte's been given the part of Lucy Binghampton in *Over the Sea*, the studio's biggest budget picture yet, though she's a complete unknown. Lionel Barrymore and Charles

Laughton are in it, too, you know. And Miss Masters is playing the female supporting role."

"Good for her," Eve said.

"Quite so and yet rather interesting," Agatha said, prodding her black-rimmed eyeglasses back up her nose. "Charlotte's never made a film before, I'm told, and she's a tad young to play the part of Lucy, don't you think? Of course, you'd already been signed to play Ruth in *The Lady Screeched*, so I suppose Orland had to find something for her. It's what he does, you know, find roles for pretty girls who are friendly to him, for lack of a better term in polite company. And it's my understanding Charlotte's been very friendly to him. I'm sure Shelia is positively seething about it. He never did do much for her while they were together, but then, she's a terrible actress."

"She thinks she's a terrific actress," Eve said. "Just like Tab thinks he is a great actor."

Agatha tittered into her hand once more. "You're absolutely correct in that assessment, Miss Spellman. As someone once said, the less talent they have, the more pride and arrogance they have."

"'The less talent they have, the more pride, vanity, and arrogance they have. All these fools, however, find other fools who applaud them.' Erasmus said that."

"Did he? Was he one of the Little Rascals? Those films always make me chuckle."

"Er, no, Mrs. Mudd, he lived in the 1500s," Eve said.

"Oh? How fascinating."

"I understand you were an actress when you were younger," Eve said.

She raised an arched, painted brow. "Now, what little bird told you that, Miss Spellman?" She looked at Victor. "As if I didn't know."

"I thought it was common knowledge," Victor said.

"Besides, you mentioned it yourself just a few moments ago," Eve said. "When you said you went from aspiring actress to gossip columnist."

"Did I say that? Well, I've had too much champagne tonight. But yes, it's true. I was an actress back in the day."

"You made a few films for Icon Studios," Victor said.

"Hmm, yes, well, I did, under the name of Kitty Manx. You saw them?"

"Er, no, I don't believe so, but I heard about them, and about you," Victor said.

"Probably better that you didn't see them. I wasn't a great actress, but I was decent, and I could have gotten better. I could have been a star, I think. I was a pretty girl once, you know, like Miss Spellman here."

"You're still a lovely woman," Victor said.

"Don't flatter me, Mr. Marvel, it's not believable. I have a mirror, and the years have not been kind. Anyway, I was forced to give up my career, everything, due to one nasty, powerful man in the industry. And now I'm a columnist." She turned her cat eyes, which looked massive behind her oversized, thick glasses, to Eve again. "Tell me, Miss Spellman, since you seem quite literate, who said 'Revenge is a dish best served cold'?"

"Hmm, I can't remember his name, but it comes from *Les Liaisons Dangereuses*, I believe, a novel first published in the 1700s."

"*Dangerous Liaisons*, of course, you're quite right. Aren't you the clever one," Agatha said. "Though most men don't like women who are smarter than they are, do they, Victor?"

"Oh, I don't know about that. I appreciate Eve's mind as much as, if not more than, her face and figure."

"Do you? Well then, you're not most men. At least, that's what I've heard, though I haven't been able to prove it. *Yet*."

"Whatever does that mean, Agatha?" Victor asked as innocently as he could.

"Oh, you know, I'm sure. But don't worry. Just don't cross old Agatha, and you'll be fine. I like you, Victor. I always have. And I do have my scruples and morals, despite what some people think."

"I appreciate that."

"You should. Take care of me, and I'll take care of you. I can be a trusted ally and a good friend, you know. Now then, what do you know about the fight Tab Rockwell had with his father?"

"Er, nothing, really," Victor said.

"Why do I not believe that?"

"It's true," Eve said. "Even Mrs. Orcott told me she didn't know what it was about."

"Marjorie Orcott is often the last to know about a lot of things," Agatha said. "Or at least she pretends not to know. I overheard her and Orland having quite a row just a little while ago about Charlotte Masters. I think Orland may have finally gone too far. After that very public argument, the guests have started scattering, like rats fleeing a sinking ship. It made everyone quite uncomfortable, though I was delighted, personally. It makes for much better copy. Surely you two heard them, even out here?"

"No, we didn't," Eve said. "We were talking with Mr. Taylor and his daughter and not paying any attention to what was going on inside."

"A pity," Agatha said. "Even the orchestra stopped playing. I thought for certain they were going to come to blows."

"How embarrassing for Mrs. Orcott," Victor said. "And on her birthday."

Agatha clucked her tongue against her teeth. "I agree. Marjorie's no fool, though. She'll never divorce him. She claims to come from money, you know. She tells people her father is the head of the First Pasadena Bank, but he's nothing more than a loan officer. And Orland had her sign a prenuptial agreement. She gets nothing if they divorce, regardless of the reason. Still, she can only be pushed so far."

"And Orland is adept at pushing people's buttons."

"Isn't he, though?" Agatha said knowingly. "Poor Marjorie's gone off to her bedroom with a sick headache, and Tab's taken to drinking at the bar all night. So, tell me, Victor, what was the fight about between Orland and him?"

"Honestly, Agatha, all I know is it caused Orland to dismiss Tab from the picture and disinherit him."

"And to appease his father, he agreed to escort Miss Masters this evening, which led to a nasty quarrel between his father and stepmother tonight," Agatha said.

"It would seem so, yes," Victor said. "Tab claims by agreeing to bring Charlotte to the party his father is going to reconsider his actions against him."

"I hope he got that in writing," Agatha said. "Orland Orcott is a liar, a cheat, and a scoundrel, as we both said earlier. My sources tell me he's gotten Tab blacklisted at many of the other major studios as well as Icon Pictures, though no one has been able to tell me why. *Yet*. Even for a man like Orland, to do something like that to his own son, the disagreement had to be quite serious."

"Er, yes, it certainly sounds like it. Tab mentioned earlier that his agent, Nora Dinsdale, is trying to arrange a screen test for him at MGM," Victor said.

"Nora's a good agent, but she'd have to be a miracle worker to pull that off," Agatha said, clucking her tongue again. "I should think Tab would have discovered by now Orland's had him blacklisted at MGM, too. The poor boy. I hope his father does reconsider."

"He most likely will. Tab's all right," Victor said.

"Personally, I think he's all wrong, at least as an actor. He and Sheila seemed rather chummy earlier tonight, I noticed. Two peas in a pod. They're both vain and untalented. What was it that Little Rascal said again, Miss Spellman?"

"Um, Erasmus. He said the less talent they have, the more pride, vanity and arrogance they have."

Agatha beamed. "Exactly. That's Tab and Sheila to a T. Well, no matter. Fools like those two always lose out in the end, though they always blame someone else for it. It makes for good copy in my column, at least. By the way, Victor, someone tossed the name of Tony Bolt my way earlier this evening. Do you know him?"

"Uh, no, I'm not familiar."

"I'm told he's a fitness model for those trashy magazines, you know the ones. They pretend to be about men's fitness, but we all know better. Someone linked Mr. Bolt's name to Tab's."

"Did they?" Victor said.

"They did. And when I mentioned Mr. Bolt to Orland, I thought he was going to have a seizure. His face turned such an interesting shade of eggplant, but he wouldn't say a word, and Marjorie was clueless, as usual."

"Sorry I can't be of more help," Victor said.

"No matter, I'll sniff it out. I have a nose for these sorts of things, you know."

"You're good at your job, Agatha."

"Better than most people realize," she said. "But then, my job is all I have, isn't it? I'm an old maid, never married, except to my career. And speaking of my career, this affair is definitely winding down, far earlier than expected, and I need to go find a nice, quiet corner to make a few notes while things are still fresh in my mind. Won't you excuse me?"

"Of course, always a pleasure," Victor said.

"It was nice meeting you, Mrs. Mudd," Eve said.

"Mutual, I'm sure, dear. Ta ta," Agatha said, slipping back into the house with catlike stealth, which belied her size.

"What a swell party," Victor said with a heavy sigh after she'd gone.

"What a mess," Eve said. "Let's go in."

"All right." They crossed the terrace and stepped back into the grand salon, which was surprisingly void of most of the guests. The musicians in the corner were packing up their instruments, and the waiters were collecting empty glasses and full ashtrays.

"Should we say our goodbyes, too, Victor? It seems most of the other guests have left or are leaving," Eve said, "just like Mrs. Mudd mentioned."

"Yes, nothing like a nasty fight between the host and hostess to put a damper on an evening. Anyway, I suppose it is getting late."

"We'll be the last to arrive and the last to leave, it seems, though here come Griff and Sheila from the entrance hall," Eve said.

"And Tab from the bar, with Charlotte trailing behind," Victor said. "She looks miserable."

"Where have you two been?" Griff said as he and Sheila approached.

"We just came in from the terrace," Eve said. "But I'm about ready to call it a night. We heard about the big quarrel between Mr. and Mrs. Orcott, but we didn't witness it."

"It was a doozy," Griff said. "A knock-down, drag-out fight, three rounds. No clear winner, but the boxers went off to their respective corners and the spectators fled. And speaking of that, I think I should get you home, Sheila."

"Already? I've been having a swell time. Let's stay a little longer."

"But everyone's leaving, and I'm done in."

"I'm tired, too," Charlotte said, taking Tab's arm as the two of them joined the group. "I'd like to go home myself. This has been an awful night."

"Why don't I call you a cab, Charlotte? I'm not ready to leave just yet, either," Tab said. "I think I should stick around and see if Marjorie needs me. She was pretty upset and angry, and rightly so."

"Oh," Charlotte said quietly. "Because of me, you mean."

"I didn't say that," Tab said.

"It doesn't matter. I want to go home. Please. Stay here if you want, just call me a cab."

"All right, Charlotte. I'll use the phone in the study."

"I thought I saw a telephone in the reception room," Griff said, "near the bar."

"I know, I used to live here, remember? But it's too loud in the reception room. I'll be right back, excuse me," Tab said, walking off a bit unsteadily.

"I'm sorry about everything that happened this evening, Miss Masters," Victor said.

She smiled wanly at him. "Thanks. It started out okay. I did a lot of dancing, had imported champagne, and met some nice people. But then that horrible argument between Orland and his wife about me made me want to crawl in a hole. I just about died. She said some nasty things about me in front of everyone."

"Er, yes. I can imagine you'd be upset," Eve said.

"Yes," Charlotte said. "Mrs. Orcott went upstairs, presumably to get some aspirin, but that was half an hour ago or more and she hasn't been seen again. I've been asking Tab to take me home ever since."

"I doubt Mrs. Orcott will be back down tonight," William said as he came up to the group, his daughter Lydia on his arm.

"Probably not," Griff said. "Where have you two been? I thought you'd left with the others."

"We wouldn't have left without saying goodbye," William said. "I was just resting a bit in the library. But then Agatha Mudd came in. She said she wanted to be alone and didn't want to be disturbed, so we wandered back out here."

"Ah, yes, she was going to make a few notes," Eve said. "For her column in the morning."

William grimaced. "Naturally. I hope she keeps my name out of it. She asked me a few rude questions about my appearance, my health, and rumors she'd heard."

"There's no such thing as bad publicity, Dad," Lydia said. "Isn't that what they say?"

"That, unfortunately, is not true," William said.

"Well, I like publicity of any kind, and I'm sure she'll mention my name," Sheila said. "With Griff's, of course."

"She most likely will," Griff said.

"Mrs. Mudd asked me all about my new picture," Charlotte said. "The role Orland got for me. I don't know what will happen with all that now." She looked like she might cry at any moment.

"Orland got me a role in Gary Cooper's new film," Sheila said.

Charlotte's brown eyes blazed. "He got you a bit part as a consolation prize. I heard you were the one who told Mrs. Orcott about Orland and me tonight."

"So what if I did? They gave you the leading lady role. You're in over your head, Charlotte. The critics are going to rip you to pieces."

"Hasn't seemed to bother you much so far. The critics hated you in the few films you've made."

"I'll bother *you* if you don't watch your mouth. You're all upset about the way Mrs. Orcott spoke to you, well, what did you expect? You're sleeping with her husband."

"Only after he got tired of sleeping with you, Sheila."

"Ladies, please, this is not the time or place," Victor said.

"I agree," William said. "If you'll all excuse me, I need to use the lavatory. Lydia, why don't we peruse what's left to eat in the dining room when I've finished? Maybe there's something we can take home."

"All right, Dad."

"Fine, I'll be back in a moment," William said. He walked away slowly toward the gentleman's lavatory off the reception room as Tab approached from the double doors to the salon.

"The cab should be here in five minutes, Charlotte," Tab said.

"Fine, I'll get my purse from the ladies' room and then wait for the taxi outside. Away from her."

"Away from who?"

"Never mind. Just away. Away from everyone. Good night. Excuse me, please," Charlotte said. She turned and stalked off down the hall toward the ladies' room.

Tab sighed. "I feel sorry for her, yet I don't. She knew what she was getting into, or she should have. God, I could use a cigarette and some fresh air. I think I'll go out on the terrace for a bit."

"I could use a cigarette, too," Sheila said. "Mind if I join you?"

"Not at all, if Griff doesn't mind," Tab said. "He is your escort, after all."

"Go ahead," Griff said. "I don't mind, and I don't smoke."

"Then you're not doing it right," Sheila said with a giggle.

"Just don't be long, okay? I really do want to get going," Griff said.

"Oh, don't worry, it's not that late," Sheila said. "Come on, Tab." The two of them walked off side by side back toward the drawing room, leaving Victor, Eve, Griff, and Lydia in the entry hall.

"I wonder what's keeping Dad," Lydia said, glancing at her wristwatch.

"Oh, he'll be along, I'm sure. How's he honestly doing, Lydia?" Victor said.

She rolled her head about her delicate neck and took a breath. "I know you've known Dad a long time. He likes you, so I suppose I can be honest. He gets tired easily, and he has some pain. And then there's the other issue that Mr. Orcott alluded to earlier."

"His incontinence," Griff said. "He told us about it at the reading."

"Yes, it bothers him a great deal. He finds it humiliating. Dad wore double pads under his tuxedo pants tonight just to be safe. He said he wasn't very comfortable, but at least he felt more confident."

"Poor William," Eve said.

"I hate seeing him like this," Lydia said. "I just don't know what to do sometimes. I was so happy when he got this part, and he was, too. We could use the money. Things have been pretty tight since he got sick. We had to move to a much smaller house. But then, the last few days especially, he's retreated back to where he was before he got the role, thanks mostly to the way Mr. Orcott's treated him. I just don't know how else to help him."

"Your father is lucky to have you," Victor said.

"I'm lucky to have him," Lydia said.

"I'd say you're both lucky. What's that you're holding, Lydia?" Victor said.

Lydia glanced down and laughed awkwardly as she noticed a bit of twine she was clutching in her hand. "Oh dear, I forgot I was still hanging on to this."

"A piece of string?" Eve said.

"Hmm? Oh, yes. I found it in the garden earlier. I want to put it in my purse for safekeeping and surprise my father with it later. Did you know my dad collects string? He delights in finding new pieces, gathered here and there from waste bins, the sidewalk, and sometimes stolen from packages he comes across, I hate to admit. It's one of his few remaining pleasures in life. That and acting, of course. He's happiest in front of a camera, where he can be someone other than himself."

"And now he will be again," Eve said.

"Yes, if Mr. Orcott doesn't destroy him before the film is even started. It breaks my heart."

"What breaks your heart, Lydia?" William said, coming into the entry from the reception room.

"Oh, hello, Dad. The, uh, thought of all that leftover food in the dining room going to waste."

"Agreed, so let's go see what we can manage to sneak out of here."

"Sure, let's," Lydia said with a forced smile. She took his arm to steady him, and they walked off down the hall together.

"And then there were three," Victor said.

"Four, actually," a wheezing voice said from above.

Eve, Victor, and Griff looked up toward the balcony, where Orland Orcott was standing.

"Oh, Orland, what are you doing upstairs?" Victor said.

"Just checking on my wife. She said she had a headache and was going to lie down for a bit, but she's not in her room. I'm not sure where she's gone off to. Have any of you seen her?"

"I haven't in some time," Eve said.

"Nor I," Griff said.

"That makes three of us. We were just preparing to leave," Victor said.

"Fine, go, everyone else has," Orland said, beginning his descent down the curved staircase with the wrought iron railing and balustrades. "I'm sure you all witnessed the debacle."

"Ah, Victor and I were on the terrace," Eve said. "We didn't see or hear it."

"But you heard about it, and so did Agatha Mudd, no doubt. I can't wait to read tomorrow morning's newspaper. Where's Sheila? Lucky for her I haven't seen her since before the argument. She was with you tonight, wasn't she, Griff?"

"Er, yes, sir. She's outside on the terrace having a cigarette. As soon as she comes back, we'll head out, too. I'm pretty tired."

Orland wheezed and coughed, breathing heavily as he reached the bottom step, a cigar in one hand and a whiskey in the other. "I'd like to have a word or two with Sheila before you leave. This is all her fault. Her and her big mouth. And what the hell were you thinking bringing her here tonight, for Christ's sake?"

"I honestly wasn't aware of any relationship with the two of you, Mr. Orcott, I swear," Griff said.

"Hmm, well, we'll discuss this on Monday. Poor Charlotte is so upset. Marjorie was most unpleasant and called her a number of awful things. Things a lady should never say, especially about another lady. Where is she now? Where's Charlotte? I want to apologize to her for my wife's behavior."

"She's getting her purse," Victor said. "Tab called her a cab so she could go home. He wanted to stay for a while in case Marjorie needed anything. Your wife was upset, too, obviously."

Orland belched. "Upset? She was angry. Utterly ridiculous and embarrassing to put on a scene like that in front of everyone, and to treat poor Charlotte like that. Maybe I should offer to drive Miss Masters home myself."

"Personally, Mr. Orcott, I don't think that would be a good idea after everything that's happened," Eve said.

Orland stared down at her. "Maybe you're right, for once. I'll send Charlotte some flowers in the morning and ask her to come see me at the studio on Monday. Poor thing."

"Ah, there you are, Mr. Orcott," said a white-jacketed older man as he whisked in through the double doors from the salon.

"What is it, Clarence?"

"A telephone call for you, sir."

"What? At this hour? Who is it?"

"They wouldn't give a name, but they said it's quite urgent and personal."

Orland scowled. "Why do I have the feeling this has something to do with my son getting into trouble? All right, I'll take it in my study where I can talk in private. Bring me a bromide in a peppermint tea. I don't feel so well."

"Yes, sir," Clarence said. "Is there anything else you need, Mr. Orcott?"

"Have you seen Mrs. Orcott?" Orland said, moving slowly away toward the salon and his study.

"Uh, no, sir, not recently. Not since, the uh, the…"

"The fight, I know. There's nothing else I need right now besides that bromide. Once all the guests and the caterers have left, see to locking up for the night. I'll be up for a while."

"Yes, sir," Clarence said, hurrying away toward the kitchen wing.

At the double doors to the salon, Orcott turned his large body briefly to look at Victor, Griff, and Eve. "Don't forget I want to talk to Sheila before you leave, Griff. And I'll see you all Monday morning on set. Know your lines, or there will be hell to pay."

"Sure, Orland, we'll have them memorized," Victor said, but Orcott didn't respond. Instead, he turned again and went through the doors, puffing on his cigar in between sips of his whiskey.

"I'm exhausted," Eve said.

"Yes, me too," Griff said. "And now Orcott wants to talk to Sheila, and I must admit I still don't know all my lines."

"You will," Victor said.

"I hope so," Griff said, glancing at his watch. "How long does it take Sheila to smoke a cigarette? I want to get out of here as soon as Orcott's finished giving her what for."

"She's with Tab, remember?" Victor said. "They're probably gossiping like schoolgirls about everything that's happened."

"More than likely. I'm so sorry I ever brought her here tonight. If only I'd known."

"I'd love to see Sheila's face when Orland confronts her about spilling the beans to Marjorie," Victor said as Clarence hurried past them, carrying a silver tray with a teacup on it.

"Perhaps I should get her home before that happens," Griff said. "She deserves whatever he has to say to her, but another confrontation tonight will delay us until dawn, I'm afraid, and I'm beat."

"Orcott would be furious if you two snuck out on him," Victor said, "but I suppose I could tell him Sheila was taken ill, and you had to get her home."

"He'd never believe it," Griff said, "and it would only make things worse in the long run, so better to get it over with, I guess. Is anyone else still here?"

"William and Lydia haven't left yet," Eve said.

"And I think Agatha's still in the library," Victor said. "I didn't see her leave, and she's usually the very last one out the door, never one to miss a thing."

"Doesn't surprise me," Griff said.

Charlotte emerged from the powder room in the hall clutching her purse and a handkerchief, her eyes red. She hurried past them and went through the front doors without a word.

"Poor Charlotte," Victor said.

"Wait a minute. You and Orland keep saying that, but Mrs. Orcott is the one who's been wronged here, Victor," Eve said. "Charlotte is just as guilty as Mr. Orcott. Tab and Sheila were both right about that."

Victor nodded sheepishly. "Okay, that's true, I admit. Sorry. What a mess."

"You can say that again. Well, I'll go powder my nose, I suppose, since we have a bit of time to kill until Sheila finally comes back inside. If you two will excuse me," Eve said, moving off gracefully down the hall.

Victor and Griff stood together but apart, careful not to get too close in case Agatha or anyone else outside their circle might see. After a few minutes, Eve returned.

"Still no Sheila?" she said.

"Nope, and no Tab, no William, no Lydia, no Agatha, and no Mrs. Orcott," Victor said.

"I suppose I should go out and round Sheila up," Griff said.

"Yes, otherwise we could be here all night," Victor said. "And Orland will be back out soon." As his words escaped his full lips, a sound boomed forth, like nothing any of them had heard before.

"What was that?" Eve said, startled.

"Thunder, maybe," Victor said, looking toward the front windows.

"But we were out on the terrace just a bit ago, and there wasn't a cloud in the sky," Eve said.

"It sounded like it was coming from the back of the house. Maybe fireworks?" Griff said.

"That would be strange. If Orland was going to shoot off fireworks tonight, he would have done it while most of the guests were still here," Victor said.

"That's true," Griff said.

"Oh, hello, there, you three," Agatha said, emerging from the library via the reception room as she pushed her oversized black rimmed glasses back up her nose again. She was breathing heavily. "What on earth was that dreadful noise?"

"None of us are sure, but it sounded like it might have been out on the terrace, Mrs. Mudd," Griff said.

"More likely the study, if you ask me. There's a door to it from the library where I was, but it's locked. It sounded as if it came from in there," Agatha said.

"Hmm, well, let's go have a look in the salon," Victor said.

The four of them, along with a handful of curious servants, including Clarence and various waitstaff from the catering company, hurried into the salon, where the lights were still blazing and the string quartet was finishing packing up. The musicians didn't seem to be bothered by the noise or interested in what had caused it.

William and Lydia came into the salon from the adjacent doors to the dining room, while Tab and Sheila hurried in from the terrace, looking puzzled. "I take it you all heard it, too?" Tab said.

"Yes," Victor said. "We thought it might have come from outside. Fireworks or something."

"We were on the terrace getting some fresh air when we heard the noise. It made me spill my drink, and I dropped my cigarette. We weren't quite sure where the noise came from, but Tab said we should go back inside and see what had happened. When we got there, you all were already there. I mean here. The noise scared the you know what out of me," Sheila said.

"As if my headache wasn't bad enough," Marjorie Orcott said, coming in from the entry hall. "What on earth is going on?"

"Oh, hello, Marjorie," Tab said. "No one seems to know. Where have you been?"

"I was lying down in my room. I got up a bit ago and went to the guest room, as the noise from down here was distracting. I'd just gotten up and was going to come downstairs when I heard whatever that was." She looked down at Tab's feet, shaking her head. "Tab, you're tracking mud on the floor. What have you been up to?"

Tab glanced down at his wet, slightly muddy shoes. "Sorry, Marjorie. The ground is still pretty soggy from the rain this morning. I thought I saw Chowder out in the yard, so I went to investigate, but it was just a squirrel or something. When we heard the noise shortly after that, we hurried back inside, and I didn't think to wipe my feet."

"Chowder?" Eve said.

"The cat," Marjorie said. "She's not allowed outside."

"I know," Tab said. "That's why I wanted to retrieve her if it was her. I thought perhaps she'd snuck out with the party going on. Where is she, anyway?"

"She was in the study," Marjorie said. "And she hopefully still is. That noise must have frightened her terribly."

Victor did a brief head count. "Everyone's here except for Mr. Orcott."

"He was taking a call in his study, remember?" Eve said.

"Yes. Odd that he wouldn't have come out after a sound like that," Victor said. He went over to the study door in the center of the far wall of the salon and wrapped on it with his knuckles.

CHAPTER FOUR

Late Saturday evening, August 12, 1939
The Orcott mansion

"Orland? Mr. Orcott? Are you in there?" Victor said as he pounded on the door. He rattled the brass knob and tried turning it, but the door was locked. He looked over his shoulder. "Agatha, you said there's a door into the study from the library?"

"Yes, but it's locked, too. I tried it when I first heard that awful sound."

"Let's double-check. Maybe it was just stuck," Griff said.

"I know a locked door, Mr. Fenwick," Agatha said, "but suit yourself. And by the way, I'd like to have a friendly chat with you yet tonight since you're still here."

"Uh, sure, Mrs. Mudd, but let's find out what's happened to Mr. Orcott first."

"Yes," Victor said. "Let's double-check that other door, Griff."

"I think we should all go," Marjorie said.

"Fine by me," Victor said. He looked at the butler. "Clarence, keep the other staff here, would you?"

"Certainly, Mr. Marvel."

"Thanks."

"The most direct route is through the reception room," Marjorie said, leading the nine people across the salon and into the reception room, then the library.

"It's that door there, on the left," Tab said as they entered.

"Considering that's the only other door in the library except for the one we just entered, that would make sense," Eve said.

Victor and Tab hurried over to it, knocking and trying the knob, but that door was just as locked as the other one.

"Any other doors into the study?" Griff said.

"Just those two," Tab said.

"I don't suppose there's a key lying around?"

"My father has the only key. Besides, it's probably deadbolted from inside. Maybe we can break one of them down."

Victor looked at the door doubtfully. "We can give it a shot, but they both seem pretty solid."

"It's worth a try," Tab said, backing up. "Stand aside, everyone. I'm the youngest and strongest here. No offense, Griff." Tab took a run at the door and threw himself against it with his shoulder, but the door didn't budge. "God damn it, that hurt," he said, wincing. "My apologies for the language, ladies, but it did."

"No offense taken, Tab," Eve said. "Are you okay? Are you hurt?"

"Just my pride and my dignity," Tab said, rubbing his shoulder. "Victor was right. We have to figure out another way in."

"What about the windows?" Agatha said.

"Good thinking, Mrs. Mudd. There are two windows in the back, overlooking the lawn off the terrace," Tab said. "Those are the only ones. Come on, Victor, Griff, let's see if we can't get in that way."

"All right, let's go," Victor said. "The rest of you stay here in the library. We'll unlock the door once we get in."

Tab, Griff, and Victor hurried out the library and retraced their steps to the closest set of French doors off the salon.

Clarence, Victor noticed, was still there along with a handful of other staff, but most of the others, including the musicians, must have gotten bored and left.

"Is everything okay, Mr. Rockwell?" Clarence said.

"What?" Tab said. "Oh, yes, fine. Maybe, I don't know. I can't talk at the moment, sorry." He hurried out the French doors, Victor and Griff behind him, onto the flagstone terrace, and then he turned right onto the lawn and stepped over some small, low shrubs to reach the two windows of the study.

"They're pretty high off the ground, at least six feet to the bottom sill," Victor said. "The drapes are open on the one, though—give me a boost so I can see in, Griff."

"You'll hurt yourself, old man, let me do it," Tab said. He took off his tuxedo jacket, handed it to Victor, and used the window ledge to hoist himself high enough to peer in. "Oh God," he said as he dropped back to the ground shaking. Even in the dim light of the terrace, Victor could tell he was pale and in shock.

"What did you see, Tab?" Griff said.

"My father. Blood. A lot of blood. He's dead, I'm sure of it. Awful."

"We have to get in there," Victor said.

"Yes, yes, definitely," Tab said. "See if that other window is unlocked." He shoved on the bottom of the one he'd just peered into. "This one is, so that one probably is, too, but check it anyway."

"Right," Griff said. "Give me a hand, Vic." Victor boosted Griff up, which was not an easy task, considering Griff weighed 205 pounds and stood six foot one. The window, as they had feared, wouldn't budge. "It's locked, too, but I can see in through a gap in the curtains," Griff said. "You're right, God, it's awful." Victor dropped Griff, who hit the ground hard with a thud. "Ow, dammit."

"Sorry," Victor said. "Are you all right?"

"Yeah, the ground is soft from all the rain, but something poked me in the behind," Griff said. He reached behind him and retrieved a stretched-out wire coat hanger. "What is this doing out here?"

"A coat hanger?" Victor said, taking it from Griff and examining it in the light from the window. "It's not rusted, so it hasn't been out here long. And there's a piece of twine tied to it. How strange."

"Probably from the groundskeepers, forget it," Tab said, looking around quickly. "We need to get inside, and I don't see any other way." He picked up a large rock from a nearby flower bed and hurled it through the window, the glass shattering into pieces and long shards, most of them falling into the room. Tab wrapped his right hand in his handkerchief. "Help me up, Griff. I can reach in and unlock it, then slide the frame up."

"Sure," Griff said, moving back over to the first window, "but be careful."

"I will," Tab said. "Steady, steady." Standing with one foot in Griff's cupped hands and one foot propped against the wall, he reached in through the broken glass and unlocked the window, sliding it up as more shards and pieces fell from the frame, some of them barely missing Griff below.

"Jesus, Tab," Griff said. "Watch it."

"Sorry. Can you lift me a little higher? I can almost climb in." Griff gave him one final boost, and Tab fell in through the opening, landing on the floor with a thud. Tab got to his feet quickly and helped

Griff up, who then leaned out to assist Victor, who was now holding both Tab's and Griff's tuxedo jackets.

"Ah, guys, why don't you just unlock the door to the salon? I'll come in that way," Victor said.

"Oh, right, good idea," Tab said. He opened the door near him while Victor came back through the French doors and over to the study door from the salon, which was now open.

Victor stepped inside, at once noticing a strong, unpleasant odor. He closed the door to keep Clarence and the others from seeing. Straight ahead were Tab and Griff, their backs to him. As he approached the two men and handed them their tuxedo coats, he took in the scene. It wasn't pretty. It was gruesome, in fact. The remains of Orland Orcott's head were scattered across the surface of the oak floor, staining it dark. His body was covered in more blood and gray matter. His left hand clasped a gun. Nearby was what appeared to be a shattered teacup, its contents spilled on the floor, mixed with the gore.

Victor felt his stomach do a flip-flop, and his face went white. For a moment he thought he might be sick, so he forced himself to look away from the grisly scene.

A cool breeze blew through the open window, but it wasn't enough to dissipate the disgusting smell that hung in the room.

"Oh, my God," Tab said quietly. He looked as if he wanted to rush toward the body, but his feet remained firmly planted in place and his body trembled, his face white.

"What the hell happened?" Griff said.

"It appears he shot himself," Victor said. "I think we'd better call the police. Is there another phone, Tab?"

"Hmm? What?"

"We need to call the police. Is there a phone besides this one?"

"A phone? Oh, uh, there's another extension in the library, through that door there."

"That's right, thanks. I'll be back in a moment. Don't touch anything." He then crossed quickly to the library door, turned the deadbolt, and opened it, closing it behind him as he entered the library. Eve, William, Lydia, Agatha, Sheila, and Marjorie were standing there, all anxiously awaiting word.

"What was that noise?" Eve said. "It sounded like broken glass."

"We had to break one of the windows to get in."

"Is Orland in there?" Marjorie said.

"He is, Marjorie."

"Is he all right? What happened?"

"There's no easy way to say it, I'm afraid. He's dead. I'm so sorry," Victor said.

"What? Dead? Are you sure? How?" Marjorie said.

"A gunshot. I wouldn't recommend any of you going in there. I'm going to call the police," Victor said.

"Of course, I suppose that would be the thing to do. The phone is on the table by the windows," Marjorie said. "May I see him? See his body?"

"Let's wait until the police get here. It's not a pleasant sight, I'm afraid."

"Oh, I suppose. This is unbelievable. Where are Tab and Griff?"

"Right here," Tab said, entering the library with Griff behind him. They had both put their tuxedo coats back on. Griff yanked the heavy door closed once more.

"My God, you two are a sight. You look like you've been in a fistfight," Eve said. "And you've cut your hand, Tab."

"Yeah, I think I've got some glass in my posterior as well. We both climbed in through the broken window," Tab said. "Victor came in through the door."

"Practical, Mr. Marvel."

"I'm afraid I'm too old to be climbing in through broken windows."

"But I'm afraid I still don't understand what's going on. You said Orland was killed by a gunshot. How?" Marjorie said.

"It looks like he killed himself," Victor said.

"Suicide? Really? There's a surprise," she said quietly. "I would have thought someone else shot him. I need a drink, and I need to sit down."

"I'll join you," Tab said. "But I won't be sitting down."

"Fine. You should put some disinfectant on that cut, and, uh, on your posterior."

"I've found whiskey makes a fine disinfectant. I'll worry about my rear end later."

"Suit yourself." She glanced down at the parquet floor. "All *three* of you are tracking mud throughout the house now. I'll have to have the maids mop the floor."

"Sorry, Mrs. Orcott," Griff said. "The ground is wet."

She dismissed it with a wave of her hand. "It's all right, no matter, that's why we have staff. Did you see Chowder in there?"

"The cat? Uh, no, but he may be hiding. I noticed the closet door next to the fireplace was open. He's probably in there," Griff said.

"*She's* probably in there," Marjorie said.

"I do seem to recall seeing a ball of orange and white fluff on the floor in the corner of the closet," Victor said.

"The poor little thing," Marjorie said. "Well, she feels safe there, I'm sure. She'll come out when she's ready. Come on then, Tab, I need a gin and tonic."

The two of them walked over to a concealed bar behind a fake panel of books and poured what looked like two strong drinks, one straight whiskey, as Victor stepped over to the telephone. As he dialed, he noticed Agatha had taken out her notebook and was scribbling furiously. William and Lydia sat on one of the couches by the fireplace, their heads close in quiet conversation, while Sheila paced back and forth, chain-smoking. Griff left to use the lavatory and clean himself up after wiping his shoes clean with his handkerchief. Tab didn't bother.

"I can't believe this, Vic," Eve said, coming up to him as he hung up the phone.

"I can't either, actually. I called the police. They're sending over a squad, an ambulance, and a detective."

"Does Bel Air have its own police department?" Eve said.

"No, it's part of L.A. I remember learning that when I did research for my role as a detective in the Phineas Hart movies I made a few years ago," Victor said. "The police detective who assisted me in my research was most obliging. In fact, he happened to be on duty. They said they would send him over, along with a squad car and an ambulance."

"And we can't leave until they get here, I imagine, so now we wait," Eve said. "I hate waiting."

"Me too," Victor said. "If patience is a virtue, I'm not feeling very virtuous."

"I'm tired, nervous, excited, and sick to my stomach all at the same time. Mr. Orcott doesn't seem like the type of man who would kill himself," Eve said. "And Mrs. Orcott certainly was calm and collected, wasn't she?"

"Now that you mention it, she was. But they weren't exactly on the best of terms."

"Still, he was her husband. She must have felt something for him."

"God knows what. I guess we'll see what the detective has to say."

"Yes, I suppose so. What's his name?"

"Garnett. Steve Garnett."

"He must have made an impression on you," Eve said, and then lowered her voice to a whisper. "Is he, you know…"

Victor shook his head. "No, he's not. He's married, three kids. In his late forties. Nice man, knows his stuff, and he happens to be a fan of mine."

"No wonder you like him."

"I always appreciate my fans. And he's quite a movie buff in general."

"I look forward to meeting him," Eve said.

"He'll probably be here soon. In the meantime, I think Marjorie and Tab have the right idea. I could use another drink, too. Join me?"

"Sure, why not? It sounds like it's going to be a long night."

Chapter Five

Sunday morning, August 13, 1939
Victor Marvel's home

Victor awakened slowly. It hurt to open his eyes. Had the previous night been a dream? A nightmare? Or was it real?

"Hey, you awake?" a deep voice said from somewhere nearby. It sounded familiar. Victor opened one eye and focused. The voice belonged to Griff, sitting up in bed beside him, the sweat on his bare chest glistening in the sunlight through the French doors.

"Ugh, yes. Good morning," Victor said, groaning, his voice hoarse. "Geez, it's so bright in here."

"I opened all the curtains. It's getting late, after ten already."

Victor rubbed his eyes, yawned, stretched, and forced himself to a sitting position. "My tongue feels like sandpaper, and my head is pounding."

"I didn't feel the greatest at first, either," Griff said. "I still don't, though I'm a little better."

"Is Orcott dead?" Victor said, scratching his head.

"What? Of course he is. Why wouldn't he be? What kind of question is that?"

Victor yawned again and shook his head as if trying to clear away the fog in his brain. "I thought it might have all been a dream or a nightmare. It's unreal."

"Your breath is unreal. Get up and brush your teeth. Since it's Sunday and Rose has the day off, I'll make us some breakfast."

"I gave her the whole week off, actually. She went to San Francisco to visit her sister."

"Oh, I didn't know she had a sister there. I must say you look rough this morning, Vic."

"Thanks a lot," Victor said, belching. "Excuse me."

"You're excused. You definitely drank too much last night. We both did. There's a glass of water and two aspirin on your nightstand. I took a couple earlier."

Victor picked up the two aspirin and downed them in one swallow along with a swig of water. "You're the best, Griff."

"I know."

Victor forced a smile and looked over at Griff. "Why do you look so good if you're hungover, too? And why are you still in bed?"

"The advantages of being younger, I suppose. I've been awake since about eight thirty. I got up, peed, opened the drapes, took some aspirin, and got back into bed. I didn't want to disturb you as you were sleeping so soundly. And snoring a bit, I might add."

"Sorry."

"It's okay."

"So, you've just been sitting there watching me sleep for an hour and a half?" Victor said.

"Yeah, and I've thinking about last night."

"Oh? What about it?"

"Lots of things. Everything. I've been going over everything that happened. Over and over and over."

"Sounds productive. It was a crazy evening, that's for sure." Victor reached across and ran his index finger down the center of Griff's chest. "I wish I could have danced with you at the party."

"Me too, but not a chance of that, unfortunately."

"Yeah, the world we live in."

"You know, since Rose is off all week, we could always put on a record in the living room later on and dance the night away."

"Not quite the same," Victor said, "but still, it's a capital idea. I'll lead."

"If we ever get out of bed."

"All right, all right. Do I have time for a shower before breakfast?"

"Sure. I haven't showered yet, either."

Victor threw back the covers and got up with a groan, stretching the full length of his naked body in a shaft of sunlight. "Oh, really?"

"Really," Griff said with a wicked grin. "We could shower together if you're feeling up to it."

Victor grinned back. "That sounds like the best cure for a hangover ever invented. I'm definitely up for it. If not now, I soon will be once you get your naked self out from under those covers."

"That, Mr. Marvel, is a deal," Griff said, clambering out of bed and striding off toward the adjoining bathroom as Victor watched his cute, white behind wiggle back and forth and up and down. At the door, Griff turned and looked at him. "You coming?"

"Not yet, but I will be, I'm sure. Turn the water on, hot."

The shower was over far too soon for either man's liking, but each of them had more or less finished, and Victor found the persistent ringing telephone in the bedroom hard to ignore. He gave Griff another passionate kiss, opened the shower door, and hurried to the nightstand, a towel hastily wrapped about his waist.

"Hello?" Vic said.

"Good morning, Victor, it's William Taylor. I hope I'm not disturbing you."

"Oh, good morning, William. I just got out of the shower, but I can talk for a bit."

"Okay. I didn't sleep very well last night. Neither did Lydia. I suppose you didn't, either."

"Actually, I did. But I had a few more drinks after I got home, and I'm feeling it this morning. Griff tossed and turned, I guess."

"Is he there?"

"Yeah, he spent the night. His place is being fumigated starting tomorrow morning, so he's moving in here for a few days. He dropped Sheila off after we left Orcott's and came over."

"What about your housekeeper?"

"Rose has the week off. She's visiting her sister up north. But she's worked for me for five years. I think she knows the score."

"Still, better to err on the side of caution."

"I know. That's why I gave her the week off when Griff asked if he could move in temporarily."

"Good thinking. How is Eve doing?"

"She was pretty shaken up and exhausted when I took her home last night."

"Understandable."

"Yeah. I'll give her a call later."

"So, uh, what's going to happen to the picture?" William said.

"What picture?" Victor said, turning his head to watch Griff, who had emerged from the bathroom and was now slowly toweling off his naked body.

"The film, the movie, *The Lady Screeched*. Will it still be made?"

"Hmm? Oh, that. Yes, certainly. Orcott was only the director, and no matter what *he* believed, directors, even him, *are* replaceable. The producer, Dick Sharp, or perhaps old Mr. Rainier himself will assign someone else to direct. The film will be made, though it might be delayed a bit."

"That's pretty much what I figured, and I'm glad to hear it," William said. "I can use the money."

"Hmm? What was that?"

"I said I'm glad to hear it because I can use the money. I haven't worked in over two years, and I've had a lot of medical bills."

"Oh, sure. Don't worry about it, William. Shooting will probably only be delayed a week or two, I'm willing to bet. They'll bring in a different director, and it will all be swell. Probably better."

"Couldn't be much worse than it was with Orcott," William said.

Victor watched as Griff tugged on a clean pair of white underwear from a stash he kept in one of Victor's dresser drawers. "I'm sure it will be better, William. In fact, I'd say things are looking really good right now."

"I'm glad you're confident. Lydia and I are both nervous about everything. I never thought Orcott would kill himself like that."

"Say again?" Marvel said. Griff had pulled on a pair of black over-the-calf socks and was now buttoning up a crisp white dress shirt.

"I said, I never thought Orcott would kill himself like that. Are you okay? You seem distracted this morning, Victor."

"Sorry, William, something caught my eye," Victor said, winking at Griff, who was now tugging up gray suit pants from a spare suit he kept in the closet, along with one of Vic's ties and a black leather belt.

"Uh-huh, and I bet I know what that something, or *someone*, is," William said. "So, I take it we won't be expected at the studio Monday morning."

"Correct. I'll make some phone calls and see if I can figure out what they want us to do and when they do want us to report, if they don't call me first. To be honest, when I heard the phone ringing, I figured it was the studio. I'm sure they know every sordid detail by now."

"You can say that again, along with everyone else in this city. It's on the front page of the morning edition. And you should see the 'Slinging Mudd' column Agatha wrote."

"I can just imagine. I haven't read the paper yet today."

"Well, it's a doozy. Her headline was all about Orcott blowing his brains out, of course, but then she got into who was all there. She was complimentary about you, Griff, and Eve, anyway. She didn't mention me by name, but she did say, and I quote, 'and a former leading man, assigned to a supporting role in the Icon Studios upcoming picture that Orland Orcott was set to direct, is looking far less like a matinee idol these days and more like a tired and worn-out old man. Sources say it's for his part in *The Lady Screeched*, but this reporter wonders if there's more to it than meets the eye.' "

"Ouch, sorry."

"It's okay, at least she didn't use my name."

"That's something, anyway," Victor said, tucking the phone under his chin so he could help Griff with his tie. Griff kissed him on the forehead and left when Victor had finished, presumably headed to the kitchen. "You can thank Eve for telling Agatha your appearance was for the movie, by the way."

"Oh, really? That was nice of her," William said. "She's a good egg."

"One of the best. Agatha seemed impressed with her. I think she liked Eve."

"And Agatha likes you, you lucky bastard. Anyway, Agatha goes on to mention Charlotte Masters in her column, along with Tab and someone by the name of Tony Bolt, who she mysteriously linked to Tab."

"Oh boy. Anything else?"

"That's the gist of it."

"Okay, thanks. I'll read it over breakfast. Are you and Lydia going to be home later?"

"Sure, we don't have any plans today, why?"

"I'm just still thinking, that's all. Would you mind if I stopped over for a visit sometime this evening?"

"You're always welcome, Vic, you know that."

"Thanks. If I can't make it, I'll let you know. Gotta run for now."

"Okay, bye."

"Bye." Victor hung up the receiver, finished drying off, and quickly dressed, putting on blue serge slacks, black socks, wingtips, a white dress shirt with gold cuff links, and a red paisley tie, held in place with a gold tie bar. With a final glimpse in the full-length mirror, he grabbed a sport coat and hurried out the door and into the hall. Victor descended the broad, tiled staircase of the surprisingly modest Spanish-style house to the first floor and proceeded to the kitchen at the back of the house. Griff, wearing a floral apron that belonged to Rose, was busy frying up eggs.

Victor stifled a laugh at the sight of him. "Oh my, if your female fans could only see you now."

Griff grinned. "I don't think they'd mind. Women like a domesticated man, I'm told. Anyway, coffee's brewing. Pour the orange juice, make some toast, and set the table."

"Yes, sir," Vic said, setting about to perform the duties.

"Oh, I brought the newspaper in, too. It's on the table."

"Thanks."

"You're welcome. What did William want?"

"To be reassured the movie would still be made and to tell me Orcott's suicide made the front page, speaking of the newspaper. Also, we're mentioned in Agatha's column—flatteringly, apparently."

"She must have done an all-nighter to get that in the morning edition. It was late by the time we left Orcott's house."

"Very late. She probably phoned some of it in to the night editor's desk while Detective Garnett was questioning the rest of us," Victor said, removing the toast and placing it on a plate on the table next to the orange juice.

"That makes sense."

"Yeah, and speaking of Detective Garnett, I'm thinking I'd like to swing by the station and have a chat with him after breakfast."

"About what?" Griff said.

"About last night. Something just doesn't feel right to me. I'll call after we're done eating and see if he's in and can spare a few minutes."

"What doesn't feel right?" Griff said, finishing up the eggs and serving them.

"Orcott killing himself. It seems out of character."

"I agree, but what does it matter? He's dead, and I can't say I'm brokenhearted about it, and I doubt anyone else is, including his wife and son," Griff said.

Victor took a seat as Griff removed the apron and sat down opposite him at the breakfast table. "You're probably right, but I'd still like to talk to Garnett. Want to come along?"

Griff shook his head. "I would, but I need to get home and pack a few things and get the house ready for the fumigators tomorrow morning. I'll swing back here after lunch."

"Okay, let yourself in and make yourself comfortable."

"I will. I have lines to study for when we eventually do make this picture. Eve has hers down pat already, but I'm still struggling. Maybe I'll go over them out by your pool and do a few laps, too."

"All right. Leave your tuxedo and things from last night here. I'll have them cleaned and pressed and sent over to your place next week when they're ready."

"Fine, the fumigators should be finished by Wednesday."

"You're welcome to stay as long as you like. Rose won't be back until next Sunday afternoon. The eggs are delicious, by the way."

"Thanks. Since I cooked, you can clean up. And don't you dare leave the dirty dishes in the sink for Rose to do when she returns."

Victor smiled. "I won't, I promise, though I'm not sure what good having a housekeeper is if you can't have her clean up after you."

"You keep her plenty busy, and no one wants to come back to a week's worth of dirty dishes piled in the sink. It will be bad enough for her as it is. You're not the neatest person in the world, you know."

Victor chuckled, wiping his mouth with a blue checkered napkin. "Guilty as charged, Mr. Fenwick. Let's finish eating and then I'll call Detective Garnett. And yes, after that, I'll do the dishes, and I promise to try and keep the place tidy."

CHAPTER SIX

Sunday morning, August 13, 1939
The police station

Victor watched as Griff drove away from the house in his new, baby blue Alfa Romeo, then called the police station and asked to speak with Detective Garnett. Luckily, he was at his desk, and he told Victor he would be available to talk anytime within the next two hours or so.

Victor hung up the phone and did the dishes. Leaving the frying pan to soak in the sink, he put on his suit coat, grabbed his hat, and headed out the kitchen door. The morning was beautiful and sunny, as most mornings in LA are, so he drove his Cadillac convertible with the top down to the West Los Angeles Community Police Station on Butler Avenue. It was an unassuming two-story brick building, and, surprisingly, he found a place to park almost directly in front. He left the top down and went up the steps into the lobby and general room of the station, removing his hat once he got inside.

The desk sergeant, a burly middle-aged man with wide-set eyes and one long eyebrow that looked like a wooly caterpillar, looked at Victor blankly and spoke in a monotone. "How may I help you, sir?"

"Good morning, I'm Victor Marvel. Detective Steve Garnett is expecting me."

The burly man gave Victor no indication that he recognized Victor's face or his name. He must not have been a moviegoer.

"Hang on." He picked up a telephone and dialed a number, waited a moment, and then said into the receiver, "Some guy named Marvel to see you, Detective. Victor Marvel. Okay, gotcha." He replaced the receiver and stared blandly at Victor. "He said he'll be out in a minute. Have a seat. Or don't. Your choice."

"Thank you," Victor said, but the sergeant appeared not to have heard. Victor looked around the general room, which was fairly busy for a Sunday morning, and tried to find an out-of-the-way place to sit. After making a few rounds of the space, he decided to lean against a Coke machine that had an Out of Order sign affixed to it and observe the other people in the room while he waited. Victor enjoyed doing that, and often used the interesting ones as character studies for parts he played.

A few cops, he noticed, were milling about, drinking coffee and chatting with members of the public, some of whom were apparently not so law-abiding. A thin, younger man with a maniacal look in his dark eyes was handcuffed and had been placed on a beat-up wooden bench against a wall. He wasn't wearing shoes, and he had a fat lip that looked sore and tender. He had probably been sitting there since very early that morning. When he grinned at Victor, he saw he was missing a couple of teeth, though Victor couldn't tell if the loss was recent or not. Another man, this one not handcuffed, looked terrified as one of the cops talked to him quietly at a desk. Victor wondered what the cop was saying to him.

After about five minutes, a fairly attractive, forty-something, sandy blond-haired man appeared, dressed in a rumpled brown suit with a green tie. His eyes were bright if a tad bloodshot, and he smiled at the sight of Victor. "Good morning. Sorry to keep you waiting, Mr. Marvel."

Victor straightened up and shook the detective's proffered hand firmly. "Not a problem at all. Thanks for seeing me, Detective, and please call me Victor."

"All right, thanks, and I'm Steve, of course. I know you've told me that before, but old habits, and all that. I mean, you being a big movie star and all…"

"Honestly, Steve, I'm just your average citizen who happens to make movies for a living."

"Yeah, sure, I know, but it's still pretty nifty. Anyway, I must admit I was surprised you wanted to see me this morning. I take it this has something to do with what happened last night."

"Yeah, though I'm not exactly sure what."

"I'm not sure, either. I spoke with everyone, including all of the household staff, and took statements. It got fairly late."

"I know. Is there someplace private we can talk?"

Garnett nodded. "Sure, follow me. Want some coffee? It's rotgut, but it keeps you awake. I haven't had much sleep lately."

"I'm fine, thanks, and sorry to hear about you not getting to sleep."

Garnett set off down a narrow hall as Victor followed behind. "Hazard of the trade," he said over his shoulder. "Orcott's suicide created a mountain of paperwork for me, and then there was the press to deal with. VIP deaths are always a pain in the ass, no offense."

"None taken. I understand."

"Thanks." He stopped in front of a door marked *Interrogation Room 2*. "This one should be empty. We can talk in here." Steve opened the door, flicked on a bright overhead light, and ushered Victor inside, closing it behind them. "Please, have a seat."

"Thanks," Victor said. He set his fedora on the worn wooden table and took a seat across from Steve. Someone had scratched a limerick into the surface of the table, and he shifted his hat to read the rest of it aloud. "'There once was a mayor named Shaw/who thought he was above the law./He cheated and lied,/and oh how he cried/when they forced him to withdraw.'" Victor looked over at Steve and chuckled. "Someone didn't care for former Mayor Frank Shaw."

"Nope. He did some good work, but his alleged mishandling of public funds forced him from office. Hopefully, Mayor Bowron will do a better job." He glanced down at the limerick and shook his head. "We need to get this table sanded down and restained."

"Good idea," Victor said. He looked around as he loosened his tie and shirt collar. The room they were in was a small cubicle, with barely enough space for the table and two armless chairs, and it was about ten degrees warmer in there than it had been in the previous room. There were no windows, but a large mirror on the wall was behind the chair the detective was sitting in. Victor wondered if it was a two-way mirror, like the one in a movie he'd once been in.

As if reading Victor's thought, Garnett said, "I'm sorry it's not more plush, but it's private, anyway. And yeah, that's a two-way mirror, but don't worry, we're not being observed."

"Okay, good. That's good. What I want to discuss is private."

"So I gathered," Steve said, unbuttoning his suit coat and making himself somewhat comfortable. "So, what can I do for you?"

"Well, I was hoping you had some information about what happened to Orcott."

Steve cocked his head quizzically. "Information? Not much to tell,

Victor. I'd say it's pretty much an open-and-shut case of suicide. Mr. Orcott was shot in the head at close range. The murder weapon was in his hand. Death appears to have been instantaneous. I'll know more after I see the autopsy results, but the bullet blew most of his brains all over the place. It was quite a mess, as you saw for yourself."

"You can say that again. I almost threw up, to be honest."

"Yup, it wasn't a pretty sight. It's amazing how much stuff our body holds. Did you know there are about 60,000 miles of arteries, capillaries, and veins in the human body? That's the equivalent of two and a half times around the world."

"That's a fascinating fact to pull out your hat, Steve. How do you happen to know that?"

Steve shrugged. "My old man wanted me to be a doctor like him, and I went to school for it for a while, but it was just too much."

"Too much?"

"Too much studying, too many tests, and it seemed like it would never end. I thought being on the police force would be easier. There are days I could kick myself."

"Yes, I can imagine it can be pretty stressful."

"To say the least."

"Believe me, being a movie star isn't all it's cracked up to be, either."

"I suppose. Walk a mile in my shoes, eh?"

"Right. Uh, is there any information on the gun that was used last night?" Victor said.

"Sure, it was a .38 Smith and Wesson. Appears to have been just one shot fired, but that was obviously more than enough. The bullet most likely lodged somewhere in his skull, or what's left of it. If it's in there, the coroner will find it."

Victor shivered, in spite of the room being quite warm. "Brutal. Did the gun belong to Mr. Orcott?"

"Yes. His son, uh, damn, I forget the son's name. I should have brought the file."

"Tab Rockwell," Victor said. "He's an actor, too."

"Yeah, I learned that last night when I got his statement. Can't say I've seen anything he's been in, and you know I go to the movies whenever I can. The wife likes them, you know."

"Sure, Steve, I know."

"Yeah, well, anyway, what were we talking about?"

"I asked you if Orcott killed himself with his own gun."

"Oh yeah, sorry." He wiped some sweat off his brow with his handkerchief and rubbed his eyes. "Dammit, I'm tired. But yeah, he did use his own gun. We checked the serial number, and it was registered to Orland Orcott. Also, Mr. Rockwell confirmed last night his father kept a revolver in the top right drawer of the desk he was sitting at when he shot himself. I checked the desk once the body had been removed."

"Oh?"

"Yes, it's standard procedure. There wasn't anything unusual, just a blotter, an inkwell, a calendar, the telephone, and a writing pad on the desktop, all spattered with dried blood stains. In the drawers were pencils, blotting papers, typewriter paper and ribbon, stationery, postage stamps, sealing wax, envelopes, a fountain pen, extra nibs, and whatnot. In one of the drawers, there was an empty space where the gun had most likely been kept. All that was there now was a cleaning rag and a box of ammunition," Garnett said. "Oh, and by the way, that drawer was jimmied."

"What? Someone broke into the drawer where the gun was kept?" Victor said, both of his perfectly shaped brows rising dramatically.

"Yup. Recently, too. The minute wood scraps on the floor matched up."

"Hmm, so it could have been murder."

"Why? When someone wants to kill himself, he doesn't much care if he damages a drawer to get at a gun."

"But surely Orcott would have had the key. Why would he have forced the lock on his own drawer?"

Steve shrugged, rubbed his eyes again, and lit a cigarette. "Want one?"

"No, thanks. I don't smoke."

"Suit yourself," Steve said, leaning back in the wooden chair. He looked worn out and in need of a solid eight hours of sleep. "Who knows? Maybe he lost the key, or it was upstairs, or he was just angry, depressed, and frustrated and didn't want to mess around with a key. Sometimes the shortest distance between two points is blunt force. You and several others said in your statements that he seemed agitated by the argument with his wife earlier last night."

"True, but I knew Orland Orcott fairly well. He wasn't the type to kill himself, especially over a fight with his wife."

Garnett took a long drag on the cigarette and blew the smoke up toward the ceiling light, where it swirled about. "I got the impression from just about everyone who was there last night that Orcott was kind of a jerk. No one seemed all that upset that he was dead, including Mrs. Orcott. But regardless, he was by himself in a locked room, and he was holding his own gun. Three witnesses, including you, all told me the same thing."

Victor sighed. "Yeah, I know. You're right, of course."

"I'm planning on reporting it as a suicide unless I get the coroner's report back and there's something in it I'm not seeing, which I doubt."

"Suicide makes the most sense," Victor said, "but it just doesn't seem right."

Steve took another drag and stared at the cigarette between his nicotine-stained fingers. "I really should quit these. My wife doesn't like them."

"Orcott smoked like a chimney, mostly cigars."

"My wife would never abide me smoking cigars."

"I don't think Mrs. Orcott liked them, either, but I'm sure Orland didn't give a damn. He could be a real son of a bitch."

"Yeah, I got that impression," Steve said.

"But I don't believe he'd shoot himself. The whole thing just makes me curious."

Garnett glanced at his wristwatch and then back at Victor. "I know you're a curious fellow, Victor. I remember that from all the questions you asked me a couple of years ago."

"I probably drove you nuts, but I appreciated you helping me out with my research for the three Phineas Hart films."

"I was glad to do it. And I appreciated the invite to watch the filming, and the tickets to the premieres. Mrs. Garnett was thrilled, and to be honest, I was pretty tickled, too."

"I'm glad, and I would be happy to do that again for you. We're getting ready to start filming *The Lady Screeched*, starring Griffin Fenwick, Eve Spellman, and myself."

"The wife's a big fan of Mr. Fenwick, and of you, of course. She was tickled pink to get that autographed picture of you."

"I could get her one of Griff, too, and of Miss Spellman and William Taylor, along with an invite to the studio to watch us film one day."

"In return for?" Steve said.

"Any other information about Orland Orcott's death that you have or will get."

"That's a sucker's trade, Victor. I got nothing for ya. It was suicide."

"But you told me the lock on the drawer was forced."

Steve ground out his cigarette in a cheap metal ashtray perched precariously on the edge of the table and leaned forward. "Look, I remember the stock market crash of '29, when a lot of folks went crazy. Believe me, none of them thought twice about whether they were going to land on some innocent schmuck walking down below when they jumped out of that window, or what was going to happen to their wives and kids, and they sure as hell didn't care if they broke the window on their way out and down. And the ones that shot themselves, well, those who weren't successful I'm sure never thought about the chance they could blind or cripple themselves because the shot missed the brain and landed in their neck, but that happened, too. When someone's got suicide on the brain, so to speak, they don't think clearly."

"When someone's got murder on the brain, they don't think too clearly either, Steve. Besides, a friend of mine who's a Broadway actor in New York told me people didn't really jump out of windows when the market crashed."

"Maybe they did, maybe they didn't, but it doesn't matter. Whatever the reason, people aren't thinking straight when they want to kill themselves."

"Fair enough. Was there a suicide note?"

Garnett snorted through his large, hairy nostrils. "Not that we found, and me and the boys went over the room with a fine-toothed comb last night. Not every suicide leaves a note, though. In fact, a lot of 'em don't."

"Okay."

"Honestly, Victor. What makes you think it was anything *but* suicide? It sure as hell wasn't an accident."

"It could have been an accident, now that you mention it. Maybe he was cleaning it and it discharged as he looked down the barrel."

"Unlikely. The gun was fully loaded. Only an idiot would clean a gun without emptying the chambers first."

"Hmm. You said you searched the room thoroughly. What about the fireplace? Could someone have hidden up there after shooting Orcott?"

"The chimney's too small, I checked. No one came in or out that way either," Garnett said, his thick arms now folded across his even thicker chest. "It could use a bit of sweeping, though, pretty dirty up there."

"I must say you're nothing if not thorough, Steve."

"Thanks."

"So, no one could get in the room and no one could get out. He was shot in the head at close range, in a room by himself, locked from the inside. If it wasn't suicide, how could it be murder?"

"It couldn't, Victor. I'd bet beer money on it."

"It's a big old house, though. What about secret doors or compartments, or trap doors in the floor or ceiling?"

"You've been watching too many of your old movies."

Victor smiled. "After playing Detective Hart three times, I guess I got the investigation bug."

"You definitely did. But yeah, we checked for secret doors, too. Two of the walls are outside walls, another one is shared with the salon, and the other with the library. The ceiling, floors, and all the walls are solid."

Victor whistled softly. "Like I said, you're thorough, and you know your stuff, Steve."

"Thanks. Lots of experience over the years."

"But why would Orcott lock himself in like that and shoot himself with a big party going on?"

"Beats me, these rich types do all sorts of queer stuff. And you all stated the party was winding down when it happened. Maybe he was, too, in more ways than one. Anyway, I'm beat, and I've still got lots of things to get done before I can go home to Sally and the kids. Is there anything else you needed?"

Victor shook his head and picked up his hat off the table. He jostled the wooden chair back, which scraped against the linoleum, and stood up. "No, I guess not. Thanks for taking the time to speak with me. And I'll see to it you get some autographed photos and an invitation to the studio for you and Sally."

"I appreciate it," Garnett said, getting to his feet also, buttoning his suit coat once more, and shaking Victor's hand again.

"My pleasure. But please do let me know if you find anything else out and if the coroner's report reveals anything unusual."

Steve frowned slightly. "I'll see what I can do. That's generally private information until entered in the public record and the death certificate is issued, but considering it's you, well, I might be able to divulge a thing or two, depending."

"Thanks. I don't want you to get into any trouble, though."

"It's fine. The chief's a big fan, too. It would help if you could manage a few personalized autographed photos for him, too, though. The name's Stanley Claggot."

"You got it. One 'T' or two?"

"Two 'G's, one 'T.' "

"Perfect. I'll see if I can't get Chief Claggot a studio pass, also. See you later, Steve, I can find my own way out."

Chapter Seven

Sunday afternoon, August 13, 1939
The Orcott mansion

Victor left the police station and climbed behind the wheel of his car. The Orcott mansion wasn't all that far away, and it was still fairly early in the day, so he decided to drop by and pay his respects to Tab and Mrs. Orcott. On the way, he pulled into A.K.'s Drive-In. The carhop, on roller skates, recognized him, asked for an autograph, and comped his fifty-cent bill for a cheeseburger, fries, and a chocolate milkshake. He left a dollar tip along with the autograph.

The gates to the Orcott estate were closed when he arrived, so he pressed the intercom button, let the unseen person behind the tinny voice know who he was, and waited as the gates swung slowly open. As he did on the night of the party, and a few times before that, he drove slowly up the drive to the main house, stopping before the massive front doors. No white-jacketed young men were there to park his car this time, though. He shut off the engine, climbed out, and went up the steps. Before he could ring the bell, one of the doors opened.

"Ah, Mr. Marvel," the uniformed man said. He was perhaps in his early fifties and impeccably groomed, with black hair peppered throughout with salty white.

"Oh, hello, yes, Clarence, isn't it?" Victor said.

"That's right, sir. They told me you were at the gate."

"Of course. Is Mrs. Orcott in?"

"Is she expecting you, sir?"

"No, but I was hoping to speak with her for a few moments. If it's a bad time, I can come back or telephone."

Clarence considered for just the briefest of moments before

speaking. "I'm not sure if she will be up for visitors at the moment, considering."

"I realize it's soon, but would you mind terribly checking with her since I'm here?"

He nodded almost imperceptibly. "Certainly, Mr. Marvel, do come in." He stood aside and Victor entered, removing his hat. He waited just inside while Clarence closed the door behind him. "May I take your hat, sir?"

"Oh, no, thank you. I won't be here all that long. I don't wish to intrude."

"I'm sure the family appreciates you paying your respects, Mr. Marvel. I'll let Mrs. Orcott know you're here."

"Thank you, Clarence. I'm sorry about Mr. Orcott, by the way."

"It was a surprise, certainly, sir," Clarence said, though he appeared to be the type of person who was never surprised and rarely showed any emotion.

"Yes, it certainly was," Victor said. "By the way, Mr. Orcott asked you to bring him a bromide in some peppermint tea last night, didn't he?"

"That's right, sir, just after I told him he had a telephone call. He often had a bromide and peppermint tea when he was agitated. It helped his stomach, you know."

"Right, and I'm guessing he was agitated rather frequently."

"Indeed he was, Mr. Marvel, and he certainly was last night."

"Do you know who it was on the telephone? It was late for a casual call."

"Yes, it was most unusual. I was quite surprised when I heard it ringing. I'm afraid I've no idea who was on the line, though, Mr. Marvel. I asked for a name, but the caller refused. All he would say is that he needed to speak with Mr. Orcott immediately, and it was most urgent and personal."

"You're sure it was a man?"

"It sounded like a man, sir, but no, I wouldn't swear to it. It was a bit muffled."

"Okay. Which door did you enter the study from when you brought him the tea and bromide?"

He cocked his head ever so slightly. "Which door? Why, the one off the salon, sir."

"All right, and when you entered the study, did you notice anything unusual?"

"Unusual? No, sir, not that I can think of."

"What *did* you notice, then? How did the room look?"

"The same as always, Mr. Marvel, why do you ask?"

"I, uh, just want to make sure I didn't miss anything when I gave my statement to the police detective last night. You didn't notice anything unusual? No furniture out of place or anything?"

"No, sir. Mr. Orcott was on the telephone at his desk when I came in. He seemed quite annoyed and irritated by whoever it was he was speaking to, and his voice was loud. The drapes on both windows were drawn, the closet door to the left of the fireplace was closed, and the overhead light and the desk lamp were both on. Quite typical of how it always was in the evenings when he was in there. There is one thing that seemed odd, though, now that I think about it."

"What was that?"

"The cat, Miss Chowder. Normally when she's in the study with Mr. Orcott, she's perched on the armchair in the corner, napping or just casually observing through half-closed eyes. But last night she was pacing about the room, back and forth, and meowing. She went round the desk a couple of times, over and back from the closet, the door to the library, and the windows, and jumped up on the desk at one point."

"Sounds like she was agitated by something, too," Victor said.

"Yes, sir, not like her at all. She's usually a quiet, well-behaved little kitty."

"Hmm. Maybe Mr. Orcott's voice and mannerisms upset her. So, besides the cat, though, everything seemed normal?"

"As far as I could tell, yes, sir."

"And you gave Mr. Orcott the tea?"

"He motioned for me to leave it, so I set it on the desk and left."

"The door was unlocked when you first entered?"

"Yes, sir."

"What about the door to the library?"

"I'm afraid I couldn't say, Mr. Marvel. It was closed, but whether or not it was locked would have been impossible for me to tell."

"Naturally, sorry. After you left the tea, did the door to the salon remain unlocked?"

"Again, I do not know, sir. I closed it behind me, of course, but I'm not sure if Mr. Orcott got up and locked it immediately or not, though of course at some point he must have locked both doors."

"Yes, that makes sense. And he opened the drapes on one of the windows and the closet door at some point, too."

"Is that so, Mr. Marvel?"

"Er, yes. When Griffin Fenwick, Tab, and I were outside after we heard the shot, we noticed the drapes on the window nearest the door to the salon were open, and after entering the room, we saw the closet door was open, too, yet you said they were all closed when you brought the tea and bromide."

"That's correct. Had they not been, I would have noticed and would have said so."

"I'm sure."

"I wasn't aware of the drapes or closet door being opened after I left, Mr. Marvel, but I didn't go back in the study after I brought Mr. Orcott the tea."

"I understand, Clarence."

"Thank you. Was there anything else, sir?"

"Just one more thing. While you were in the study, you must have overheard some of what Mr. Orcott was saying into the telephone."

"Naturally, Mr. Marvel. It would have been impossible not to. As I said, he was speaking quite loudly. But in my position, I always respect the privacy of my employers. It's expected."

"I'm afraid it's important, Clarence. I suspect there may be more to Mr. Orcott's death than we're being led to believe, and so does the police detective."

Clarence looked almost mildly surprised. "You don't say, sir. Well, even if I wished to disclose his conversation, I doubt it would do much good. Mr. Orcott only said things like 'What do you mean by that' and 'I don't like what you're implying,' and just before I left the room, he said something like 'You want me to hold the line? For how long?' "

"Fascinating. So, he didn't indicate whether or not he knew the person he was speaking to."

"No, sir, he did not. Is there anything else you require at the moment, Mr. Marvel?"

"Uh, no, thank you, that will do it."

"Very good. I'll announce you to Mrs. Orcott and see if she's willing and able to see you. If you'll just wait here a moment."

"Certainly," Victor said.

Clarence turned on a practiced, well-polished heel and stepped away briskly through the reception room and the library beyond.

While Victor waited, hat in hand, he studied the entrance hall, noting the oil paintings, the Spanish tile, the intricate wrought iron railing on the curved stair, and the crystal chandelier glistening overhead. The center table held a fresh bouquet of callas, zinnias, and China asters, most likely cut from the garden that morning, and the air smelled fresh and perfumed. It was as if last night had never happened. He was sure the interior of the study was a different story, however.

After just a few moments, Clarence returned, his pace slow and practiced. “Mrs. Orcott will see you, Mr. Marvel, if you will kindly follow me.”

“Lead the way, my good man.”

Clarence turned once more and walked back across the entrance hall into the reception room and the library door on the opposite side. With a white-gloved hand, he knocked firmly.

“Come in,” Victor heard Marjorie say.

Clarence opened the door and stepped inside. “Mr. Marvel to see you, ma’am.”

“Fine, fine, show him in, please.”

Clarence stepped aside as Victor entered, but he remained at the open door, hands behind his back, awaiting further instruction.

In this room, too, Victor noticed, everything seemed back to normal. The muddy footprints had been wiped away along with all traces of the chaos and tragedy of the night before.

Marjorie Orcott was seated on one of the low, dark green velvet sofas that flanked the fireplace, and Victor stepped over to her. She gazed at him as he approached. She was an attractive woman, of course, but also sensible, smart, and savvy. Not the kind of woman Victor imagined would marry a man like Orcott. Her hair, the color of a raven, had been let down so that it fell upon her soft shoulders. Her lips were full and crimson, and her skin was almost luminescent, a delicate shade of ivory. She was wearing a knee-length black dress with a beaded hemline in violet. On her left breast was an unusual brooch, outshone only by a dazzling diamond on her left ring finger. Next to her on the sofa, a small, plump, orange and white cat was stretched out, looking at him suspiciously through half-closed eyes.

“Victor, good afternoon. This is a surprise.”

“I’m sorry to intrude, Mrs. Orcott.”

She waved away the thought with her ringed hand. “Not at all. I welcome the distraction.”

“Still, I’m sure this must be a difficult time for you.”

“I’m still in a bit of shock in many ways, to be honest. And please call me Marjorie. I’d like it if you did. We’ve known each other for a while now, albeit not well.”

"All right, thank you, Marjorie. I believe we first met just after your marriage to Mr. Orcott."

"Yes, nearly six years ago, hard to believe. Orland threw that big party for us after the ceremony. You were there with some pretty young woman, but I can't recall her name."

"I can't either, to be honest," Victor said. "I remember how lovely you looked, though."

"Thank you, that's kind." Her crimson lips formed a soft smile, and she closed her eyes for just a moment. "I should have known then."

"Known what?"

She opened them again. "About my husband, of course. It was a reception of sorts, since our wedding was small. Halfway through the evening, Orland vanished into thin air, and so did one of the young starlets he'd invited from the studio. He claimed later he was just giving her advice on her career." She chortled. "She was taking what he was giving, but I'm sure it wasn't advice."

"I'm sorry."

"Don't be. As I said, I should have known right then. Now, have a seat, please. May I offer you anything? Coffee, tea, or a cocktail?"

"No, thank you," Victor said, settling into the other green velvet sofa, which faced her. He set his hat on the marble coffee table. "I'm fine."

"That will be all then, Clarence," Marjorie said.

"Yes, ma'am." He stepped back out and closed the door quietly.

"He's a good man," Victor said.

"Clarence? Yes, one of the best. I adore him. He's worked here over fifteen years. Now that Orland's gone, I intend to give all the household staff raises. That's something he never allowed me to do while he was alive."

"That's admirable of you, Marjorie."

"They've been underpaid for far too long. I'm just righting a wrong."

"Still, it's considerate, especially with the economy the way it is. That's a beautiful cat, by the way," Victor said. "I take it that's Chowder."

"Yes, the one and only. Cats fascinate me."

"In what way?" Victor said.

"Oh, cats are marvelous creatures, and quite beautiful. They're very misunderstood, though, and very mysterious. You can try and force them to do things, but sooner or later they do what they want, don't they? Cats can't truly be owned, you see, not like people, or some people anyway. Cats will be with who they want to be with, eventually."

"I suppose that's true. They're different than dogs."

"Dogs are loyal to anyone who feeds them, but cats are independent. I envy that. She started out being mine, but somehow, and for some reason, she was attracted to Orland."

"That happens sometimes."

"Of course, that's what I'm saying. Cats will be with who they want to be with."

"Curious."

"She's a curious cat. She's polydactyl, as you may have noticed."

"Poly what?" Victor said.

She smiled again. "Polydactyl. She has extra toes on her feet, which makes her extra special."

Chowder looked up at her and blinked, putting one of her big paws up on her leg.

"It's as if she knows we're talking about her," Marjorie said.

"Perhaps she does. I love all animals, cats, dogs, rabbits, horses, you name it. Cats, though, I will admit, are among the easiest to care for."

"Agreed. Chowder is quite independent, yet make no mistake, she, like all cats, still craves affection and attention."

"Oh, yes, I'm well aware. I've had several cats of my own over the years as well as dogs. So, was your husband fond of her?"

"I'm not sure Orland was fond of anything. Well, that's not entirely true. He was fond of cigars, scotch, and pretty young women, unfortunately. As for Chowder, here, Orland enjoyed showing her paws off to people. She was a source of amusement to him." She scratched Chowder under the chin and the cat closed her eyes, leaning into Marjorie's palm.

"She seems rather fond of you now."

"Yes, I wonder if she's aware Orland's not coming back. She was most distraught last night and this morning. So many people in and out, all the noise and commotion. Animals are very sensitive to that, you know. She's calmed down now, thankfully, but she's still not herself. I found her hiding in the closet in the study last night after everyone had finally left, and she was cowering under my bed this morning. Normally she's the first one up in the household, even before the staff."

"It had to have been quite traumatic for her, no doubt. The sound of the gunshot alone probably took three or four of her lives."

"It didn't do much for me either, Victor."

"I'm sorry, I don't mean to imply that it wasn't traumatic for you also. Of course it was."

"It was a shock for everyone, I'm sure. No one expected Orland to lock himself in his study and shoot himself."

"I've been wondering why he felt the need to have both doors locked."

She shrugged and arched her back. "My husband was a strange man. He liked solitude, privacy, and secrets. The study was his domain. I'm told he had taken some sort of a telephone call, so he probably didn't want to be disturbed by an errant party guest wandering in half-drunk."

"Yes, he had a telephone call from someone who said it was urgent and private. Do you know who could have made that call or what it was about?" Victor said.

"I'm afraid I have no idea. It's so strange. The detective asked me that same thing last evening, but as I told him, I can't imagine anyone calling Orland at that time of night. I suspect that whatever it was about it must have upset him so greatly that he took his life."

"That's certainly a plausible theory. You were upstairs when he, uh, shot himself, weren't you?"

"That's right. I heard what appeared to be a loud pop. I didn't think much about it at first, but then I heard raised voices in the salon. So, I got up and went downstairs to see what was going on. Everyone was gathered outside the study door off the salon. Someone, I think it was a man from the catering company, said it sounded like a shot from inside the library, and Tab said Orland wasn't answering the door. Then you, Tab, and Griff ran outside, broke the window, and got in, or something to that effect, anyway. I may not have all the facts exactly correct."

"That's fine. Do you know any reason your husband might want to kill himself, aside from the possibility of the phone call driving him to it?"

She shook her head. "The detective asked me that, too. No, I'm afraid I don't have a good answer to that. Perhaps we'll never know for sure what the reason was. I think Orland was a man of many secrets and many torments, though. I will say it surprised me he would take his life."

"It surprised me, too, to be honest, Mrs. Orcott. Marjorie, I mean."

"But who knows what goes on inside someone else's mind?"

"That's true," Victor said. "I imagine a few people were not all that upset by the news of his passing, if you'll forgive my saying so."

A look crossed her face that might have been a smile she was trying to hold back, might have been a grimace. "Indeed not. My husband wasn't a popular man. Many people disliked Orland and several outright hated him. In fact, I can't think of many who cared for him. Though what that has to do with him killing himself I couldn't answer. But let's just say I'm not expecting a large turnout at the funeral." She sat up and reached out a hand to him, which he took briefly. "I do hope you'll be there, though."

"Certainly, Marjorie. I'm sure Miss Spellman and Mr. Fenwick will wish to pay their respects, too, along with Mr. Taylor, of course."

"That's kind. Kinder than he was to them, or to you, I'm sure."

"We had our differences with Mr. Orcott, certainly. By the way, were you aware your husband kept a gun in the study?"

She withdrew her hand and stroked the top of Chowder's head once more. "A revolver, yes. He was a bit paranoid. I don't much care for guns myself."

"Nor do I, actually. Do you know where he kept it?"

"I insisted he keep it locked up in his desk. Why?"

"The fatal shot was fired from his gun."

"Yes, I figured that. Ironic in a way, that a gun he had for protection he used to end his own life."

"Do you happen to know where he kept the key to the drawer it was locked in?"

"No, he never shared that with me. Probably on his key chain, though I'm not certain. Why?"

"I was just curious. I recall seeing Mr. Orcott sign many a document in my days in his office. He was right-handed, wasn't he?"

"Yes. Orland told me once that when he was a child he was forced to learn to write with his right hand. In all other things, though, he uses his left. Used his left, I should say."

"Including shooting a gun?"

"If it came to that, yes."

"And apparently it came to that last night," Victor said. "The gun was in his left hand. By the way, I heard you and Orland fought at some point during the party."

Marjorie rolled her eyes about and sighed. "Ugh, that. That police detective, oh, I've forgotten his name but I have his card somewhere, was nice enough but tiring. He asked me about that fight over and over, too. It was nothing, really. Certainly nothing out of the ordinary. Orland and I quarreled more often than not."

"About his, uh, indiscretions?"

"And other things. Last night was involving his latest indiscretion, Charlotte Masters, which I only just learned about."

"That's what I was told."

"You mean you didn't witness it yourself? I thought everyone at the party saw the whole thing."

"Miss Spellman and I were on the terrace at the time."

"I see. Well, you missed a doozy of an argument. Orland had promised me he was through with philandering, but it turns out it was just another of his lies. He even had the audacity to invite Miss Masters, the little bitch, to my birthday party last night. Oh, he thought he was being clever having Tab escort her, but he wasn't clever enough."

"That had to be very distressing for you to discover."

"It's funny, I should be used to not believing a word he says, used to knowing he's a liar and a cheat." She sighed and closed her eyes again momentarily. "Still, he loved me, or at least he loved the idea of being married to me. I brought him respectability and stability. Each time he had one of his little affairs, he gave me something as a token. A necklace, a car, a trip, a birthday party."

"Did you love him?"

"I must have, once. I didn't know who he was when we first met. I wasn't attracted to him so much physically, though he *was* better looking then, but he was also a fascinating man. He knew so much and was quite clever and powerful. After we married, I found out what he was, but by then it was too late."

"Er, yes, you mentioned the party where I first met you."

"Some party. I was the blushing bride, but not because I had lost my virtue, because I had lost my husband."

"Was it your first marriage?"

"Yes, and his second. I've never met his first wife, though I should like to someday, perhaps, now that Orland's dead. As terrible as he was to me, I regret that fight with him last night. I regret that the last words we spoke to each other were in anger. I feel guilty about that."

"I understand, Marjorie. Regret isn't a place you want to stay, though. You go there, you do your time, and you move on. Guilt can serve a purpose, but it serves no purpose here that I can see. I think you've done your time in the last six years."

"That's kind of you to say, Victor, thank you. I'll let you know when the funeral is. It would be nice to have at least one or two friendly faces there." She laughed lightly. "It would be nice to have at least one or two people there, period."

"You may be surprised by the turnout," Victor said.

Marjorie nodded as Chowder got to her feet on the sofa and stretched, arching her back and swishing her tail. "Maybe. What was it someone once said? Give the people what they want and they'll turn out in droves, or something like that."

Victor chuckled. "Er, yes. Eve Spellman would probably know exactly who said that."

"Miss Spellman's a smart cookie. Hang on to her, for what it's worth. I'm told she's one of the few people to ever say no to Orland. And I'm sorry, by the way, for how my husband treated you. And Griff, and Mr. Taylor, and virtually everyone else, including her."

"Thank you, Mrs. Orcott, and I'm sorry for how he treated you."

"Thank you, and again, Marjorie, please."

"Sorry, I forgot. Thank you for seeing me today, Marjorie," Victor said, getting to his feet as he picked up his hat.

"Certainly. Shall I ring for Clarence to show you out?"

"I think I can find my way. Have a good afternoon."

"Likewise, Victor. Good luck with the picture. I'm sure it will be terrific."

"Once we find a new director," Victor said, and then instantly wished he hadn't.

"Yes, of course," Marjorie said quietly. "Good day."

"Good day," Victor said. He strode over to the door and out into the reception room, where he bumped into Tab.

"Victor. What are you doing here?"

"Just paying my respects to your stepmother. How are you?"

"I'm okay, considering," Tab said. He was dressed in a black suit with a black tie. He looked tired.

"Sure, I understand."

"I was just going in to see how she's doing," Tab said, "and if she needed anything."

"She seems to be holding up all right for the moment."

"She's a strong woman. She had to be to stay married to my father for six years, but I imagine she'll have good days and bad. This morning, she was trying to make funeral arrangements on the telephone. She asked me if I thought it should be a closed casket." Tab shook his head. "I said I imagined so, since he shot himself in the head."

"Yes, well, I'm sure she wasn't thinking clearly, and she didn't see into the study last night while your father's uh, body, was still there. Listen, since I'm here, is there someplace private you and I can talk before you go in to see your stepmother?"

"Talk? About what?"

"About last night."

"Not sure what else there is to say, but we can go into the salon if you want. I don't think anyone's in there at the moment."

"Sure, that would be fine," Victor said. They walked from the reception room into the large salon. Here, too, no remnants of the party remained. The furniture had all been put back into its usual places from what he remembered from previous visits. The area rugs had been returned to their spots on the floor, and everything had been wiped down, polished, and cleaned. Tab directed them to two small, upholstered chairs near the closest set of French doors.

"Have a seat," Tab said as he settled gingerly into one of the chairs.

"Thanks," Victor said, balancing his fedora on his knee as he took the other chair.

"How's your posterior, by the way?"

"I had Clarence extract a shard of glass nearly an inch long last night. It's okay."

"As I said to Marjorie, Clarence is exceptional."

"I agree. So, what's this about?"

"To be honest, I'm not sure. You and Sheila were on the terrace when the shot was fired, correct?"

"That's right. I'd been looking for what I thought was Chowder, and Sheila was laughing at me as I foraged in the shrubbery. When we heard the noise, we went inside and saw all of you."

"Sure, I remember," Victor said. "And we determined your father was the only person missing, and that he had taken a phone call in his study."

"Yeah. We knocked but there was no answer, and both doors were locked from the inside. I got the urgent feeling something was seriously wrong, that perhaps he'd had a heart attack or something. That's when

I figured we'd better get inside. I thought maybe he wasn't even in the study, that he'd figured out a way to get out with the doors locked as kind of a joke on us."

"But it was no joke."

"Not at all," Tab said, shaking his head. "I didn't want to waste a second in getting up there to the window once we'd gotten outside, so I hoisted myself up with Griff's help. You confirmed the other window was also locked, so I smashed the glass and reached through to unlock it. I used my handkerchief to protect my hand, but even so I cut myself a bit." He looked down at the bandages on the knuckles of his right hand. "Then I slid the window open far enough to get through." Tab shuddered once more, putting his hands to his face. "It was horrible. I don't know exactly what happened next. It's all kind of a blur, mixed up."

"After that, you helped Griff up, then you opened the door off the salon to let me in. We called the police from the library."

"Did I? Did we? Is that how it all happened? I honestly don't remember."

"That's understandable. Do you know any reason he would have killed himself, Tab?"

He lowered his hands away from his face and Victor noticed his eyes were red and somewhat puffy. "Are you playing at being a dick, Vic? Because that police detective asked me pretty much all the same things last night."

"Sorry, I don't mean to rehash what he's already asked you. But I can't think of any reason your father would take his life, so I was just wondering if you had any thoughts about it."

"Thoughts? I've had a lot, actually. I've barely slept. On the surface, I agree with you. It doesn't seem like he'd have any reason to, but I was probably closer to him than anyone, including Marjorie. No one knows, or I guess I should say *knew* Orland Orcott like I did. He wasn't a happy man, you see, not really, not at all. He desired things, craved things, obsessed about them until he got them, thinking somehow whatever it was would bring him happiness or peace or something. His latest obsession was wanting to win an Academy Award for best director. He had high hopes for *The Lady Screeched*, but the cast he desired never materialized."

"I understand you were signed to play Jasper Crockett initially. That would have been a big part for you."

"Yeah, well, it didn't work out. Originally, he wanted Tyrone Power or Errol Flynn in the Crockett role, and was hoping for Humphrey Bogart for Cabot, Eddie Quillan for Beaumont, and Joan Crawford as Ruth. When he couldn't get Power or Flynn, he signed me on but was still hoping for the rest. Then he and I had a disagreement of sorts, and I was off the picture."

"Yes, you mentioned that last night."

"That's when he signed Griff. He still hoped against hope for Bogart, Quillan, and Crawford, but that didn't happen. When the studio handed out a shoestring budget, my father had to expect he couldn't afford that kind of star power. He had to take what he could get, no offense, Vic."

"None taken. With Griff came me, and with me came Eve Spellman."

"Right, and William Taylor at the last minute. And that all spelled the end of any chance at best director, in my father's mind. He was furious. Do you know he cleared a space for the Oscar on the mantel of his study?"

"No, I didn't. A bit premature, don't you think?"

"That's how he was. He wanted it so badly. There's not a thing on the mantel right now. It's funny, though. When he did finally obtain something or someone he desired, it never brought him the happiness he thought it would. So, he grew tired of them, even despised them until he moved on to something else."

"You think he may have committed suicide because he was unhappy?"

Tab raised and then dropped his shoulders. "I wouldn't put it past him. My father may have sought death as a way to find peace. He told me once he feared nothing but death, desired nothing but relief, and paradoxically believed relief could only come from death. And in taking his own life, he may have also sought to punish those he disliked or was angry at."

"Like his wife?"

Tab grimaced. "Yes. And me, unfortunately. Marjorie's a lovely woman. He didn't deserve her, and she didn't deserve to be treated the way she was by him. I've moved back here temporarily as of this morning, at least until after the funeral, just to help her out and support her as best I can."

"I'm sure she appreciates that. Not to be indelicate, Tab, but you mentioned your father was angry with you, and you brought up the argument between the two of you a couple of times."

"Yeah, the one that led to me being replaced in *The Lady Screeched* and banished from the studio. It's not exactly a secret."

"That's right, it's not a secret, but it wasn't the first time he blew his top at you, was it?"

"Hardly. He always got over it, though, and he would have again if he hadn't killed himself."

"But this time the argument was because he discovered the truth about you, wasn't it? About you and a man named Tony Bolt," Victor said, watching him closely.

"Who told you that?"

"Does it matter?"

"Not really, but I can make a pretty good guess who blabbed. Sure, Dad found out, and he put most of the blame on Tony as if he seduced me or something. Dad hated Tony, and he told me he was going to destroy him."

"That's awful," Victor said.

"That's how my father was, but I think he was more bluster than action. There's nothing between Tony and me. We're just friends, more or less. I hired him to do some personal training, that's all. He wants to break into show biz, naturally, so I told him I would see what I could do."

"Sounds like an amicable arrangement. Personal training in exchange for a possible screen test."

"Oh, I paid him, too, of course, for his services. He knows his stuff."

"No doubt. So, how did your father find out?"

"One of his many young women told him she thought I was funny."

"Why would she think that?"

"Because she made a pass at me. Several passes, actually, when my father wasn't around. I turned her down flat every time, so naturally she assumed I'm a homosexual because she felt she was irresistible."

"Was that Sheila?"

"No, another woman. Dad cheated on his mistresses, too. Anyway, when she told my father, he hired a private dick to trail me. It was one of the afternoons I went to see Tony. Don't ask me how the dick did it, but he actually got photographs of us in the middle of a training session, even though Tony's place is on the second floor. There is a fire escape, but you would think one of us would have seen or heard him if he was out there taking pictures."

"Maybe from a building across the street," Victor said. "If he had a telephoto lens and a good camera."

"Yeah, maybe."

"So, you and Tony didn't have a relationship?"

Tab scoffed. "Hardly. He's not my type, at least out of bed he's not. I prefer a more sophisticated man. Besides, Tony isn't exclusive with anybody. He even sleeps with women if they're willing to pay him, though he prefers men. I told my father Tony was just my personal trainer, but he didn't believe me, and the photos made it look worse than it was. Anyway, none of that had anything to do with my father killing himself. He took his life because he was truly, deeply unfulfilled and bored with life, I'm sure of it. He was a very, very unhappy man, and he loathed himself more than anyone else did, and that's saying a lot."

"Interesting theory. You think it more likely it was suicide rather than murder?"

"Murder? He was alone in a locked room, wasn't he?"

"Apparently, yes."

"Then I'm sorry, but I don't see how murder would be possible, Vic. I think the very public fight with Marjorie last night might have driven him over the edge. Perhaps he finally realized, when she threatened to leave him once and for all, what an ass he'd been, and he knew he could never recover from that."

"Perhaps. Anyway, thanks for talking to me. I'm sorry for your loss."

"Thanks, but to be honest, it wasn't much of a loss. I know that sounds cold, but he wasn't your father."

Victor stood and Tab followed suit. "That's true, he wasn't." Victor extended his hand, which Tab grasped weakly.

"Sorry, Victor, but my right hand is still pretty sore from the broken glass last night."

"Oh, of course, I understand. I'll see myself out."

"Okay, I'm sure Marjorie will let you know when the funeral is."

"Thanks, yes, she said she would." Victor stared at Tab for just a moment longer, then turned and crossed the salon to the double doors and into the entry hall and the front doors just beyond. Clarence was nowhere in sight, so he pulled the door open and stepped outside, putting on his hat as he closed the door behind him.

Chapter Eight

Late Sunday afternoon, August 13, 1939
Victor Marvel's house

Victor put his car in the garage next to Griff's and went through the wrought iron gate in the privacy wall onto the terrace.

"Hello, there," Griff said, looking up at him from his chaise lounge near the pool. "Welcome home." He was wearing a blue and white floral swimsuit, the sweat on his body glistening.

"Hiya, handsome, and thanks. Did you get all packed up and moved in?"

"I did. I brought two suitcases and all three of my potted houseplants. Thanks for making room for my things in the bedroom closet and such. I'll try to be a good houseguest."

"You're welcome, and you're the perfect houseguest. Who could ask for anything more?"

Griff grinned. "Sweet talker."

"It's all true."

"Likewise. Eve telephoned while you were out, by the way. She wanted to know if we'd like to meet her for lunch tomorrow at the Brown Derby."

"Sure, that's fine with me. What time?"

"Noon."

"Sounds good."

"I figured it would, so I already told her yes. How did it go at the police station?" Griff said, setting the script he'd been studying on a nearby table.

"Okay. Detective Garnett and I had a pretty decent conversation."

"I'm glad, but you're back later than I thought," Griff said as Victor walked closer and stooped to give him a kiss.

"I know, sorry. How are you doing on the lines?"

Griff rolled his eyes and groaned. "Ugh, I may need cue cards."

"You'll be fine."

"Thanks for the vote of confidence."

"Always. And you definitely don't need to worry about that swimming suit scene in the film. You look amazing," Victor said, looking at Griff's tanned, toned body.

"Aw, thanks, Vic. I thought I'd do a few laps and get some sun. Trying to memorize this part is driving me nuts."

"Can I help?"

"Maybe. Having someone to read with me would make it easier, but I believe I'm finished for now. It's getting late and the terrace and pool are now almost completely in shade."

"Yeah, so I see," Victor said, taking off his suit coat and tie and loosening his collar. "But it's still plenty warm out here."

"True. So, what did the detective say? What did you two talk about all this time?"

Victor hitched up his trousers and sat down on a lounge chair next to Griff. "Not much I didn't already know. He's convinced Orcott killed himself. The room was locked up tight, no secret or trap doors, and no one hiding in there. He even checked the chimney."

"Wowzer. But you're still not convinced?"

Vic shook his head slowly. "I don't know, but I hope to find out. After I finished talking to Garnett, I drove back out to the Orcott place. That's partly why I'm late getting home."

"Oh? What did you go out there for again?"

"To have a look around and to speak to Mrs. Orcott."

"And?"

"She was subdued and reflective as expected, I suppose. She was dressed in black, but she wasn't exactly mournful."

"That's not surprising."

"No. She thinks her husband killed himself because he was unhappy."

"Unhappy? Orcott? Huh, I never thought of him that way. He delighted in making other people miserable."

"That he did. I talked to Tab while I was there, also. He said pretty much the same thing as his stepmother, His father was deeply dissatisfied with his life. Tab believes it was a suicide, too, and maybe there's something to it. Maybe unhappy people enjoy making other people unhappy until they can no longer stand it. Until they themselves can no longer function."

"The old misery loves company thing, eh?"

"Who knows?" Victor said. "It makes sense, in a way."

"Now it sounds like you're trying to convince yourself."

"I just want to know for certain one way or the other."

"Why?"

"Why? I don't know. I'm just curious, I guess. I feel like the truth, whatever it is, should be known."

"That sounds like something you'd say. So, what's next?"

"What do you mean?"

"I mean, you want to know the truth, so let's figure it out. Either we'll prove he was murdered, or we'll prove it was suicide. We *are* gumshoes, after all."

Victor laughed. "Only in the movies. But I do enjoy playing detective, onscreen and off, and I think I'm good at it. I appreciate your support, Griff, I really do."

"You always have my support."

"And you mine."

"Thanks."

"Am I being an idiot, though, Griff? I mean, I wonder sometimes if I'm just wishing there was more to it. I sometimes feel like I see things others don't, and then I wonder if they were real."

"You think you saw something related to his death?"

Victor rubbed the back of his neck and frowned. "No. Maybe. I'm not sure. I guess I just wonder if maybe there is more to it. It won't hurt to do a little more investigating, I suppose."

"Okay, which leads us back to my original question. What's next?"

"That, my handsome roommate, is a very good question. What would Crockett and Beaumont do? Or Phineas Hart?"

"Talk to the suspects, of course," Griff said.

"Good thinking. And who are the suspects?"

Griff leaned forward in his lounge chair. "Hmm, I imagine the top suspects would be those still left in the house at the time of the shooting, excluding the employees of the catering company and the household staff, I suppose."

"I'm not so sure you can exclude them. Remember when I played

Detective Hart in *Harts and Clubs* a few years ago? The killer ended up being a florist at the wedding who took the job just to murder the father-in-law."

"That was a movie, Victor, but point taken. Still, let's focus on the people we know. If we eliminate all of them, then we can look at the others."

"Fair enough. So, there was Marjorie and Tab. Eve was with us at the time, so I think she's okay."

"Right, though she hated him as much as anyone, if not more."

"She did, that's true."

"Definitely. Sheila Burton was also there, and William and his daughter, Lydia."

"Correct," Victor said.

"Oh, and don't forget Agatha Mudd was still at the mansion, though she doesn't seem to have that much of a motive compared to the others," Griff said.

"I'm not so sure. She had some rather interesting things to say the night of the party."

"Oh? Like what?"

"She intimated to me it might have been Orland Orcott who had something to do with her pregnancy and subsequent loss of her acting career fifteen years ago. At least that's the way I took it."

"Wowzer, I guess it wouldn't surprise me if he did. Okay, so we'll keep her on the list."

"Yes."

"Ugh, I'm trying to remember. What was the line your character says to mine about motives and opportunity?"

"'Every suspect, Crockett, in order to be considered a suspect, has to have a motive, an opportunity, and the means to carry it out.'"

"Yeah, that's right. Gee, I wish I had your memory for lines. So, maybe besides the list of names we should list what their motives, opportunity, and means would be."

"That's a good idea. Have a pencil?"

"Sure," Griff said. He leaned over and picked up his script and a pencil. "I can write on the back of the last page. It's blank."

"Okay. So, make a list of everyone we just named, starting with Marjorie Orcott."

"Got it. What's her motive?"

"She found out her husband lied to her yet again and he was having an affair with Charlotte Masters. She was humiliated on her birthday at a party in front of virtually everyone she knew."

"That's a good motive. And her means and opportunity?"

"Unknown at this time. Again, the locked room being the stumbling block. That, unfortunately, will be the case with every suspect for the time being."

"Okay, so what about Tab? I suppose his motive is his father finding out he's a homosexual and blacklisting him at every studio in town."

"Yes, put that down."

"Right," Griff said, scribbling on the page. "And Sheila Burton hated Orcott because he dumped her for Charlotte Masters."

"Yup."

"Agatha Mudd we got already," Griff said, scribbling more. "But gee, you really think Mr. Taylor or his daughter could have done it?"

"I don't like to think so, but it's possible. William hated Orcott for the way he humiliated him, but I'm sure he hated him more for what he did to Lydia, if he believed it. And whether it was true or not, Lydia hated Orcott for spreading vicious gossip about her that not only damaged her reputation but hurt and upset her father."

"Valid points. That makes six good suspects, and they were all more or less out of sight at the time of the shooting. So now what?"

"I think we should stop by William Taylor's house for a chat."

"All right, when?"

Victor got to his feet. "No time like the present. I told him this morning that we might be dropping by this evening. We can stop for Chinese food or something afterward for dinner."

"Sounds good to me. I just need to shower and get dressed."

"Okay, and I have to use the bathroom, shave, and freshen up."

Griff got to his feet also, tucking the script under his arm and the pencil behind his ear. He grabbed his towel, grinned at Victor, and said, "Last one in has to use the hall bath." He sprinted toward the house like a gazelle as Victor laughed, picked up his suit coat and tie, and slowly followed.

CHAPTER NINE

Sunday evening, August 13, 1939
William and Lydia Taylor's house

"This is it, I think," Victor said, pulling his Cadillac over to the curb in front of a small house squeezed between other small homes on tiny lots. Many of them were unkempt, but William's was clean and tidy, the yard freshly mowed and the flower beds weeded.

"Haven't you been here before?" Griff said.

"Not to this place, no. He used to own a larger house up in the hills, but that was, well, before. He and Lydia have lived here for the last year or so. She gave me the address when I sent flowers for his birthday a few months ago."

"Not the kind of place I would have pictured him in," Griff said.

"It's a rental, I believe. I'm sure it's just temporary until he gets back on his feet."

"Sure. Let's go say hello, then." He and Victor got out and walked up the flower-lined path to the front door.

At the sound of Victor's knock, Lydia swung open the door. She was dressed in a full red skirt and a yellow, short-sleeved blouse embroidered with colorful parrots. She was barefoot.

"Oh, Victor, Griff, what a surprise."

"Good evening, Lydia. Didn't your father tell you we'd be stopping by for a brief visit?" Victor said.

"No, he never mentioned it, but with all that's happened he probably just forgot. You're always welcome, though, you know that. Please, come in." The front door opened directly into the living room. The tiny kitchen was visible through an arched doorway on the back wall.

"I hope we're not catching you at a bad time," Griff said.

"Oh, no, not at all. We finished dinner a while ago and were just listening to the radio." She walked over and turned it off. "But there's not much good on tonight. Dad's in the bathroom, but he'll be right out. Won't you sit down?" she said as she perched on the arm of the overstuffed chair next to the console radio.

"Thank you," Victor said. He and Griff took a seat on the sofa, balancing their hats in their laps.

"Oh, where are my manners?" Lydia said, springing to her feet. "Please, let me take those for you." She scooped up the fedora and the Homburg and hung them on hooks on the back of the front door next to a dusty black derby Victor recognized as William's. "May I get you two anything? Coffee or iced tea?"

"No, thank you, Lydia, we're fine," Victor said.

"Okay. If I'd known you were coming, I'd have baked something," she said, sitting back down into the chair.

"I'm glad you didn't go to any bother," Griff said.

"Me too," Victor said. "We just wanted to stop and say hello. That's a lovely blouse you're wearing."

Lydia smiled. "Oh, thank you."

"And that looks like real silver jewelry," Victor said. "That necklace, the bracelet, and those silver and amethyst bird earrings all look like the real deal. They're so shiny. Are they new?"

"Uh, yes, fairly recent. You have a good eye, Mr. Marvel." She glanced down nervously at herself. "And oh, my goodness, I just realized I'm not wearing shoes. I must look a fright."

"Not at all, you look lovely," Victor said. "Where did you find a blouse with embroidery like that, though, and that jewelry, in the midst of the Depression? It all looks like something from the studio costume department on the *South of the Border* picture I was in once."

"Um, yes, well, I happened to be in Tijuana in May, and I picked it all up there. Everything was incredibly affordable."

"What on earth were you doing in Tijuana, Lydia?" Griff said.

"Oh, uh, you know, picking up some, uh, medicine for my dad that I can't get here," Lydia said, fiddling nervously with her necklace.

"Did your father go with you?" Victor said.

"No, I didn't exactly tell him I was going. He worries so much, you know, so I told him I was going to visit a friend in San Diego. He thinks I got the medicine from my friend there. Please don't mention it."

William appeared from a small hall off to the left just then. "Mention what? I thought I heard voices. Hello, Victor, Griff, how nice of you to stop by. To be honest, I forgot you said you might be coming this evening."

"Yes, you did forget, Dad," Lydia said, springing up from her seat once more. "Well, let me just go freshen up and put on my face."

"You're fine, Lydia, honestly. We're all friends," Victor said as he and Griff got to their feet.

"Thank you, but I'll just be a minute." She dashed off into the hall.

"I hope we're not disturbing you, Mr. Taylor," Griff said.

"It's William, please, Griff, and you're not disturbing us at all. Sit, sit." He shuffled over to a wooden kitchen chair at a small round table in the corner of the living room and sat down also. The table, Victor and Griff noticed, had a large ball of string upon it, made up of various odd pieces strung and wound together.

"Wouldn't you be more comfortable in the armchair or sitting here on the sofa?" Victor said. "I can sit in the kitchen chair, I don't mind."

William waved him back down. "No, it's fine, really. I don't usually sit on the upholstered furniture anymore. Wood chairs, uh, suit me and my condition better."

"Oh, of course," Victor said, feeling awkward.

William shrugged. "Don't be embarrassed. Like you said, we're all friends here."

"Thanks, William."

"Certainly. No secrets between us, it seems."

"How are you feeling, William?" Griff said.

"Fair. The doctors say I'm more or less okay now physically, except for the incontinence issue. I still get fatigued so quickly, though, and I still have some pain issues. My physician tells me I need to gain weight and build my muscles back, but it's a struggle. Still, Lydia does her best to fatten me up and whip me into shape."

"She makes a good nurse, I'm sure," Victor said. "You'll get there, William, day by day. You just have to be patient."

"I try, I do, but she'll tell you my patience is sometimes in short supply."

"I can imagine," Griff said. "I'm glad your doctor said you're okay otherwise, but aren't you still taking medication? For the pain and whatnot?"

William shook his head. "No, I'm fine. I just get tired once in a while, and an upset stomach, that's all. I use a mustard plaster now and then, and some licorice root for the indigestion."

"Both good home remedies, William," Victor said. "I've used those myself."

"Yeah, they do the trick," William said, nodding, his thin strands of hair plastered to his skull. "So, what brings you two way out here? It's a long drive from your neighborhoods."

"Yes, well, I've been doing some thinking about Orcott's death," Victor said.

"Me too," William said. "I've been thinking I'm glad he's dead."

Victor crossed his legs and fidgeted with a piece of lint on his trousers. "Yeah, about that. You said you didn't believe your daughter would do anything with Orland to ensure a part in his movie for you."

"Lydia would never."

"But Orland certainly insinuated she did."

William scowled. "Orcott was an ass. What are you getting at, Victor?"

"Easy, William, easy. I'm sure his accusations had to be upsetting."

"That's putting it mildly. He insulted my daughter and sullied her reputation with lies. He was a despicable person."

Victor raised his hands, palms facing William. "Of course he was, I agree. We all agree. I'm sorry, I didn't mean to rile you. I know it's a sore subject, but I just feel like there's more to his death than meets the eye."

"What is that supposed to mean?"

"I wish I knew, to be honest," Victor said, dropping his hands back into his lap.

"Knew what?" Lydia said, coming back into the living room. She had put on black leather pumps and a little makeup, and had tied back her hair with a blue satin ribbon.

"We were just talking about Orland Orcott," William said. "Victor believes there's more to his death."

"Oh," Lydia said quietly. She took a seat in the upholstered armchair once more and smoothed out her skirt. "Why? Like what?"

"I just think it might not have been suicide," Victor said.

"You're crazy, you know that, Victor?" William said. "That detective last night said he killed himself."

"I know."

"So what? You think it might have been an accident?" William said.

"It's possible," Griff said.

"Or do you think he was murdered?" Lydia said, staring at Victor.

"I think that's also possible, Lydia," Victor said.

"You're a brick shy of a load," William said. "He'd locked himself in. Besides, even if somebody did murder him somehow, who cares? He was a loathsome human being."

"He was a human being," Victor said softly.

"Not much of one," Lydia said.

"I'll grant you that," Victor said. "You were both in the dining room of the mansion at the time the shot was fired, weren't you?"

"Yes," Lydia said. "We thought we'd see if there was some food left we could bring home."

"We're not proud, and anything left over would have gone in the garbage anyway," William said. "But as it was, it was pretty picked over by the time we got there. There wasn't much left. The staff might have taken the leftovers for themselves."

"That could be," Griff said.

"As I recall, the dining room has French doors onto the terrace, double doors into the salon, double doors into the hall off the entry, and a single door into the butler's pantry," Victor said.

"If you say so," William said. "Beats the hell out of me."

"Dad, language," Lydia said.

"Well, it does. Who cares how many doors there are or where they go?"

"No one, I suppose," Victor said. "By the way, you were cast in *The Lady Screeched* back in March, weren't you, William?"

"Yes, that's right, just after Eve, I believe. I think I was the last person to be cast. Why?"

"Just trying to think things through," Victor said, glancing at his Rolex. "I suppose Griff and I should get going. We haven't had dinner yet and it's getting late."

William got slowly to his feet. "To be honest, I'm tired, anyway. I might go to bed early. Thank you for stopping over, though I'm not sure what this was all about."

Victor and Griff stood, as did Lydia.

"This was an awfully short visit," Lydia said, smoothing out the folds in her skirt. "Do come again when you can stay longer."

"We will, Lydia, thank you," Victor said.

"Let me get your hats." She handed the fedora to Victor and the Homburg to Griff.

"Thanks," Griff said.

The three men shook hands. "Let me ask you something, Victor," William said.

"What's that?"

"You said you think there's more to Orcott's death than meets the eye. You know, it pained me to be even remotely civil to him, and I only did so because I needed the work. You hated him just as much as anyone else, and so did Griff here, I'm sure, so why do you care?"

Victor paused just a moment before answering and then nodded slowly. "That's a good question, William. I wish I had a good answer for you. I guess I just figure that if somehow it wasn't suicide, people should know the truth."

"Why?" Lydia said, crossing her arms. "It wouldn't bring him back to life."

"No, but if it was murder, don't you think that the murderer should be brought to justice?" Victor said. "People can't take the law into their own hands. Besides, Orland didn't commit a crime."

"I beg to differ. He committed adultery, that's a crime."

"Not really, William. Not in California, anyway. And it's certainly not something he should have been killed over."

"*If* he was killed," William said. "Stop stirring the pot and let it rest, Victor. It's for the best."

"Sure, William, that's something to think about," Victor said. "Well, thank you both again. Good night."

Lydia tugged the front door open for them, and the two men stepped out onto the stoop, the night air still and humid. "Good night," she and William both said.

Victor and Griff went down the walk and climbed back into Victor's car.

"Chinese takeout for dinner?" Victor said, starting the engine and looking over at Griff.

"Sure, that sounds good. Know a place?"

"Yeah, Liu's Restaurant, not far from my house." Victor pulled away from the curb, did a U-turn, and drove slowly down the narrow residential street.

"Fine with me. What did you make of all that?" Griff said.

"Of William and Lydia? Clearly, they both hated Orland."

"And with good reason."

"Yeah," Victor said. "It seems everyone had a good reason to hate him, including us, as William pointed out."

"Orcott was not a likable person. Still, some people disliked him more than others."

"Like William and Lydia," Victor said.

"Yeah, and Orcott's wife, Tab, Sheila, and Mrs. Mudd. I feel sorry for William and Lydia the most, though."

"Me too. But maybe with Orland gone, they'll be able to move on."

"I hope so," Griff said. "Did you find anything out tonight, talking to them?"

Victor brought the car to a halt at a stop sign and glanced briefly over at Griff before proceeding through the intersection. "Maybe. I hate to say it, but I wonder what Lydia was really doing in Tijuana."

"What do you mean?"

"Well, she said she went down there to get medicine for her father, but he said he's no longer taking anything."

"Yeah, but maybe he was lying. If she's buying something illegal over the border, I doubt he'd admit it," Griff said.

"True. Still, William was signed on to the picture toward the end of March, which means Lydia probably went to see Orcott in early March."

"That would make sense."

"And then, nine to ten weeks later, Lydia took a solo trip to Tijuana."

"I'm not following you, Vic."

"Well, I could be totally mistaken, but other women who have found themselves in the family way have gone there for an abortion."

"You mean you think she was expecting?" Griff said.

"It's a possibility. And it's also possible that if she did sleep with Orcott to get William a role in *The Lady Screeched*, Orcott could have been the father of her baby."

"Wowzer, you believe Lydia would do that? Sleep with him, I mean, and then get an abortion?"

"I honestly don't know what I believe, Griff. Tijuana is a convenient place to go for that sort of thing, and while she was down there for a few days, she may have treated herself to some inexpensive jewelry and a new blouse, though William and Lydia are hard up financially."

"Yeah, that's why the part in the movie was so important to them," Griff said.

"Right. I know she felt the role in Orcott's picture would mean a lot to her father emotionally, too. Still, it does seem out of character for her."

"Not that either of us really knows her," Griff said.

"Point taken. If it's true, that's all the more reason the two of them are suspects."

"Is that why you brought up all the doors in the dining room?"

"It is. I was just thinking they could have easily slipped out without anyone seeing them and then gone back in, only to make an entrance after we were all in the salon. I couldn't help but notice the large ball of twine, either. He collects it, remember?"

"Yes, odd hobby."

"And remember that hanger that was outside the study window? It had a piece of string tied to it, and Lydia found a piece of string on the terrace, or so she claimed when I asked her about it."

"What's the connection?" Griff said.

"I wish I knew. Maybe nothing."

"And if they were involved, how would they or anyone else have gotten into the study?"

Victor took a sharp corner and sighed, drumming the fingers of his left hand on the steering wheel. "Good question. Maybe I'm all wet about this. Maybe Orcott did shoot himself."

Griff reached over and put a hand on Victor's thigh. "I think he might have, to be honest, but we'll see this through one way or the other."

"Thanks, handsome. You know, we're forgetting one other suspect."

"Oh? Who?" Griff said.

"Tony Bolt. He had a motive for wanting Orcott dead, too. Orland said he would destroy Tony."

"Gee, but Mr. Bolt wasn't at the party."

"Not that we know of, but that doesn't mean he wasn't," Victor said.

"True. He may have been one of the caterers or something, or maybe we just never noticed him. I mean, we've never met him."

"Not yet," Victor said. "I'm thinking I should swing by and pay him a visit sometime tomorrow, maybe in the morning. What say you? Want to tag along?"

"I say I'd like to, but I'm still stumbling over my lines, and shooting will probably start soon once a replacement for Orcott is found. I'll stay home at your place and practice, I think."

"Sure, that's fine."

"Don't forget we're meeting Eve at the Brown Derby at noon for lunch, too."

"Oh, that's right. Might be easier if I go right from Tony's place to there. Would you mind picking up Eve? I could meet you both as soon as I finish."

"Of course, I'd be happy to."

"Great, thanks. And I promise to help you study as soon as I can. Maybe we could run lines after dinner tonight."

"If you don't mind, that would be helpful," Griff said.

"I don't mind at all. And there's Liu's restaurant. I'm in the mood for some fried rice and egg rolls. Come on, let's get some takeout and go home."

"I like the sound of that, Mr. Marvel."

"I thought you didn't care for fried rice?"

"I don't, wise guy. I'll get the crab Rangoon. I was talking about the going home part. With you."

Victor grinned widely. "My home is your home, handsome. Always."

Chapter Ten

Monday morning, August 14, 1939
Tony Bolt's apartment

The address listed in the phone book for Tony Bolt was a small, unassuming three-story painted brick building, rather grandly named Royal Apartments. It was on a sketchy part of Hollywood Boulevard, sandwiched between a drugstore and a five-and-dime, but Hollywood Boulevard was a busy street, and it was broad daylight, so Victor felt okay leaving his car parked out front. He put the top up and locked the doors, though, just in case. He quickly scanned the directory next to the entry, and then, noting the lock on the front door was broken, shoved it open and entered the narrow, dark hall. Immediately an odor hit his nostrils that reminded him of a damp crypt he'd once been in. It wasn't pleasant. As his eyes adjusted to the dim light, he saw four units per floor, two in the front and two in the back. According to the directory, Tony Bolt's place was 2B, so Victor climbed the creaky wooden stairs on the left side of the hall to the second floor, which smelled just as bad as the first. Apartment 2B was in the front, on the right as he came up the stairs and turned to the front of the building.

Victor wasn't exactly sure who or what to expect when he knocked, but he definitely didn't expect the man who opened the door. He was about five-eleven, in his early twenties, and all muscle, head to toe. His hair was short, dark, and curly, and his eyebrows thick and solid. He wore a white T-shirt that looked like it was two sizes too small for him, which was probably why he chose it. It hugged every ripple, both nipples, and all of his abs. It also made his ultra-tan skin stand out in contrast. He was wearing blue jeans that looked like the seams and buttons might burst at any moment. There was a prominent bulge in his fly, and he was barefoot. His feet, Victor noticed, were of considerable size.

"May I help you?" the muscle man said. His voice was not as deep as Victor had expected, but deep enough to penetrate directly to Victor's loins.

"Uh, um, yes, I'm uh, looking for Tony Bolt."

"You found him. What do you want?"

"I was hoping to chat with you for a few moments, Mr. Bolt."

Tony cracked his knuckles and looked Victor up and down. "Who are you? You look familiar."

"I'm Victor Marvel."

Tony's tawny brown eyes lit up with recognition. "Oh, yeah, of course, the movie star, that's where I know you from. Wow. I've seen several of your films. They were great."

Victor smiled. "Thank you, I'm glad you enjoyed them. As I said, I was hoping to ask you a few questions. Do you mind if I come in for a moment? I won't keep you long."

The big guy stepped aside. "Suit yourself, I can spare a few minutes. I'm expecting a client, but not for another hour or so. Come on in."

"Thanks." Victor entered, just brushing up against Tony as he did so. Tony didn't seem to mind. He closed the door behind him. Victor removed his fedora and glanced about. It was a small studio, with a full-sized, unmade metal bed, a kitchenette piled with what Victor assumed were the breakfast dishes and maybe the dinner dishes from the night before, a single closet, and a bathroom. Two windows above the bed overlooked the busy street below, a fire escape just visible through the one on the left. The décor in the apartment was mostly barbells, dumbbells, fitness posters, and magazines.

"You can hang your hat on the bedpost if you want," Tony said.

"Uh, sure, thanks," Victor said. He walked over to the metal bedstead and hung his fedora on the post of the footboard. The mattress had a deep sag in the middle.

"Can I get you something to drink, Mr. Marvel? I don't drink alcohol, but I have water and milk, oh, and some orange juice, fresh squeezed. I know a guy with an orange tree. He gives me a bag, and I squeeze them myself."

"No, thanks, I'm fine," Victor said. "I bet you have the grip of a python."

Tony stared at his hands for a moment and grinned. "Yeah, I'm a good squeezer."

Victor imagined the oranges would be pulverized in seconds in Tony's hands, and he imagined he'd like to watch. "I bet you are."

"Yeah, well, uh, I don't get many visitors, Mr. Marvel, I mean, not like you. Most of the folks that come over are only here for one thing, and I'm guessing that's not why you're here." He cocked his head like an overgrown puppy. "Or is it?"

"Uh, sure, right, I mean, no. Uh, what one thing would that be, just out of curiosity? The thing most people come here for, I mean."

"I call it personal training sessions, one on one, though I've been known to do two or three folks at the same time for an additional charge. Personal training is how I make most of my money right now."

"Horizontal personal training?" Victor said.

Tony stared at Victor for just a moment and then laughed from his gut, which looked like it was made of ribbed cast iron. "I get it, that's a good one, Mr. Marvel. Yeah, horizontal personal training."

"On your bed," Victor said. "I couldn't help but notice the mattress is well broken in."

"Yeah, I should buy a new one. It's been bothering my back a bit lately."

"Maybe you can deduct it as a business expense."

Tony laughed again. "You've got a good sense of humor, Mr. Marvel. I like you. You're a handsome man, too."

"Thanks, and likewise, I must say."

"Aw, thanks. I try to keep in shape. It's important in my business, you know."

"Of course. I'm sure your horizontal personal training clients appreciate that."

"They do. They're not all horizontal, though," Tony said.

"No?"

"Nope. I had a guy once, an accountant from Burbank. He was a fairly little guy. He wanted to hang upside down from the rod in my closet while I flogged him. Takes all kinds."

"I can imagine. I think," Victor said, trying to picture it. "He wanted to hang upside down?"

"Yeah. It worked out okay until the closet rod broke and he came crashing naked onto the floor."

"Oh, my, that's fascinating. You should write a book of your exploits."

Tony grinned broadly. "I could, you know. But I'd never name names."

"No, that wouldn't be good," Victor said.

"Nope. So, what can I do for you?" Tony said, leaning forward, closer to Victor. His breath smelled like oranges.

"Oh, yes, well, I, uh, I just want to chat for a bit, if that's all right." Victor found that he was having a hard time not letting his mind wander, and his palms felt sweaty.

"Just chat? Okay. That makes sense with a guy like you. I did have an actor here once, though, not all that long ago. Big name, married to a gorgeous woman. I'm sure you know him, and you'd be surprised, I bet. But like I said, I don't kiss and tell, no sir. If I did, I wouldn't get any more clients, see? Folks like their privacy."

"Discretion is the better part of valor, they say."

"Sure, I've heard that expression."

"Right, well, uh, is there someplace we could talk?" Victor said, taking in the tiny flat once more with one swoop of his eyes.

"Yeah, sure. Have a seat at the kitchen table. Sorry, my place is kinda small."

"It's fine," Victor said, taking a seat in one of the two wooden chairs at a round table, which was only about five feet from the end of the bed. He glanced at the black-and-white photographs that covered the table surface. "Oh, uh, oh, my. Are any of these you, Mr. Bolt?"

"Sure, they're all me," Tony said proudly as he sat down in the other chair, which creaked under his weight. "In some, I dyed my hair blond, and in others I let my chest hair grow out and I grew a mustache, but they're all me. Even the one where my head is shaved."

"Yes, I see that now. Very, uh, artistic and athletic."

"Thanks. I was just reviewing them when you knocked. I like that one there," he said, pointing with a thick index finger. "The one where I'm wearing that leopard print posing strap, and the one next to it, too, where I'm just in a basic jock. Those two are my favorites. They really oiled me up in those photo shoots."

"Er, yes, I see. Your skin is glistening."

"Yeah, thanks, my butt looks good, too. It's the oil and the lights, you know. Usually, it takes a long hot shower and a lot of scrubbing afterward, though."

"To get all that oil off? I imagine. You'd be all slippery and warm, and wet, and, uh, stuff," Victor said. Their knees were just touching under the table.

"You got that right. Anyway, if you know anyone at the studio that might be interested in my pictures, please let me know. I want to be in the movies, legit movies, as an actor. I have a regular portfolio, too, you know. Headshots, with me in a suit and tie, that kind of thing."

"Ah, that's good. I imagine most casting directors would want your regular portfolio, but some may prefer the latter, I'm sure. Regardless, I'll be happy to do you—I mean, I'll be happy to do *that for* you, Mr. Bolt," Victor said. He was sure his face was red, and he was perspiring. "Ask around, that is. Um, Bolt is an interesting last name." Victor felt it was surprisingly hot in the tiny apartment, though Tony didn't seem to notice.

"Yeah. I was born Anthony Bianchi. I changed it when I moved out here to California. It sounds better, don't you think?"

"It does have a certain style to it. I like it, and it suits you."

"Gee, thanks, Mr. Marvel. So, what did you want to talk to me about?"

"Hmm? Oh, well, I, uh, I understand you know Tab Rockwell."

"Tab? Yeah, I know him. Why?"

"I suppose you heard about his father's death."

His expression changed ever so slightly. "Sure I did. It was on the radio and in the newspaper. Big news. Sad."

"How did you meet Tab, by the way?"

"Through this dame named Sheila."

"Sheila Burton? The actress?" Victor said.

"Yeah, you know her? I suppose you would, you being a movie star and all. Say, what's Clark Gable really like?"

"I'm afraid I don't know Mr. Gable. We've never met. Sorry."

"Oh. I just figured you all knew each other. I'd give him a HPTS for free."

"Sorry, a HPTS?"

Tony grinned. "Horizonal Personal Training Session. I hope you don't mind my using that from now on."

"Oh, no, that's fine, just keep my name out of it, please."

"Sure, not to worry, like I said, I don't kiss and tell about nothing."

"That's good to know, Mr. Bolt."

"You can call me Tony, if you want."

"Thank you, Tony. So, you met Tab through Miss Burton?"

"Yeah, that's right. She's okay. Smarter than she acts and not bad looking, though she's had work done. Not that there's anything wrong with that."

"I agree. How did you meet her?"

"On a film shoot. We were both in a movie together. That was before she got signed at Icon, of course."

"A film shoot? I thought you said you wanted to get into movies, Mr. Bolt, I mean Tony, but you're already an actor?"

"Well, the films I make right now don't exactly require acting, exactly, Mr. Marvel."

"They don't?"

"Not much, anyway. I just have to take my clothes off, see?"

"Oh, I see. Those kinds of movies," Victor said, wondering where he might get a copy of one for him and Griff to screen in private sometime.

"Right. My best work was in *Bolt Upright and Hard*, but I'd like to do more. I know I can do more. I want to be a legit actor, for a big studio. I mean, gee, Sheila got her big break and signed to a contract, when am I going to get mine?"

"How *did* Sheila get signed at Icon?"

Tony leaned back, the chair creaking accordingly. "She told me Orland Orcott saw one of her special films. He arranged to meet her, and I guess she did what she had to do to get a contract."

"Ah, I see."

"I'm willing to do what I have to do, too," Tony said.

He stood up and casually unbuttoned the top button of his jeans, revealing just a glimpse of what looked like a jockstrap underneath. "Do you think you could help me, Mr. Marvel? No charge. I mean, I couldn't help but notice how you've been looking at me, and you never moved your knee away from mine under the table. How about I give you a free HPTS, and you help me get a part in a movie? What do you say?"

Victor swallowed hard, forcing his eyes back up to meet Tony's. "That's a generous offer, Mr. Bolt, I mean Tony, but I'm afraid I don't have much clout with the studio anymore, and besides, as attractive as you are, I'm involved with someone."

Tony shrugged his massive shoulders and sat back down, though he didn't bother to rebutton the top button on his jeans. "Oh, okay. It was worth a shot, right? I'd still appreciate it if you'd ask around for me, though. You're welcome to take some of my publicity photos to show folks if you want, the ones on the table or the ones from my regular portfolio. Or both."

Victor picked up one of the photographs off the table and stared, wetting his parched lips. "That's tempting, but if anyone expresses interest, I'll let you know and you can send the photographs over directly."

"Okay, that would be swell, Mr. Marvel, thanks."

Victor set the photograph back down and looked across the table at Tony once more. "You're welcome. So, you met Tab Rockwell through Sheila Burton."

"Yeah, that's right. After she started, uh, getting to know Mr. Orcott, she met Tab at Orcott's house one day. He told her he wanted to get in shape, build up his upper body. He thought it would help his film career. So, she introduced him to me."

"Because you're a bodybuilder or because you give personal training sessions?"

"I can do legitimate training, too, you know. I work out at Ned's Gym. I've helped a few guys get built. If you're interested, I could maybe do something for you, too, on the level, I mean."

"Thanks, but I'm okay. I have a gym I go to."

"I figured. Even with that expensive suit on, I can tell you work out. You take care of yourself for an older guy. A lot of men don't."

"Thank you. I did some pretty physical labor in my youth, and I've tried to keep myself in shape. In my business, it's important to take care of the mind and body also."

"Sure, that's why I do it, too. Tab said he could make things happen for me, though, in the legitimate movies."

"And you were willing to do whatever it took?"

Tony shrugged his massive shoulders. "I've done worse, and Tab's a handsome man. Not that I'm saying anything happened."

"Right, you don't kiss and tell. But if Tab was going to assist you, why did you ask for my help just a little bit ago?" Victor said.

"The more connections and friends on the inside, the better, I figure. And you, Mr. Marvel, are a pretty big name in this town. And you do have what they call clout."

"But not as much as I used to, as I said just a bit ago."

"Maybe not, but you know producers, agents, and directors. Movie people who could help me."

"Sure, that's true, I suppose. Did you ever meet Orland Orcott, Tony?"

"Tab's old man? Nah, but I heard about him. I was hoping Tab could fix it with him so I could maybe get a screen test on one of his films. That's one of the things he said he'd do."

"But I understand Mr. Orcott wasn't too happy with you," Victor said. "Tab told me his father was angry about the two of you."

"Yeah, I didn't know about that until, well, until I did. And now he's dead. Tab said his old man threatened to ruin me after he saw some pictures of the two of us. Him being dead kind of changes things, doesn't it?"

"I suppose it does," Victor said. "By the way, where were you Saturday night?"

"This past Saturday night? I was here, why?"

"Alone?"

"I had a fellow over for a while. We finished, he left, and I had dinner. Pork tenderloin, green beans, cottage cheese, and a glass of milk."

"That's a pretty good meal for someone living in a studio apartment during the Depression."

"The fellow tipped me well. He's a regular. I do okay for myself, but most of my earnings go into the bank. I have a fairly big savings account. I'm not an idiot, Mr. Marvel. I know eventually when I get older, men aren't going to want to hire me, and if I don't get a movie contract soon, I want to have enough money saved up to maybe open my own gym or something. That's my fallback plan."

"That's very wise. So, after your, uh, client, left, you were here alone the rest of the evening?"

"Yup. I fell asleep pretty early, I think. I was beat."

"I see. Well, I think that's all my questions for now." Victor stood up as Tony did the same, his jeans still unbuttoned. "I wish you luck, Mr. Bolt. Tony."

"Okay, thanks. It was great meeting you. Have a good rest of your day, Mr. Marvel."

"Thank you and likewise. You know, I just thought of something. I hear RKO is planning on making a new Tarzan film next spring. I'm willing to bet you'd look great in a loincloth. In fact, I *know* you'd look great in a loincloth."

"Oh yeah? Tarzan? I could play that. Not too many lines, you know?"

"Quite true. It seems like a tailor-made role for you. Give Carson Brickmore a call over at RKO, and tell him I sent you. Maybe send him a couple of those photographs on the table, too, along with a legitimate headshot."

Tony beamed, his whole face lighting up. "Carson Brickmore at

RKO, about the new Tarzan movie. Got it. Gee, thanks, Mr. Marvel. You're okay. I knew you was okay. Funny and handsome, too." He reached out and grasped Victor's hand in a bone-crushing shake.

"Yikes, I was right about you having the grip of a python," Victor said, wincing as he wrenched his hand free.

"Oh, geez, I'm so sorry. I got carried away in all the excitement. Are you okay?"

"Yes, it's all right, nothing broken. I don't think. I'm fine."

Tony looked relieved. "Good. I gotta be careful about that."

"A wise idea. Don't forget to buy a new mattress."

"Thanks, I won't. And if you ever change your mind about a HPTS, let me know."

"I'll do that. Now if you'll excuse me, I have to meet some friends for lunch, and it's already well after eleven. Goodbye." He picked up his fedora off the bedstead, strode to the door, and went out, resisting the urge to take one last look over his shoulder at Tony Bolt, who was, no doubt, filling the entire doorframe in which he stood, his jeans still bulging and the hint of jockstrap still visible.

CHAPTER ELEVEN

Monday afternoon, August 14, 1939
The Brown Derby restaurant

Victor put the top down again on his shiny, cherry red Cadillac and climbed in behind the wheel. He steered the car south to Wilshire Boulevard and then east to the corner of Wilshire and Alexandria. Since it was lunchtime, he had trouble finding a parking spot in the lot of the Brown Derby, but luckily, he knew the doorman at the Ambassador Hotel across the street, who was more than happy to let him use the valet service there. Victor tipped generously, of course, and hurried back across Wilshire, dodging traffic. At five minutes after twelve, Victor entered the infamous Brown Derby, taking off his fedora and smoothing his dark hair as he glanced about the crowded restaurant.

"Good afternoon, Mr. Marvel," the maître d' said with a smile he'd perfected over many years on the job. "How nice to see you again."

"Hello, Stuart, thank you. I'm meeting Eve Spellman and Griffin Fenwick. Have they come in yet?"

"Yes, sir, they're expecting you. Won't you follow me, please?" He led Victor to a center banquette with a round table which was covered in a starched white tablecloth. Two armchairs were opposite the banquette. Griff was sitting in one of the armchairs, and Eve was looking quite comfortable on the brown leather banquette. Victor joined her, sliding in and setting his hat beside him. Stuart handed him a menu, poured a glass of ice water, and returned quickly to his station by the front door.

"Hello, there. Sorry to keep you two waiting."

"Not at all, Vic," Griffin said. "We just got here maybe five minutes before you."

"Good. I see it's busy and loud in here, as always."

"Yes, it's a popular place," Eve said. "Griff got the last spot in the lot."

"I noticed. I had to use the valet at the Ambassador," Victor said, glancing at the menu. "Thanks for picking Eve up, by the way."

"Sure, happy to," Griff said.

"Do you two know what you're having?" Victor said, closing his menu and setting it aside.

"I do," Eve said, nodding. Her oversized white drum-shaped hat bobbed back and forth.

"Me too. My usual, I think," Griff said.

"Okay, let's order. I'm hungry." Victor gave a nod to a waitress hovering nearby.

"Hello, Mr. Marvel, Mr. Fenwick, Miss. May I take your orders?" she said as she approached them, pad and pencil in hand.

"Hello, Shirley," Victor said. "This is Miss Eve Spellman. Remember her, she's going to be a big star. She has the leading female role in an important upcoming Icon picture."

The waitress looked suitably impressed. "How do you do, Miss Spellman? Gee, that's terrific, congratulations. What may I bring you?"

"I'll have a Cobb salad and black coffee, please."

"Same," Victor said. "Can't mess with the house specialty."

"I'll have the grilled salmon," Griff said. "And an iced tea."

"Coming right up." She turned quickly and maneuvered back toward the kitchen.

"Next time you come in, Eve, she'll remember your name," Victor said.

"Thanks for that, Vic, but I'm not exactly the new kid at the studio."

"I know, but you're going to be great in this film, I can tell. It's going to open doors for you, just wait and see. Soon your caricature will be up there on the walls of this place along with mine and Griff's."

Eve looked around at the black-and-white drawings of just about every star in Hollywood, including the famous German shepherd Rin Tin Tin. "That would be nice," she said. "I'd get a kick out of that. So, what have you found out so far, if anything, Victor? Griff's been filling me in on your thoughts and the conversations you've had since Saturday night."

"I see. Well, I'm glad you're up to speed. I talked to Tony Bolt in his apartment this morning."

"Griff said you were coming here from his place. He's the fitness model, right?" Eve said.

"Yeah, for lack of a better term in polite company. He's certainly built, and a good-looking man. He was wearing the tightest T-shirt I've ever seen."

"Really? And you didn't invite me along?" Eve said.

"Sorry. He plays for our team, Eve, but it sounds like he's more than willing to switch hit temporarily for the right opportunity."

"Oh, one of those," Eve said.

"He's willing to do whatever it takes to break into show business," Victor said.

"And you didn't invite *me* along?" Griff said with a wicked grin.

"Wise guy," Victor said. "I made it known I was seeing someone, as are you, and I wished him luck."

"I'm just pulling your leg, Mr. Marvel. I'm quite content with the person I'm seeing," Griff said.

"I'm glad to hear it," Victor said, nudging him playfully and discreetly with his foot under the table.

"This is all heartwarming, but what exactly did Mr. Bolt have to say?" Eve said. "Or did he just pose and flex for you?"

"Very funny. He told me he met Tab through Sheila, and he had met Sheila on a film shoot," Victor said.

"A film shoot?" Griff said. "So, he's already in the biz?"

"In a manner of speaking. The films he's made to date involve being naked."

"Oh, blue movies," Griff said.

"And Sheila was in them?" Eve said, raising a painted-on, arched brow.

"That's what he said, or implied at the very least. Mr. Bolt told me that's how Orland found her originally. He watched one of her blue movies and arranged a meeting."

"Ugh. Why am I not surprised he'd watch those things?" Eve said.

"I don't think there's anything wrong with them, as long as it's between consenting adults," Griff said.

"I agree, though sometimes people can be coerced, which I don't agree with," Victor said.

"Definitely not," Eve said.

"That's not the case with Tony and probably not Sheila, either."

"Tony? You're already on a first-name basis?" Griff said.

"He told me I could call him Tony, that's all."

"How interesting."

"Not as interesting as you're imagining, I'm sure. Anyway, I recall Orcott telling me once he has a screening room near the swimming pool in one of the outbuildings on his property," Victor said. "He told me he used it to show special friends his films at Icon before they were released and to show other films at parties and such."

"Other films indeed," Griff said.

"Yeah," Victor said. "Those must have been some parties."

"It all sounds sordid. And you said Shelia introduced Mr. Bolt to Tab?" Eve said.

"Yes. She met Tab through his father, and Tab told her he wanted to get in shape and bulk up, so she thought of Tony Bolt. Tony said he could help him, and it seems Tab said he could help Tony."

"In what way?" Eve said.

"Help him to break into pictures."

"In exchange for a little bedroom time. That old song and dance," Griff said.

"It's been done to death in this town, and probably always will be."

"You're right, Victor, sadly," Eve said. "Do you believe he had something to do with Orland's death?"

"I don't know. Tab did say his father told him he'd destroy Tony after he found out about the two of them. And he claims he was home alone most of Saturday night."

"So, no alibi," Griff said.

"No. And I can't help but wonder if Sheila was involved somehow with him, given their history."

"She *was* at the party that night, after basically inviting herself, and she certainly was angry with Mr. Orcott for dumping her and taking up with Charlotte Masters," Eve said.

"And Mr. Orcott knew about her past in the blue movie industry. Maybe he was holding that over her head to keep her quiet about their affair and other things she probably discovered about him."

"That would certainly give her a motive. But how would she have been involved in his death? I still don't get how it's not suicide," Griff said.

"I don't either, and I could be all wrong, but I want to talk to her," Victor said.

"To Sheila?"

"Yes, sooner rather than later. And I think it might be helpful if you come along, Eve," Victor said.

"Me? Whatever for? We're not exactly friends, or even friendly."

"I'd just like a woman's perspective on what she says."

"I doubt she'll say much of any consequence. She has about as much depth as a sidewalk puddle after a rainstorm."

"Nonetheless, I want to chat with her," Victor said. "Join me?"

"Okay, I guess it can't hurt, physically, anyway. So, when?"

"After lunch, if that works for you."

"I'm available."

"Great, I'll see if Sheila is, too."

At that moment, Shirley returned bearing their lunches, which she placed in front of each of them. "A Cobb salad and a black coffee for you, Miss Spellman, and also for you, Mr. Marvel, and the grilled salmon and an iced tea for you, Mr. Fenwick. Is there anything else?"

"Yes, actually, Shirley, would you bring me a telephone, please?"

"Right away, Mr. Marvel." She tucked her tray under her arm and disappeared once more, returning with a white Bakelite telephone, its cord neatly coiled. She undid the cord and plugged the end into a jack between their booth and the neighboring one. "Here you are, sir."

"Thank you."

"You're welcome. I'll be back in a bit to check on you all," Shirley said, stepping away to take an order at a nearby table.

Victor took a bite of his salad and a sip of his coffee, then extracted a black leather address book from his suit pocket, turning the pages to the B's. He lifted the receiver, cleared his throat, and said to the operator, "Klondike Lake 2891, please."

"Are you calling Sheila?" Griff said.

Victor nodded.

"You have her phone number in your address book?" Eve said.

Victor covered the mouthpiece of the phone and said, "Yes, *and* her address. I called Lois at the head office of Icon earlier this morning, and she graciously gave me Sheila's home address after I sweet-talked her a little. She also told me they're trying to get Mervyn LeRoy to take over for Orcott on *The Lady Screeched*. If all goes well, we're to report first thing next Monday morning."

"That would be wonderful," Eve said, beaming, between forkfuls of salad. "I've always wanted to work with him."

"Gee, me too," Griff said. "Mr. LeRoy is a terrific director." He'd nearly devoured his salmon already.

"He is," Victor said, and then he held up a finger, indicating quiet. "Hello, Miss Burton? It's Victor Marvel. Yes, fine, thanks, and you? Good, good. Listen, I'm just finishing up lunch at the Derby and was hoping to swing by for a visit in a little bit. Oh, that doesn't matter, just an informal chat. That's right. Yes, I actually have the address. Hmm? Oh, the studio gave it to me. Yes, I know. All right, I'll see you in about an hour or so, thank you. Yes, goodbye." He hung up the receiver and took another bite of salad, nearly finished.

"I take it she was agreeable," Griff said.

"She was."

"And I noticed you didn't mention I would be coming along," Eve said.

"I thought that would be a nice surprise."

"Speaking of surprises," Eve said, finished with her salad, "look. Or don't look. Agatha Mudd just walked in."

Victor glanced toward the entrance, where Agatha was holding court with the maître d', no doubt grilling him about which stars were present and who they were dining with. As she caught sight of the three of them, she smiled and gave a little wave.

Victor smiled and waved back. "Here she comes," he said.

"So I see. My God, where did she get that awful hat?" Eve said. "Is she trying to compete with Hedda?"

"Eyeglasses are more Agatha's style. No one can compete with Hedda Hopper when it comes to hats," Griff said. "And speaking of hats, that one you're wearing is something, Eve."

"Thank you, Griff, it's nice of you to notice."

"Hard not to," Victor said as Agatha arrived at the table with a flourish.

"Well, well, if it isn't the happy couple. Or trio, should I say?"

Victor and Griff got to their feet.

"Hello, Agatha," Victor said. "Won't you join us?"

She smiled pleasantly. "Thank you, Victor, how kind of you. I will, but only for a moment. I'm supposed to be meeting Henry Fonda here for lunch, but I'm early."

"Wonderful," Victor said.

Griff held the chair next to his for her, and she sat down as Victor and Griff did the same.

"It looks like you three are all finished eating," Agatha said.

"Just about, yes. May I order something for you?" Victor said.

"Thank you, I am parched. I'll just have a tomato juice."

"Certainly," Victor said.

"With a splash of vodka and a dash of Worcestershire sauce," Agatha said. "Oh, and a celery stalk."

"Er, of course." Victor called Shirley over, and she took the drink order, poured more coffee and iced tea, cleared the three plates, and removed the telephone.

"You really should have the grapefruit cake for dessert, my dears, it's delicious."

"Perhaps another time, Agatha," Victor said.

"Oh, I know, you're all watching your weight. I am, too, but it is scrumptious. Well, I suppose you've all seen my column in yesterday's morning edition?" Agatha said, tugging off her ivory white gloves and setting them atop her black patent leather handbag.

"Of course," Griff said. "I read it every week."

"Oh, you are a lamb, aren't you?" Agatha cooed. "And what about you two lovebirds?"

"Naturally, Agatha," Victor said. "Eve and I read it together."

"Over your morning coffee? Really? Hmm." She peered at him over the top of her oversized glasses, which today were rimmed in bubblegum pink, matching her dress.

"We try to be discreet," Eve said.

"Naturally. Well, mum's the word," Agatha said. "Hmm."

"Your Bloody Mary, Mrs. Mudd," Shirley said as she arrived at the table once more and set the drink in front of her.

"Thank you, dear," Agatha said, "but I ordered plain tomato juice."

"Oh, I'm so sorry," Shirley said.

"With just a touch of vodka and Worcestershire sauce."

"Um, but…" Shirley said.

"That will be all," Agatha said, lifting the glass. "I'm dining with Henry Fonda, once he finally gets here. Do let me know, won't you?"

"Of course, Mrs. Mudd," Shirley said. She gave a slight bow and then stepped away hurriedly.

"How is your daughter, by the way, Agatha?" Victor said.

"Sylvia's fine, thank you. I try to visit her every day."

"She's fifteen now, isn't she?"

"That's right. You have a good memory, Victor. And it's kind of you to inquire about her."

"Your husband died not long after your daughter was born, I believe you had said."

Her eyes narrowed ever so slightly. "Yes, it was sudden. An accident."

"I'm so sorry," Victor said, and then he turned to Eve and Griff. "Would you two mind checking on my car for a few minutes? It's across the street in the Ambassador valet lot. I left the top down, and I want to make sure it's okay. Those pesky pigeons, you know."

"Your car?" Eve said.

"Oh, sure, Vic, I get it." Griff nodded knowingly. He got to his feet and said, "Let's go, Eve."

"Um, all right," Eve said, getting to her feet as Victor did the same.

"I'll see you two in a bit," Victor said as they walked away.

"Want to tell me what that was all about?" Agatha said as Victor took his seat once more. "Or don't I want to know? I doubt you wanted to get me alone to whisper sweet nothings in my ear."

"No, afraid not."

"I didn't think so. What is it, then?"

"I just wanted to say again I'm sorry about your husband dying."

"Thank you, but you could have said that in front of Miss Spellman and Griffin. What else is on your mind?"

"Well, you said the night of the Orcott party that you were an old maid, never married."

"Did I? I'm sure you misheard, Victor. Or perhaps I misspoke. Too much champagne, you know."

"Of course. I had a few too many also that night. I must have misheard you," Victor said. He leaned in closer to her and dropped his voice. "Or was it that you were an unwed mother in 1924, back when you were Kitty Manx, an up-and-coming actress?"

She leaned in, too, also lowering her voice. "What are you driving at Victor? And who did you hear that from?"

"Some of it's rumor, some I pieced together. Is it true?"

"I don't know what you're talking about, and if you know what's good for you and your career, Mr. Marvel, you'll drop the whole thing. Don't forget who you're speaking with. Should I choose to, I have the power to bring you to your knees with just a few strokes of my typewriter keys."

"I know that, and I'm sorry, Agatha. But I think you ended up with a child, either by force or by accident, by someone who was a powerful force in this town. That person, in order to keep you under his thumb, leaked the situation to the press, which killed your career. You went away to have the baby as Kitty Manx and came back as Agatha Mudd, resurrecting yourself as a top gossip columnist."

Agatha leaned back and studied Victor. "You're awfully clever."

"I don't know about that, Agatha, and I'm not trying to interrogate or accuse you. I just want to understand. Help me to understand, please. Of course, anything you say to me is completely confidential."

"Ha, I've heard that before. I've *said* that before."

"Well, in my case it's true."

"Hmm. I do like you, Victor, I always have. And *perhaps* I trust you, though that may be foolish of me." She paused to take another drink, and then said, "I take it, however, that your confidence includes Griffin, and possibly Miss Spellman?"

"To some degree, yes, to be honest. The three of us have few secrets from each other."

"Meaning anything I tell you will make its way to the two of them."

"If necessary, but you can trust them. They're top-notch."

Agatha set the glass down on the tablecloth. "Hmm, at least you were honest with me about that. Call me foolish, but after so many years, I feel like I need to confide in someone, and it seems you've already figured out most of it, anyway."

"Have I?"

"You know you have. You're not just a handsome face, Victor Marvel. All right, I'll put my faith in you. And, I suppose, in Miss Spellman and Mr. Fenwick."

"Thank you, Agatha. I won't let you down. *We* won't let you down. So, it *was* Orcott?"

She nodded ever so slightly, her ostrich feather hat bobbing gently. "How did you know?"

"It seemed logical, knowing him as I do, and knowing the two of you have history together, along with some of the things you said Saturday night."

She took a large drink of her Bloody Mary, nearly finishing it. "Well, you're right, all the way around."

"And I'm sorry, by the way, for what Orcott did to you back then."

"Oh, that's kind of you, but we were both adults, and we both knew what we were doing. Besides, I gained a beautiful daughter I love deeply."

"I should like to meet Sylvia sometime."

"That can be arranged. I should like for the two of you to meet also. She doesn't know about her father, of course. Not her real father."

"That's understandable. Did Orcott force his intentions on you, Agatha?"

"Did he force me? In a manner of speaking, I suppose. I wanted better roles in bigger pictures. Orland assured me I'd get them, *if* I cooperated."

"And *if* you did as you were told?"

"That's right. Only he hadn't counted on me becoming pregnant, and I hadn't, either. He was married to his first wife at the time, and furious when I told him. He denied it was his and said he would ruin me if I claimed he was the father. Then, to ensure my silence, he effectively destroyed my chances at being an actress by letting the press know I was an unwed mother. It caused a terrible scandal. Oh, the awful letters and telegrams I received, some from people I thought were my friends back in Wisconsin."

"That's terrible, but couldn't you have then gone to the press and let them know who the father was?"

"To what point? Even if they believed me, Orcott was too powerful. My career was over. He had assured me I'd never work in the movie industry again, and he hoped I'd go back to Kenosha, Wisconsin, and just disappear."

"But you didn't. You stayed in Hollywood, and you made yourself over, better than ever. You rose from the ashes like a phoenix and became something new and better."

"I did. I decided if I couldn't beat the gossip columnists, I'd join them and become the best of the best. Unlike some of my peers, I try to be fair, and I try to be honest, but I don't hold back much."

"That's why you're so good at your job."

"I like to think so. Now then, I've bared my secrets to you. Would you care to return the favor?"

Victor looked at her cautiously. "I suppose it's only fair I trust you."

"Trust is a two-way street, Victor. Or at least it should be."

"I agree." Victor looked around and leaned in once more. "You're referring to Griff and me, I assume."

"Am I?" Agatha said, emptying her glass and wiping her mouth with the cloth napkin, leaving lipstick prints upon it.

"You know you are, and so do I. You know the truth; you always do, somehow."

"Yes, well, my dear, it wasn't that difficult to determine. The way you two look at each other, the stolen glances, the subtle touches, always together at events and premieres, yet separate just enough. I've suspected you two were more than just friends for some time."

"And yet you never disclosed it or hinted at it in your column."

"You're correct, and that's only because I like you and Griff. You must be ever vigilant, though, both of you. If I can put one and one together, so can my rivals in the gossip biz. I must say, though, having Eve Spellman as your cover is brilliant. She's a lovely girl, and she seems loyal. You're at that age where you need someone like her. Griff, being still fairly young, can get away with the bachelor image, but not you."

"Eve is a terrific friend, and I owe her a great deal. Griff and I both try to be as discreet as possible. If something like this were to get out, it would ruin Griff's career."

"Not to worry as far as I'm concerned. You've always played straight with me, and you now know my big secret. I think we're even, wouldn't you say?"

"I would say, Agatha. Even Steven."

"Splendid. So, why are you bringing up this ancient history now? Because of my slip of the tongue that night at the party?"

"I wanted to know if my suspicions were correct about you and Orcott."

"But what does it matter? Especially now that he's dead, thank God."

"Maybe because he is dead, and because you and most everyone else seem happy about it."

"Happy? I can't say I'm happy, but I will say I'm relieved."

"Oh?"

"Yes, of course, it's only natural. I wasn't the first woman to be put in that position by him, nor the last. I'm glad there won't be any more now, at least as far as he's concerned."

"I understand, Agatha."

"Good. Oh, and there's Mr. Fonda, so I must dash off." She picked up her handbag and withdrew her compact, reapplying her lipstick in the mirror concealed within the lid. "There, that's better."

"Yes, and I see Eve and Griff have returned and are hovering near the maître d's stand," Victor said.

"No doubt waiting for us to finish." She dropped the compact back into her purse and snapped it shut. "I want to thank you for your discretion, Victor. In my profession, I don't have many friends. Not real ones. But I'd like to think *we* could be."

"I'd like to think that, too, Agatha. And thank you for your discretion as well."

"Of course. Just don't cross me, darling." She rose from the chair and got to her feet with amazing agility, adjusting her hat and smoothing out her skirt. "Thank you for the tomato juice. Ta ta for now, I'll be in touch. Let's do lunch sometime soon." She scooped up her gloves and her handbag once more and sailed off toward a table where Henry Fonda had been seated.

"What was that all about?" Eve said as she and Griff returned to the booth and sat down.

"Gossip, nothing more. And gossip is her business."

"Why do I not believe that's all there was to it?" Griff said.

"We all have our secrets," Victor said, "though some, I think, can be deadly. I'll fill you both in later as needed. She gave me permission." He signaled for the waitress one last time. "Let me pay the check, and then I think you and I should pay that visit to Sheila Burton, Eve. Want to come along, Griff?"

"Thanks, but I have my car here and things to do. I'll meet you back at your house later if that's okay."

"Sure," Victor said. "I shouldn't be late. It's one thirty now. I'll be home as soon as we finish at Sheila's and I drop Eve off at her place." He glanced over at Eve. "Unless you'd like to come to dinner at the house tonight. Griff's cooking, so it will be edible, as opposed to when I'm in the kitchen."

Eve chuckled. "Thanks, Vic, but two's company, as the saying goes."

CHAPTER TWELVE

Monday afternoon, August 14, 1939
Sheila Burton's house

Victor and Eve crossed Wilshire Boulevard at the corner and retrieved his car from the Ambassador Hotel valet, Victor tipping the attendant another dime as he brought it around.

"Thank you, Mr. Marvel," the young man said with a grin. He couldn't have been more than twenty or twenty-one, clean-shaven, with wavy ginger hair and deep blue eyes.

"You're welcome. Help me put the top up, will you? The lady's hair, you know."

"And don't forget my brand-new hat," Eve said, "which, I might add, you haven't seemed to notice, though Griff did."

Victor looked over at her. She was wearing a just below the knee raspberry-colored skirt, matching long-sleeve jacket cinched at the waist, white gloves, and white pumps. Atop her head was a drum-shaped, white, puffy hat that reminded Victor of a large, fluffy marshmallow, held in place by a chin strap of white velvet.

"Sorry, Eve. I did say earlier it was hard not to notice it, if you recall. I should have commented on it more thoroughly, though. It's, uh, different and unique."

"Why, thank you, Victor, how nice of you."

The young valet grinned and looked like he was about to say something, but then changed his mind as he finished securing the car's top. "There you go, Mr. Marvel. The lady's hat won't be going anywhere now."

"Good, thanks again."

"My pleasure, sir. Say, if you know of anybody at the studio looking for a dancer, I'm your guy. The name's Hobson, Hobson Hocklee. I can sing a little, too. I moved out here from Arizona to get into the movies, but I haven't had much luck yet."

"Okay, Hobson, tell you what. Contact central casting at Icon Pictures, feel free to use my name," Victor said, helping Eve into the passenger side and closing the door. "Ask for Spencer Call."

"Gosh, thanks, Mr. Marvel, I will, right away."

"Good luck to you, kid," Victor said, climbing behind the wheel. With a wave, he steered the Cadillac out onto Wilshire Boulevard.

"You were right," Eve said. "This town is full of them."

"Yes, young, hopeful, and eager. I wish I could help them all. Despite talent, or lack thereof, only the lucky ones will make it."

"It's kind of sad."

"I agree. I happened to get lucky, in more ways than one."

"Well, here's hoping Hobson Hocklee is one of the lucky ones, too. He seemed nice and he has a handsome, fresh-faced look about him. So, where are we headed?" Eve said.

Victor glanced over at her briefly. "To see Sheila Burton."

"I know that, silly, but where does she live?"

"A house off Highway 99, the old Ridge Route."

"Really? That's an odd spot for an aspiring actress to live."

"It's probably something Orcott helped her get."

"Why would he want her so far away? Wouldn't an apartment in Hollywood make more sense?"

"I suspect he liked his mistresses out of the way unless he needed them. Made it easier when the affairs ended, too, I bet."

"What a guy," Eve said. "Okay, but drive carefully. I've been on that road, and it's steep, narrow, and serpentine."

"Yes, ma'am," Victor said.

As ordered, he took it easy, driving at or just below the posted speed limit. He wouldn't admit it to Eve, but the road made him nervous, too, and he gripped the wheel tightly every time he had to take a hairpin turn. Neither one of them said much until at last Victor turned into a gravel driveway on the right and went up a short incline, just a little after two in the afternoon. At the top stood a small yellow wood-framed house surrounded by towering pine trees.

"This is it, I think," Victor said.

"It's pretty out here, if nothing else," Eve said, looking about. "It's hard to believe we're only about thirty minutes away from the Brown Derby."

"Yeah," Victor said, taking a deep breath as he got out and went around to open the car door for Eve. "I'm not used to fresh air."

Together they walked up the dirt path to the front door and knocked, as no doorbell was visible.

Presently the door opened, and Sheila, dressed in a tight white short-sleeved blouse, red shorts, and black high heels, stared out at them. She had put on her face and had her bright red hair combed out and tied back with a white satin ribbon.

"Hello, Miss Burton," Victor said, taking off his fedora.

"Good afternoon, Mr. Marvel. And Eve, this is a surprise."

"Hello," Eve said.

"Yeah," Sheila said, and then she looked back at Victor. "You said on the telephone you wanted to talk to me about something. I wasn't aware Miss Spellman would be joining you."

"Is that why you're dressed like a beauty pageant contestant?" Eve said. "Because you were expecting Mr. Marvel to be alone?"

"It's my house, I dress the way I want. I like to be comfortable, that's all."

"Of course, and high heels are *so* comfortable," Eve said.

"You look lovely, Miss Burton," Victor said.

"Thank you, Mr. Marvel," Sheila said. "At least one of you has manners. Please call me Sheila."

"All right. We just finished lunch at the Brown Derby and thought we'd say hello and see how you're doing after everything that's happened," Victor said. "Since I have to drive Eve home later, I asked her to tag along. I hope you don't mind."

"Oh, I see. Come on in, then," she said, stepping aside as they entered. "Both of you, I suppose. Have a seat. You can put your hat on the table there, Mr. Marvel."

"Thanks," Victor said as he put his fedora down. He and Eve made themselves comfortable in chintz armchairs near the fireplace. The overstuffed sofa faced the armchairs and the fireplace, and Sheila perched upon the sofa's plump cushions, kicking off her heels and curling her bare legs up under her. A newspaper, opened to the crossword puzzle, sat on the table next to her, a pencil resting atop it.

"Um, interesting place you have here, Sheila," Victor said. The cottage was decorated in early American, with lots of animal heads on the walls.

"It's okay. It came furnished, not my style, you know? I've only been here about six months. It's kind of far out of town, and that road scares me, especially after dark."

"It *is* treacherous. Perhaps you can think about moving closer in now," Victor said.

"Yeah, it crossed my mind. The lease on this place is paid up until February of next year, so maybe then I'll look for an apartment or something in Hollywood. Nothing fancy, though."

"As long as it has a double bed, I'm sure you'll do just fine," Eve said.

"Is that a crack?"

"I, uh, I hope we're not disturbing you," Victor said.

Sheila looked back to Victor. "Nope, I was just working on today's crossword puzzle in the paper. Did you read the 'Slinging Mudd' column in yesterday's paper?"

"Ah, yes," Victor said. "I saw that."

"I read it, too," Eve said.

"She didn't mention me and barely mentioned Griff."

"Well, most of the column was taken up by Mr. Orcott's unexpected demise," Eve said.

"Yeah, I suppose. At least she didn't have anything nasty to say about me. I read her column every week just to make sure. I also do the daily crossword because I'm told puzzles keep the mind sharp. You should try it sometime, Eve. At your age, you need to focus on improving your brain."

"Eve's a very intelligent woman, Sheila," Victor said.

"Yeah, I suppose she is. She hooked up with you, so she ain't stupid."

"*Isn't* stupid, Sheila," Eve said.

"Isn't what stupid?"

"That is the question, isn't it?" Eve said, raising a brow.

"You have too many martinis at the Derby, Eve?" Sheila said.

"Just black coffee."

"Coulda fooled me."

"No doubt. It's an easy thing to do."

"What's that supposed to mean?"

"It loses all meaning if I have to explain it, Sheila."

"Then don't. See if I care. Where'd you get the goofy marshmallow-shaped hat, anyway? Pick it out of a cup of hot chocolate?"

"Why do you two dislike each other so much?"

Eve looked over at him. "I don't dislike Sheila. I feel absolutely nothing toward her. She's a dull, talentless void."

"Mutual, I'm sure," Sheila said. "And I must say, it takes one to know one."

"Really? Is that the best you can do?" Eve said. "I've heard better retorts on a grammar school playground."

"God, you're especially bitchy today," Sheila said. "Someone tug your girdle strings too tight this morning?"

"I don't wear a girdle, Sheila, I don't need one. Besides, I rely on my wits more than my looks."

"And a good thing, to look at you. No wonder you're still only getting supporting and character roles. And you *do* need a girdle."

"When was your last starring role, Sheila?" Eve said.

"I'm new, just getting started. You've been at it twenty years."

"Ten."

"Sure, if you say so. I still can't believe Orland gave you the role of Ruth just because he and I stopped being friendly."

"It wasn't because of the two of you," Eve said. "Victor wanted me in the picture. I told you that before."

"That's true, I did want Eve to play Ruth," Victor said.

"But why?" Sheila said, focusing her gaze on him again now. "I mean, I know she's your girlfriend or whatever, but so what? I guess that's the only way she can get a decent role is if her boyfriend gets it for her."

"You mean that's the only way *you* can get a decent role," Eve said. "Or was the only way. I guess you're out of luck now."

"About that," Victor said.

"About what?" Sheila said, staring at him.

"I'm curious about a few things."

"Oh, yeah? Curiosity killed the cat, you know."

"And the cat, so to speak, is dead," Victor said.

"What cat?" Sheila said, a look of alarm sweeping across her face. "There's a few of them around here, strays, you know. I feed them. Did something happen to one of them? You didn't run over one, did you?"

"No, dear, he's talking about Orland Orcott," Eve said.

"Oh," Sheila said, looking relieved. "Well, sure. He's dead, we all know that. We were all there, remember? I thought you were talking about one of the kitties out here."

"We never saw a cat this afternoon," Victor said.

"They lay low during the day, mostly," Sheila said. "Orland had a cat, too, you know. Chowder. He was with Orland in the study that night, I heard. You know, when I used to visit Orland out in his screening room by the pool, the cat would sometimes be there. He followed Orland all over the place. It was kind of sweet."

"I think Chowder is a female," Victor said.

"Is he? I wouldn't know, they all look the same. I like cats, though, and that cat sure liked him."

"For some strange reason," Eve said.

"You didn't like Orland, Eve, but he wasn't all bad, you know. He could be real nice sometimes."

"I'm sure," Victor said.

"When he wanted something," Eve said.

"Yeah, but now he's gone, dead. Dead's a relative term, though, isn't it?" She put on a pair of glasses that had been sitting on the end table and stared at Victor.

"I wasn't aware you wore glasses, Sheila," Eve said.

"I don't usually. I can see well enough without them. I mean, I'm not walking into doors or anything, but I sometimes get a headache when I leave them off too long, and I can feel one coming on now. Though it might just be the company, yours excluded, Mr. Marvel."

"Uh, thanks. If you get headaches, though, you should wear them more often," Victor said.

"But you know what they say, 'men don't make passes at girls who wear glasses.' And bespectacled women don't get leading lady roles, either. And I intend to be a star one day," she said as she looked over at Eve.

"I don't need glasses, Sheila. I have 20/20 vision."

"In your case, I don't think it would matter one way or the other. I wonder who they're going to get to direct *The Lady Screeched* now. It might not be good for you, Eve."

"Or it might be very good, Sheila. There's a rumor they're trying to get Mervyn LeRoy."

Sheila looked suitably impressed. "Oh yeah? Well, we'll see how that works out."

"You don't seem too upset about Mr. Orcott's death," Eve said.

"Why should I be? He threw me over for Charlotte. Now he's dead."

"And you're delighted about that?" Victor said.

"Delighted that he's dead? No, but I'm not sad, either, if I'm being honest. It's just something to get used to. I mean, what is dead? Some say people go to heaven or hell, some say the soul is reincarnated as a newborn or an animal, some say the soul is simply transferred to an existing animal."

"You don't say," Victor said.

"I don't say anything, but some do. Mr. Kirtchner says things like that all the time."

"Mr. Kirtchner?" Eve said.

"He's one of the makeup men at the studio. Stanley is his given name, I think."

"Oh yes, Stan, I know him," Victor said.

"He's very ethereal," Sheila said.

"My, that's a big word for you," Eve said.

"He taught me that word. It means light, in a way that seems too perfect for this world. It's crazy, but right after he taught that to me, it was in the paper's crossword puzzle the next day. Isn't that strange?"

"A coincidence, certainly," Victor said. "So, Mr. Kirtchner talked to you about souls?"

"About all kinds of things when I was sitting in his chair for my last picture. He's quite intelligent. I think he likes me, you know."

"I thought you said he was quite intelligent," Eve said.

"He is, and he can do wonders with makeup, not that I ever need much. But you, Eve, well, you should see if he makes house calls. Maybe the studio dietician, too."

"Uh, let's get back to Mr. Orcott," Victor said.

"What about him? He's still dead, you know. Though perhaps his soul has transferred," Sheila said.

"Transferred?" Victor said.

"Like the crosstown bus?" Eve said.

"I mean like maybe to Chowder, the cat. Tab told me earlier this afternoon when he called me that Mrs. Cobbledick, she's the head housekeeper for the Orcotts, told him Chowder wouldn't touch his regular food this morning, but ate a piece of dried fig that had fallen on the floor. Dried figs were Orland's favorite. I tried to give Chowder one once, and he wouldn't touch it. Now all of a sudden, he gobbled it down."

"*She's* probably just under stress," Victor said, "a break from her routine, all the hubbub and strangers about, and not knowing what has happened to Mr. Orcott. Animals behave differently in times like these, just like people do. I highly doubt Orland's spirit has been transferred to the cat."

"Perhaps, perhaps not. The spirit world is very mysterious. I figured you to be the logical type, though, very reasonable, and I was right."

"Logic, Sheila, is the cornerstone of thought," Eve said.

"I know you make stuff up like that to sound smart, but it just makes you sound stupid."

"That doesn't seem very logical," Eve said.

"What's that supposed to mean? I get the impression you're insulting me again, and I don't like it. Two can play at that game, you know."

"In a game of wits, I'm sure you'd be unmatched, Sheila."

"When I figure out what you mean by that, you're going to be sorry."

Victor cleared his throat. "You said you spoke with Tab earlier this afternoon, Sheila?"

"Sure, he called to say hello and see how I was doing. Wasn't that nice of him?"

"You two have become fast friends, it seems," Eve said.

"I guess so, Tab's okay."

"You met Tab through his father, is that correct?" Victor said.

"Yeah, that's right. I'd go over to Orland's house quite a bit, always in the building out back, never the main house, even though I was only ever there when Marjorie was gone. But sometimes Tab would be there, lounging by the pool or something."

"And after you met Tab, I understand you introduced him to Tony Bolt."

"Who told you that?" Sheila said.

"I stopped by Tony Bolt's apartment this morning."

"Tony? What were you doing at his place?"

"I had a few questions for him. He mentioned he knows you and Tab."

"Tony's a nice guy, and real good looking. I haven't seen him in a while, though."

"But you did introduce him and Tab?" Eve said.

"I wouldn't say that, exactly. I mean, Tab wanted to build up his body, and I told him I knew a fella that could help, and I gave him Tony's number, that's all."

"I see. And you met Tony while working on a film? A special type of film?" Victor said.

"Tony's got a big mouth," Sheila said, her face blushing a deep pink.

"Was Tab aware of your work in blue films?" Victor said.

"Sure, so was Orland. But I don't like it being blabbed around, you know?"

"I'm sure not. I don't plan to tell anyone," Victor said.

"What about her?"

"I won't say anything, either, Sheila," Eve said.

"Yeah, like I believe that. Well, if you do, I'll yank your hair out, roots and all."

"I'd love to see you try. Of course, yours has been bleached and dyed so often it will probably fall out on its own soon. Blond, redhead, brunette, blond, now redhead again, and that's just in the last year."

"Redheads get noticed."

"Especially when it's a shade not found outside of a circus," Eve said.

"Um, were you surprised, Sheila, that Mr. Orcott killed himself?" Victor said.

She focused on Victor again. "Surprised? Should I have been? I don't know, I suppose so. Mr. Kirtchner said suicide is a selfish act."

"It can be perceived that way," Victor said. "I happen to believe it's a tragic act."

"Well, it ain't a comedy," Sheila said, her glasses sliding down her nose. "But it is funny."

"What is?"

"Oh, I don't know, just everything. The cat, Chowder, was the last living thing with him, you know? It makes sense his soul would be transferred, you see? Transferred to the cat."

"And we're back to that again," Eve said, rolling her eyes.

"You were on the terrace when the shot was fired, correct?" Victor said.

"That's right. We were on the terrace getting some fresh air when we heard the noise. It made me spill my drink, and I dropped my cigarette. We weren't quite sure where the noise came from, but Tab said we should go back inside and see what had happened. When we got there you all were already there. The noise scared the you know what out of me."

"The brains?" Eve said.

Victor tried to stifle a laugh as he stood up. "Yes, well, thank you for seeing us, Sheila. We'll let you get back to your crossword puzzle."

She tossed her head. "Okay. I do have one question for you, though, if you don't mind."

"What's that?"

"What's a six-letter word for guile?"

"How about 'deceit'?" Eve said.

"Deceit? How do you spell that?" Sheila said, picking up the puzzle and her pencil.

"I before e except after c."

"Huh, that's weird, but it fits."

"Indeed," Eve said.

Sheila set the paper and pencil down, got to her feet, and put her high heels back on. "I'll walk you two out."

"There's no need," Victor said as he and Eve walked to the door.

"It's fine, I want to make sure my cats are all okay, anyway. It's almost three thirty and they start to get active about now every afternoon." She walked to the door and extracted a cigarette from a box on the table.

"Got a light?"

"Certainly," Victor said, extracting a silver lighter from his trousers pocket. "I don't smoke, but I always carry a lighter."

"That's cause you're a gentleman," Sheila said, allowing Victor to light her cigarette. She inhaled deeply and exhaled softly, the smoke billowing about her bright red hair. "Shall we?"

"After you," Victor said. He put his lighter back in his pocket, took his hat from the rack, and stepped out after Sheila and Eve.

CHAPTER THIRTEEN

Monday afternoon, August 14, 1939
The road back

"She's going to break her neck," Eve said, as she adjusted the velvet strap of her hat.

They pulled away in Victor's Cadillac, driving slowly down the gravel path to the main road. Sheila was hobbling along behind in her heels, puffing away on her cigarette like a steam engine on a downgrade.

Victor glanced at her in the mirror. "Or at least twist an ankle."

"We can only hope. Well, whatever you do, keep your eyes on the road and don't run over any of her cats. You'd never hear the end of it, and I'd feel terrible."

"Don't worry, I'm an animal lover, too. And I'm going about as slow as I can."

"Good." They were almost to the end of the drive. Eve glanced back again. "She's still upright so far anyway."

"Gotta give her credit," Victor said.

"For navigating a gravel road, at a decline, in high heels?"

"And for caring about animals."

"Oh, well, yes, I'll give her credit for that, at least, but I swear that woman doesn't have a brain in her head."

At the end of the gravel driveway, Victor stopped and waited as a blue Rambler rambled by on the main road. Parked off to the side of the highway was a black Ford.

"Odd place for someone to park," Eve said.

"Yeah, might be an overheated radiator," Victor said. "Surprising, as it looks like a new car, but these grades are pretty steep. That's a Model 91A, if I'm not mistaken."

"Want to stop and see if they need help?"

"No, they're probably just checking a map or something. If they were having trouble, they would have raised their hood."

"Okay," Eve said.

When the Rambler had passed and the rest of the main road was clear, Victor turned left, heading back toward town.

"You know, it's curious," Eve said.

"What is? And don't say a cat."

Eve smiled. "No, not a cat. I was just thinking. Did you notice Sheila used the exact same wording and phrasing just now when she described where she and Tab were when the gun went off?"

"What do you mean?" Victor said.

"I mean that she said the exact same thing, word for word, I'm sure, just now that she said the night of Orcott's death. Both times she said, 'We were on the terrace getting some fresh air when we heard the noise. It made me spill my drink, and I dropped my cigarette. We weren't quite sure where the noise came from, but Tab said we should go back inside and see what had happened. When we got there you all were already there. The noise scared the you know what out of me.' "

"You remember every word she said?"

"It's one of my skills. It helps me memorize my dialogue. I can read or hear a line and almost instantly remember it. I may have missed a word or two, but believe me, it was almost exact."

"Hmm, that is curious. It's as if she'd rehearsed it," Victor said. "Like an actress reciting her lines."

"A bad actress. She spoke both times with almost no emotion and no feeling. No real feeling, anyway. It's why it stuck out in my mind."

"It did sound phony. But what does it mean?"

"I've no idea," Eve said. "And I wonder why Agatha Mudd didn't mention Sheila in her column yesterday. She certainly doesn't care for her. I believe she called Sheila a parasite."

"Agatha did call her that, but most of the column was devoted to Orcott's death."

"True, but I wonder if Sheila knows about Agatha's daughter and is holding that over her head to make sure Agatha never writes anything bad about her," Eve said.

"It's possible, I suppose. Even with Orland's demise, it's not like Agatha to miss an opportunity to take a potshot at someone like Sheila."

"I agree," Eve said.

"There's something else that's been weighing on my mind, too, speaking of Agatha's daughter."

"What's that?" Eve said.

"Agatha told me at lunch today Orland may have been the father, and he may have been the one to destroy her career."

"Holy moly, are you serious, Victor?"

"Yes, and I'm only telling you this in confidence because I'm trying to sort all this out. She gave me permission to share that with you if necessary."

"I wonder if Agatha didn't have something to do with Orcott's death," Eve said, holding on as Victor took a hairpin turn.

"Yes, but how?"

"Well, Agatha was alone in the library when the shot was fired, remember? She had shooed out William and Lydia earlier."

"Yes, that's right. She said she wanted someplace quiet to compose her notes," Victor said.

"Right, but how do we know that was the real reason? Once she got rid of William and Lydia, maybe she locked the door from the library to the reception room. Then she waited until she heard Orland enter the study. She went in, shot him, put the gun in his hand, and fled back to the library, locking the connecting door between the study and the library behind her. All she had to do next was unlock and exit the door from the library to the reception room, come out to the entrance hall, and innocently ask us what had happened."

"That's a plausible theory."

"I think so. She probably got the gun sometime earlier in the evening when the study was empty. The drawer was jimmied, don't forget," Eve said.

"You're right. She had motive, opportunity, and means. Good thinking."

"Thanks," Eve said.

"Agatha said I was clever, but maybe she is, too, more than I realized. The only hitch is the door between the study and the library. It was deadbolted from the study side, so Agatha wouldn't have been able to lock it from the library."

"Unless she somehow picked the lock in reverse."

"Maybe. We did find a coat hanger outside that had been straightened out." Victor glanced in the rearview mirror. "Huh."

"What?"

"That car behind us, it's the black Ford Model 91A, I'm almost positive."

"The one that was parked on the side of the road just before the drive from Sheila's?"

"Yes. It must have pulled out shortly after us and did a U-turn."

"So?" Eve said.

"So, I dropped my speed down to ten below the limit, and he's still behind us."

"This isn't exactly a road anyone in their right mind would want to pass on, Victor."

"I know, but even in the couple of straight stretches he never made an attempt to go around."

"Maybe he's just timid."

"Maybe, but also each time I've accelerated he's sped up, staying on my tail."

"Okay, that is a bit unusual," Eve said, glancing back.

"Yes, I think so."

"You think he's following us?"

"I'm going to find out," Victor said. He rolled down his window and drove the car as far off the road as possible while slowing down considerably. With his left hand, he waved out the window, indicating for the vehicle behind to pass, but it didn't. Instead, it slowed down, too, almost to a stop.

"All right, something's up," Victor said. He pulled back onto the road and picked up speed. The Ford followed suit.

"He's still sticking to me like glue," Victor said, looking again in the rearview mirror.

"Who is it?"

"I can't tell. See if you can," Victor said, gripping the wheel tightly with both hands.

Eve craned her neck around again to peer out the back, her poofy hat just clearing the roof of the car. "I can't tell, either. He's wearing a hat and sunglasses, and it looks like a coat and scarf."

"Interesting attire for August. He doesn't want to be recognized. If it is a he. Can you make out the license plate?"

"I think so. I believe it's 5L 7524, California."

"Okay, good. Remember that."

"Done," Eve said.

Victor barely touched the brakes as his car squealed around a bend, gravel flying. Eve was pressed against the door.

"Victor, slow down!"

"And let him, or her, get us? Not a chance." Another hairpin turn, this one in the opposite direction. Eve slammed against Victor, who jerked the wheel left into the oncoming traffic involuntarily. The driver of a small truck blared his horn and swerved onto the shoulder as Victor tugged the wheel again, bringing the Cadillac back into the proper lane.

"You're going to go over the edge, Victor. You're going to get us killed. It could just be one of your fans."

"Not likely. Brace yourself." Victor hit the brakes hard, the tires screaming as the car lurched to a halt sideways. The mysterious driver of the Ford hit his brakes, too, smoke and the smell of burnt rubber rising up from the tires, but his car stayed facing head-on. It started moving again, aiming right for the broad side of the Cadillac.

"He's going to ram us and knock us over the edge," Eve said, panicked.

"Hold on," Victor shouted.

Eve clutched the door handle, unsure of what else to grab. She was terrified.

Victor spun the wheel and hit the gas, the Caddy responding like the well-tuned machine it was. The Ford hit the corner of the Cadillac's back left bumper, and Eve braced herself as best she could as Victor fishtailed before picking up speed once more. The black Ford followed suit.

"Victor, watch out!" Eve yelled as a young deer sprinted across the road in front of them. Victor swerved into the oncoming lane again, which was thankfully empty this time, and the deer made it across safely. Once more Victor slammed on the brakes hard and Eve's head hit the windshield with a thwack as she flew from the seat. The Ford roared past them in the other lane, its front bumper hanging down on one end. It kept going.

"Are you all right, Eve?" Victor said.

She pried herself back upright and stared at him, pushing her marshmallow hat, now completely squished down, back into place. "I'll live. My hat slipped forward and cushioned the blow. But you'd better get out of this lane before another vehicle comes along and flattens us."

"Right, good idea." Victor released the brake and hit the gas once more, gently this time, maneuvering back into the correct lane of traffic.

"What was that all about?" Eve said.

"I wish I knew."

"Do you think he'll come back?"

"I don't know. I don't think so. Maybe they were just trying to scare us, or maybe they gave up. I should get you to a hospital."

"That's not necessary, Victor, just get me home. I want a vodka and an ice pack. I'll be fine."

"All right. But once you're back at your place, call your doctor. Have him stop out and take a look at you."

"Okay, I will, I promise. Are you okay?"

"I think so. The steering wheel might have cracked a rib, though, when I slammed into it."

"You'd better have your doctor stop over when you get home, too."

"I will. Damn. I'd like to know who the hell that was."

"So would I," Eve said.

"One of the tires seems a bit wobbly. I'll need to swing by a service station, get some gas, and have them check the car over before we go much farther."

"Sounds like a good idea. And I may use the ladies' room and throw up."

Chapter Fourteen

Early Monday evening, August 14, 1939
Victor Marvel's house

"Hello," Griff said from the living room sofa as Victor entered through the front door. "What happened to you? I thought you'd be back ages ago. It's after six, and I've got dinner all ready."

"Sorry, but something came up," Victor said, arching his back, holding his ribs, and tossing his fedora on the hat rack near the entrance.

"Are you okay? You don't look so good."

"I don't feel so good, either. I think I may have cracked a rib, or at least done some serious bruising. Nothing a stiff drink and a hot bath won't help. The Cadillac, on the other hand, is going to need some work."

Griff got to his feet and hurried over to him. "Were you in a car accident?"

"Not an accident. Someone tried to run me and Eve off the road. She said she's fine, thank God, just a little shaken up."

"I can imagine. I'm glad she's okay, but I'm worried about you."

"Eh, I'm all right. My car is pretty banged up, though. I had to stop and have one of the tires fixed just so I could make it home. It's drivable now, but I'll have to get it into the dealership soon for repairs."

"Geez, Vic. You mean someone did this on purpose?"

"That's exactly what I mean, up on Highway 99, the old Ridge Route."

"Holy cow, that's a dangerous road. What happened?"

"Pretty much what I just told you. I think it might have something to do with Orcott's death. Someone may think I'm getting too close."

"But if that's the case, Orcott's death was definitely murder."

"It would seem so," Victor said, removing his tie and kicking off his shoes, the laces still tied.

"Did you let the detective know? What was his name?"

"Steve Garnett, and no, not yet. I'm going to call him now." Victor winced as he slowly took off his suit coat and draped it over a nearby chair.

"Good. I'm going to call Dr. Hightower and have him come out and look you over. You're in pain, I can tell."

"Fine, I suppose that would be a good idea."

"The studio would insist on it. Besides, I think it's in our contract."

"Probably. Let me call Detective Garnett before you call the doctor, though. Make me a whiskey sour, would you? A strong one."

"Sure," Griff said, moving off toward the bar.

Victor walked slowly over to the sofa and picked up the telephone off the end table. He dialed the operator and asked to be connected to the West Los Angeles Community Police Station, and then he asked the desk sergeant for Detective Steve Garnett.

Victor heard a click, and then the familiar, deep, resonant monotone voice. "Detective Garnett speaking."

"Steve, it's Victor Marvel."

"Oh, Victor, hello."

"I'm glad you're still there."

"Another five minutes, and I wouldn't have been. I'm ready to go home. What's up?"

"I was wondering if I could ask you a favor."

"What kind of favor?"

"Any chance you can run a check on a license plate for me? A black Ford model 91A tried to run my convertible off the road a short while ago out on Highway 99. Nearly killed me."

"Did you file a police report?"

"No, I called you."

"You should always file a police report when things like that happen," Garnett said matter-of-factly. "Are you okay?"

"Yeah, I'm fine, more or less. Eve Spellman was with me. We were both a little shaken up, literally and figuratively, but we're okay. She hit her head on the windshield, but her hat cushioned the blow, thankfully. Believe me, I'll never make fun of women's fashion again."

"Did you take her to the hospital?"

"I dropped her home, but she promised she'd call her doctor and have him come out yet tonight. I'll check in on her later."

"Good," Garnett said. "The other driver was probably drunk."

"Maybe, but he was quite aggressive, Steve. And he was following me for a long time and wouldn't pass. I tried to lose him, but I couldn't. That's when he tried to force me off the road and over the cliff."

"Jeez, Victor, and you didn't think to call the police once it was over?"

"That's what I'm doing now, Steve. You *are* the police."

"Not the same. You should have reported it to the highway patrol."

"You're right, I should have. But I'm calling you now because I think the incident might have something to do with the Orcott case."

"In what way?"

"I'm not sure. Maybe I'm just being paranoid, or maybe I'm getting close to figuring this out."

"Figuring what out?"

"The truth about Orcott's death. Though I don't have any answers yet, maybe someone *thinks* I do."

"Victor, this is a police matter. You can't go around investigating on your own. I know you played Detective Hart in three movies, but you're *not* a police detective. Did you get a description of the driver?"

"No, he was wearing a hat, coat, and sunglasses, as if he didn't want to be recognized. I'm not even one hundred percent certain it was a man. We were talking to Sheila Burton at her house. When we left, this car started tailing us. It was like he was waiting for us." He withdrew the scrap of paper that Eve had scribbled on earlier from his pants pocket and glanced at it. "The license plate is 5L 7524, from California."

"All right, I'll call over to the DMV and see if I can get some information yet today, though it's getting late. Please leave the rest of the investigation to me, though, okay?"

"Is there an investigation in your opinion, Steve? You said it appeared to be suicide."

"Well, the coroner's report came back a short while ago on Orland Orcott. It was…interesting."

"In what way?"

"I can't say, Vic. The case hasn't been closed yet."

"Meaning it's *not* a cut and dried case of suicide."

"Well, not exactly, no."

"Okay, I understand. You know, I was thinking the other day about how you never got credit for all the assistance you gave me on the Phineas Hart movies. I might be able to get you mentioned in the credits of the new film."

"You're kidding, Victor."

"'Special thanks to Detective Steve Garnett of the West Los Angeles Community Police Station for his invaluable assistance with research.' How does that sound?"

"Gosh, that would be terrific. You could do that?"

"I think so. It would help, though, if you could share at least a little something with me about the autopsy report on Orcott."

"Oh, I see, you scratch my back, I scratch yours, is that it?"

"Listen, Steve, I think I'm on to something. Anything you tell me will be held in the strictest confidence between me and my associates, I promise. You can trust me."

"Well…"

"At least just tell me what the coroner had to say. It will be public record eventually, anyway."

Garnett sighed heavily into the receiver, which crackled in Victor's ear. "Fine, but you didn't hear it from me. Orcott's body showed no indications of any poisons, sleeping pills, or drugs in his system, not in the bloodstream or in his stomach. Nothing out of the ordinary. The remnants of the teacup were clean, too, just regular peppermint tea with a bromide."

"Oh, is that it? So, no one slipped him a mickey," Victor said.

"Nope. But they did notice something else. The way the bullet entered the brain and the estimated trajectory of the bullet don't seem to add up to suicide. The coroner thinks the gun was fired roughly five or six feet from the victim. Also, it's not common for suicides to shoot themselves in the face, I've seen my share of them. It's usually the left or right temple, or the heart, or sometimes with the barrel of the gun in the mouth. But he was shot basically in his right eye, as near as we can determine."

"That does seem strange."

"Yes. It looks like perhaps it may have been murder."

"Murder disguised as suicide," Victor said.

"Right. Somebody may have tried to make it look like he did himself in."

"Griff and I were discussing that possibility, among others," Victor said.

"There were also no powder burns or residue of any kind on his left hand or coat sleeve. It seems pretty certain that the gun was placed in Orcott's hand after he was already dead."

"You'd testify to that?"

"If it came to it, but this is off the record, Vic, remember? The case is still under investigation. I can't comment further on it."

"Sure, of course. I don't suppose any fingerprints were on the gun other than Orcott's, though? You can tell me that much, right?"

"Well, I suppose. The only prints were Mr. Orcott's. The guys in the lab tell me it definitely was the murder weapon, though. The bullet they retrieved matched perfectly."

"Good, thanks. Anything else?"

"Just one. I suppose I can share with you that he had a pocket watch in his vest pocket, with a fob attached."

"Okay, that's not so unusual on the surface."

"No, but the fob has a compartment in the back of it, and in that compartment, we found a small key."

"Interesting. I would have to bet it's the key to the desk drawer where he kept the gun," Victor said.

"I would say you're right, but we'll have to make sure. That's it for now. Honestly, I can't say another word, and please keep this all under your hat."

"Yeah, of course, Steve. Thanks again for your help."

"Oh, there is one more thing."

"Yes?" Victor said.

"For the, uh, credits in the movie. My name is spelled Stephen with a 'PH,' and my middle initial is 'F.' My mom would like it if you used my full name, Stephen F. Garnett. And I suppose you should also add Chief Claggot, just to be safe and keep me on his good side if he gets wind of any of this."

"You got it. And thanks again."

"Don't mention it, Victor. And I mean that. To anyone."

"Right, I understand."

"Good. Call me in the morning about the license plate. Goodbye."

"Goodbye." Marvel hung up the receiver and looked over at Griff, who was holding two whiskey sours.

"So, what did he say?" Griff said, handing Victor his drink.

"He said he'd check with the DMV and see what he can find out about the car and its owner. And he also said the coroner's report came back, and it doesn't appear like it was suicide. They think the gun was fired about five or six feet from Orcott, and there were no powder burns or residue on his hand or sleeve."

"So, it *was* murder, you were right. A marvelous murder."

"It appears so, and that's why someone tried to run me off the road."

"You and Eve could have been killed. You need to be careful. You should let the police handle it from now on."

"That's what Garnett said. He also said they found what they think may be the key to the desk drawer in the back of Orland's watch fob, which was in his pocket."

"Interesting. If he had the key with him the whole time, he definitely wouldn't have needed to jimmy the drawer open to get at the gun."

"Correct. But where do we go from here? It still leaves us with the question of how someone murdered Orcott when he was alone in the room and it was locked up tight, and then managed to escape practically into thin air," Victor said.

"That's the hundred-dollar question."

"Any thoughts on the case would be most welcome. I value your opinion and ideas," Victor said, taking a large drink of the whiskey sour.

"Okay. Well, if Orcott *was* murdered, and it certainly seems to be the case from what the detective told you just now, maybe someone killed him from outside the room somehow."

"Outside the room? What do you mean?"

"I figure the facts are indisputable. Mr. Orcott was in a locked room, alone. The windows and doors were locked from the inside."

"That's true."

"And once the detective got on the scene, the room was thoroughly searched."

"Right again," Victor said.

"At first, I thought perhaps there was a secret door that no one knows about. You know, like behind the bookcase or something. A movie I was in once had that as a plot device. Anyway, that would explain how the murderer got in and out without being seen, and the room locked up tight."

"Very clever, except there is no secret door, at least none that Garnett could find."

He frowned. "I know. Then I thought maybe someone was hiding in the room and slipped out through the broken window after we all left the study."

"That occurred to me, too, except there wasn't any place *to* hide. You, me, and Tab were all in there at the same time. The closet door was wide open and empty except for the cat cowering in the corner, and obviously, no one was under the desk."

"Yes, that's why I think it might have been done remotely. Someone might have rigged up the gun in the closet with some kind of remote device, or maybe something as simple as a wire leading out the far window. I know the windows were locked, but there most likely would have been enough room to run a thin wire."

Victor arched a brow. "Probably."

"Yes, well, they rig up the gun, knowing he'd probably go into the study at some point, and wait until he sits down at his desk, then they tug on the wire or however they've rigged it, and the gun goes off. Afterward, the murderer goes into the salon and joins the rest of the group, pretending to wonder what has happened. After the body's discovered, it's a simple matter for him or her to sneak back into the room and retrieve the wire or other device and put the gun in Mr. Orcott's hand. And remember the hanger we found outside with the twine tied to it? That might have been used somehow."

"But we all saw the gun in Mr. Orcott's hand when we broke in. Someone shot him and then placed the gun in his hand. And it's been confirmed that it was the same gun."

"Oh, yes. I see what you mean."

"And firing a gun remotely is extremely risky, I would think. The murderer would be taking a very big chance of hitting the intended victim. Even if Mr. Orcott always sat in the same position at his desk, all it would take is for him to stretch or bend or move ever so slightly and the bullet would miss."

"Yes, that did cross my mind, but if that's not how it was done, how was it? He was alone in the study. No one could have gotten in, and no one could have gotten out, unless the cat did it."

"Meow. Maybe she did."

"Goof," Griff said.

"Sorry. I do have a theory of my own, but I need to think on it," Victor said, taking another drink. "And I'm curious about that hanger and twine."

"Okay, well, while you're thinking on it, I'm going to call Dr. Hightower and have him stop over right after dinner to examine you.

And speaking of that, let's eat after I call him. I made chicken parmesan, if it's not tough and ice cold by now."

"I'm sure it will be fine. And after dinner and the doctor, I need to take some aspirin and a hot bath."

"Okay, I'll scrub your back."

"Deal. Just be gentle with me."

CHAPTER FIFTEEN

Early Tuesday morning, August 15, 1939
The Hollywood Athletic Club

Victor, his brown leather gym bag in his hand, left the locker room and stepped into the well-appointed lobby of the Hollywood Athletic Club on Sunset Boulevard. He fished a nickel from his trousers and entered a telephone booth near the main entrance, depositing the nickel to place a call to Detective Garnett.

"Detective Garnett speaking."

"Hello, Steve, it's Victor Marvel."

"Oh, hi, Victor. You're up early."

"Yeah, I didn't sleep well. Seems I was more banged up from that car chase yesterday than I thought. My doctor stopped out last night and checked me over. Nothing broken, but he taped my ribs just to be safe. There's a lot of bruising, too."

"Geez, I'm glad nothing was broken, but sorry that happened. What about Miss Spellman? How is she feeling?"

"I'm not sure yet, but I'm hoping for the best. She seemed fine when I dropped her off last night. I didn't want to call her too early this morning in case she was sleeping in, but I'll ring her up next."

"Good. Please give her my regards when you do speak with her, and do let me know if she's not okay. And I hope you're feeling better soon."

"I'm sure I'll be fine. I went to the gymnasium for a steam bath this morning, which seemed to help. I'm calling from a pay phone in the lobby of the club, as a matter of fact. I couldn't wait until I got home."

"Wait for what?" Steve said.

"For any information you can give me on that license plate, if you have it."

"Well, you're in luck. It's a slow morning at the Department of Motor Vehicles, and I don't have a lot on my desk at the moment. They told me the plates of the car that tried to run you off the road show it to be a Hertz Drive-Ur-Self rental. A man by the name of Albert Smith rented it yesterday afternoon. A phony name, I'm sure. He paid cash in advance. The car was found outside their lot this morning, and it was most likely left there after closing last night. It was a little banged up, especially the front fender."

"Which matches what happened on the highway. They hit my rear fender pretty hard. At least we know it was a man who rented the car."

"Yes, but that doesn't mean anything in terms of suspects," Garnett said. "I've seen this before. In order to cover their tracks, a criminal pays some schmuck to rent the car for them, usually half up front, half after they get the keys."

"But wouldn't the rental company require a valid driver's license?" Victor said.

"That's policy, yes, but a fake license is pretty easy to get, unfortunately. The only personal information on a California license is the person's name, address, eye and hair color, sex, height, weight, and date of birth, along with a thumbprint and a signature."

"That's true," Victor said.

"Yeah, and the rental place told me they were pretty busy yesterday. No one working at that time remembered this man very well, and they couldn't give more than a vague description. They said he was mid-thirties, dark hair, and brown eyes as far as they could recall, and about five foot eight, with an average build. That's a pretty generic description that would fit more than a thousand men in this town."

"Definitely. I imagine if someone did have a fake license made with those details, it would be pretty easy to find someone to be their patsy that fit them."

"Yup. A lot of unemployed men would be happy to collect a few bucks to do something like that. And once the car was rented, all they had to do was hand over the keys to whoever paid them, perhaps give the phony license back, and collect the other half of their fee."

"So, it's a dead end."

"More or less," Garnett said. "But we'll keep checking and we'll ask around, see if anyone, a neighbor perhaps, noticed the car being dropped off or who dropped it off, that sort of thing. But it's a long shot."

"Okay, I understand. I'm surprised whoever it was bothered returning it to the rental place. I would have thought they'd just abandon it along the road somewhere."

"Most likely they had left their own vehicle nearby the agency."

"Oh, sure, that makes sense. Well, thank you again, Steve, for everything."

"Sure, you're welcome. But I must caution you once more to stay out of this. Leave it to the police, please."

"All right, you know best. I'll check in with you later, though, if that's okay."

"How about I check in with you if and when I have questions or if there is something I can share with you."

"Is that a question or a statement?" Victor said.

"It wasn't a question, Victor."

"I see. Okay, it's a deal. What are you going to do next?"

"Investigate. It's what I do. You make movies, I investigate crimes. Notice I didn't say I investigate crimes *and* make movies, and neither should you."

"Point taken. I assume you're going to talk to everyone who was there the night of the party again."

"Among other things, none of which I'm at liberty to discuss," Garnett said.

"All right, Detective Garnett, I can take a hint. Enjoy your day."

"I'll see what I can do. And you get some rest and take care of yourself."

"Yes, sir," Victor said. He hung up the receiver, picked it up again, and fished out another nickel. As the coin went clinking into the phone box, he dialed a number he knew by heart and waited. After just two rings, a soft, feminine voice answered.

"Hello?"

"Eve, it's Victor."

"Oh, hello. I was hoping I'd hear from you sooner rather than later. What did you find out?"

"Quite a bit, to be honest, but more importantly, how are you feeling? Are you okay?"

"Me? I'm fine, really, I told you that last night. I slept quite soundly."

"Good, I'm glad to hear that. But did you call the doctor after I dropped you at your place?"

"Would I have heard the end of it from you if I hadn't?"

"Probably not," Victor said.

"*Definitely* not. Yes, I called Dr. Adamsky, and he came right over. He's such a sweet man, and he lives close by. He said I'm in good shape, just some mild bruises on various parts of my body. He said my stylish hat—which was brand new, by the way, and is now crushed and ruined—most likely saved me from a concussion, or worse."

"I'm sorry about the hat, but glad it saved you. But what could be worse than a concussion?"

"Dr. Adamsky told me I could have been thrown through the windshield. That would definitely have been worse."

"Oh, my God, Eve. I'm so sorry. This was all my fault."

"It wasn't, Victor. It's the fault of whoever was driving that other car."

"But I could have pulled over and stopped, like you suggested."

"True. And then what? What if this person had a gun and shot us both dead? That would be worse than being thrown through a windshield. I think."

"Well, I can't argue with that," Victor said.

"The point is, neither of us knows what would have happened had you stopped. You did what you felt was best, and I can't fault you for that. Besides, it all worked out, we're both okay." She paused briefly. "You *are* okay, aren't you?"

"Yeah, I'm good. I had my doctor come over last night, too. Griff insisted on it. The doc taped my ribs, and I also have some bruising, but otherwise, I'm top-notch."

"Excellent. That's a relief. What about your poor car, though?"

"Also scraped and battered, but it can be fixed. Since the service station fixed the tire, it's drivable at least. I'll make an appointment with the Cadillac dealership and see if I can get it in this week."

"Okay. And speaking of cars, did the detective find anything out about the owner of the car that rammed us?"

"Yeah, I just got off the phone with him, as a matter of fact. The car was a rental. Somebody using what was probably an assumed name and a phony driver's license rented it yesterday afternoon. The description of the person the agency was able to provide was generic, a man, mid-thirties, dark hair, brown eyes, average height and weight.

Garnett said it's possible that whoever the driver was got a patsy to rent the car for them."

"That makes sense. So, it could have been a man or a woman behind the wheel."

"Right. There's something else, too. Garnett said the autopsy report came back. It appears Orcott's death was most certainly not suicide. I'll go over all the details when I see you."

"Jeepers creepers, Vic, you were right."

"Well, you don't have to sound so surprised."

"Sorry, but I still don't get it. I mean, how?"

"I wish I knew."

"Me too. What's your next step? Or don't you know that yet, either?"

"Detective Garnett wants me to stay out of it and let the police handle it."

"Which, knowing you, you won't do," Eve said.

"You do know me, Miss Spellman. Griff told me I should leave it to the police, too, but ever since I played Detective Hart in *Harts and Clubs* and the follow-up films, I've felt like I could have been a pretty good gumshoe, a private dick."

"But you're not a dick, Victor, you're a movie star, and it seems someone has already tried to kill you, or at least scare you off, and me with you. I think you should listen to Garnett and Griff and just let the professionals take over before something worse happens."

"I can't, Eve. I'm in it too far at this point. I want to see it through."

Eve groaned. "How did I know you were going to say that?"

"Because as I said, you know and love me like a sister."

"All right, dear brother, so, what's your plan?"

"For starters, I want to go back to the Orcott mansion."

"The scene of the crime?"

"Sure. That's what they do in the movies."

"Again, this isn't a movie, Victor, this is real life. Besides, in the movies it's the killer who returns to the scene of the crime."

"Fine, but either way, that's my next stop."

"Okay, but why? What's at the Orcott mansion?"

"Hopefully some answers. I told you about the hanger we found outside the window the night Orcott died, right?"

"Yes, you said Griff landed on it when he fell."

"Right, and it had a piece of twine tied to it. Lydia had a piece of twine in her hand later, too. She claimed she found it on the terrace, but I wonder."

"I don't get what you're getting at, Victor."

"I'm just wondering if that hanger and twine are somehow connected to Orcott's murder. I want to poke around the bushes and see if I can find something. I just feel like there's a connection I'm missing. In any case, something's rotten. It's clear that someone, probably the murderer, thinks we're on to something, and I think they may be right."

"On to something? In what way?" Eve said.

"I think I have a good idea, but I'm not certain just yet. I'll fill you in later."

"I don't think so. I want to come, too. To the Orcott mansion."

"Whatever for?"

"I'm curious, and maybe I can help. Perhaps I can distract them while you poke about in the bushes."

"I don't like the idea of potentially putting you in danger again, Eve."

"You may not have noticed, Mr. Marvel, but I'm a big girl and I can take care of myself. What time should I meet you at the mansion?"

"You, Miss Spellman, are stubborn as a mule. If you insist on coming, why don't you meet me at my house in about thirty minutes? I'd rather we arrive together."

"Okay, but wouldn't it be easier to just swing by and pick me up on your way to the Orcott place?"

"I'm actually at the Hollywood Athletic Club at the moment. It would save time if you met me at my house. Griff is there, still trying to memorize his lines. He'll probably want to tag along, too."

"Fine, but what are you doing at the club with taped ribs and bruises?"

"Don't worry, I'm not lifting weights. I just had a steam bath, but I'm all finished, showered and dressed. I'm going to head home soon. Once you get there, the three of us can drive to the Orcott mansion together."

"All right, I'll see you in about thirty minutes. It would probably be a good idea to call Mrs. Orcott first, though. It would appear rude for three of us to show up unannounced."

"I suppose that's true."

"And besides, Mrs. Orcott and Tab may be busy with funeral arrangements and whatnot, and not receiving callers."

"Fine, I'll telephone and ask if we can stop out. If there are any problems, I'll let you know. Otherwise, I'll see you at my house."

"Good manners are always in style, Victor."

"Yes, ma'am. Oh, and Eve?"

"Yes?"

"Remind me to buy you a new hat."

Chapter Sixteen

Tuesday morning, August 15, 1939
Victor Marvel's House

The next call Victor made was to Don Lee's Cadillac dealership on the corner of Seventh and Bixel Streets. They assured him they could make the repairs and that they had an appointment available first thing Wednesday morning. Victor told them he'd get it there at opening. With that taken care of, he used his last nickel to telephone the Orcott mansion. Clarence picked up on the second ring.

"Orcott residence."

"Yes, good morning, this is Victor Marvel. Is this Clarence?"

"Good morning, Mr. Marvel. Yes, it is I. How may I help you?"

"I was wondering if Mrs. Orcott and Mr. Rockwell were at home and receiving visitors."

"Mrs. Orcott is home, Mr. Marvel, but Mr. Rockwell is out. He left just a short time ago."

"Oh, I see. Did he mention where he was going?"

"No, sir, he did not. He seemed in a bit of a hurry."

"Did he say when he might be back?"

"I'm sorry, Mr. Marvel, but he didn't mention anything to me. Perhaps Mrs. Orcott knows."

"All right, may I speak with her, please, Clarence?"

"She's having her breakfast on the terrace at the moment, I'm afraid, but I can let her know you telephoned and wish to talk to her."

"Fine, do that."

"Of course, sir. Did you wish to leave a number?"

"No, she has my home telephone exchange. I'm out at the moment, but I'll be back at my house shortly."

"Very good, she shan't be long as the groundskeepers are working today. They started on the west side but will be making their way toward her soon."

"The west side? Isn't that the area beneath the windows to the study?"

"That's right, sir. Mr. Lynch, the head groundskeeper, said it was quite a mess back there from the three of you the night of Mr. Orcott's death."

"I can imagine. Sorry about that, Clarence, but it couldn't be helped. The ground was so wet."

"Oh, I completely understand, sir, and I explained that to Mr. Lynch. Odd, he told me he found twine tied to a branch near the windows. The end of it had been torn or cut."

"Really? How strange. As if something had been tied to the bush and was hanging from a branch?"

"It would appear that way, sir, but it's quite puzzling."

"Yes, quite. I recall Mr. Rockwell was looking for Chowder out in the bushes before Mr. Orcott was shot."

"So I understand, sir. Of course, as it turns out, she never left the house and was in the study with Mr. Orcott. I certainly could have told him that if he had asked. I've never known her to go outside."

"Interesting. By the way, do you happen to know where Mr. Rockwell was yesterday afternoon?"

"No, sir, not exactly. He went out for a drive. He often does. He didn't return until nearly dinnertime and went straight to his room for a shower."

"He must have been hot and sweaty," Victor said.

"I couldn't say, Mr. Marvel."

"And even if you could, you wouldn't."

"No, sir. Was there anything else?"

"Just have Mrs. Orcott telephone me when she's free, please. I should be home in thirty minutes or so. Oh, and ask Mr. Rockwell to call me when he returns as well."

"Yes, sir, goodbye."

"Goodbye." Victor hung up, exited the phone booth and the Athletic Club, and walked slowly to his car in the lot while he pondered the significance of a small piece of twine. It was a beautiful morning, so he kept the top down and turned the radio up, singing along to the Andrews Sisters and Bing Crosby as he drove home.

Before long, he swung his Cadillac through the gates of his

property. In the driveway of his house, behind Griff's Alfa Romeo, Victor noticed a brand new, sporty black BMW 335 that he didn't recognize. He parked behind the BMW and got out, his ribs aching. Slowly he went up the walk to the porch, and then into the living room, which was empty. He could hear voices coming from the rear of the house, so he hung up his hat, went into the hall, and from there into the kitchen, where he saw Griff and Tab seated at the kitchen table drinking coffee. Tab had the movie script in front of him.

Griff looked up and smiled. "Oh, hi, Vic. How was the club? How are you feeling?"

"Hello. The club was fine. I've still got some pain, but I'm doing okay." He looked over at Tab. "Tab, this is a surprise."

"Good morning, Victor," Tab said, setting down the script he'd been holding.

"Tab offered to come over and help me run my lines. I told him not to bother, that you said you could help me once you got home, but he wouldn't take no for an answer. I hope you don't mind."

"Um, no, not at all." Victor looked at Tab again. "I just wasn't expecting to see you here this morning."

"I called right after you'd left for the Athletic Club, apparently," Tab said. "I was hoping to talk to you, and I was surprised when Griff answered as I didn't know he was staying here."

"Just while his place is being fumigated," Victor said.

"Yeah, that's what he said," Tab said. "Anyway, he told me he was struggling with his lines for the new movie, so I told him I'd stop over and read with him while I waited for you to return."

"I see," Victor said.

"I mean, I was obviously familiar with the script anyway, so why not?" Tab said.

"Generous of you," Victor said, looking at his boyfriend. "How's it going, Griff?"

"I'm getting there," Griff said. "We were just going over the garden scene, since that's what we're shooting first thing Monday morning."

"Makes sense," Victor said. "Break it up into scenes in the order they're being shot and take them one by one."

"Yes, that was Tab's idea. Want some coffee? I made a whole pot."

"Thanks," Victor said. He walked slowly over to the stove and poured a mug from the percolator, taking a sip as he turned back to the two young men. "What did you want to talk to me about, Tab?"

"Hmm?"

"You said you called this morning hoping to speak with me, and you drove over to wait until I got home."

"Oh, yes, you're right, I did. Griff told me about your car accident yesterday, by the way. I'm so glad you're okay," Tab said.

"Me too, but it was no accident. What else have you two been chatting about?"

"Nothing but the movie, really. I can't get anything out of Griff," Tab said. "He only told me about the incident with you and that other car because I asked why you weren't home, and he let it slip that you were at the Athletic Club having a steam bath because you were in pain. And from the way you're moving, I can see that is definitely still the case."

"Just some bruised ribs, I think. I'll be fine, but I should take some more aspirin."

"That's a good idea," Griff said. "Want me to get you some?"

"No, thanks. I'll go up in a bit and let you two run lines some more."

"Okay," Griff said.

"Tab," Victor said, "you still haven't told me why you called me this morning or why you're here."

"Oh, well, I just wanted to check in and see how you were doing and if you'd had any more thoughts about my father's death. I've heard you've been asking a lot of questions."

"Who did you hear that from?"

"Marjorie, Sheila, and Tony, for starters. You've been busy."

"So have you. How are the funeral arrangements coming along, by the way?"

"Marjorie has it all set for this coming Sunday at the Blessed Sacrament Church, followed by interment at Forest Lawn. It will be a simple service. I'm sure she'll be calling you later today to let you know the details."

"Simple is sometimes the best," Victor said.

"I agree," Tab said.

"Though whoever killed your father had a complex, fairly well-executed plan."

"You still think he was murdered?" Tab said.

"I'm pretty certain, yes, and I think I know who did it. I telephoned your father's house before I left the club, by the way."

"Oh? Why is that?"

"I wanted to speak with you and your stepmother, but Marjorie was having breakfast on the terrace, and you had just left, in a bit of a hurry, I'm told."

"I wouldn't say that."

"Clarence did. I imagine after you telephoned here and found out I was out, you thought you might get some information out of Griff. If not, you'd just wait until I got back because you suspect I know something."

"What are you driving at?" Tab said, getting to his feet. "I was just curious and trying to be helpful to Griff, here."

"Big of you. You know, I can't imagine too many people knew your father kept a gun locked in the drawer of his desk in the study. In fact, if I had to guess, I'd say only you and Marjorie were aware of that. Possibly Clarence."

Tab shrugged. "I have no idea who knew about the location of his gun."

"I also imagine not too many people knew he shot with his left hand. He wrote with his right because he was forced to do so as a child. Most folks would have assumed he was completely right-handed."

"My father killed himself, Victor. He knew where the gun was kept, and he used his left hand to pull the trigger. He was alone in a locked room."

"That's what the killer wanted us to believe," Victor said. "But I think someone broke into Orland's desk sometime during the night of the party and stole his gun. You couldn't tell the lock on that drawer had been forced when it was closed. Neither Griff nor I could tell, anyway. And we have only your word that the window you tried was locked."

"And your point is?"

"Let's assume Mr. Orcott didn't notice the broken drawer when he came in to take the call. He probably had his mind on whoever was waiting to talk to him on the telephone. Clarence told me that Orland was quite agitated."

"That would make sense," Griff said. "He most likely came in to answer the phone and never paid any attention to the drawer."

"Yes, but then what?" Victor said. "According to Clarence, Chowder was upset that night also. She was acting up, pacing back and forth, and meowing behind and around the desk and over by the closet while Orland was on the call."

"As if she knew someone had broken into the drawer, maybe," Griff said.

"Maybe. Or perhaps something else. Mr. Orcott was irritated with whomever he was talking to on the phone and Chowder was restless, perhaps pawing at the closet door. So, Orland, when he finally hung up, spun around in his chair, annoyed at the cat, and that's when he was shot."

"But how?" Griff said.

"Are you saying the cat shot him?" Tab said with a nervous chuckle.

"No, I don't think even a polydactyl cat could pull a trigger on a gun," Victor said.

"I was joking, but actually, I suppose that's a possibility, in a way," Tab said. "Maybe my father set his gun on the mantel next to the closet and Chowder jumped up there, knocking it off. It discharged and unfortunately killed my father. That makes sense."

"You think fast on your feet, Tab," Victor said. "But I'm not buying it. The key to the drawer where the gun was kept was found in your father's watch fob, which he had on him. There was no need for him to break into the drawer."

"Who knows?" Tab said. "Maybe one of the servants broke in and took the gun, but when they heard my father coming, they set it on the mantel and fled out the library door."

"Agatha Mudd was in the library. She would have seen them."

"Maybe it happened earlier in the evening. Or perhaps my father forgot where he'd placed the key to the drawer. He could be forgetful at times."

"So," Victor said, "you believe that at some point during the night he forgot the key was in his watch fob in his pocket, so he broke the lock, removed the gun for some unknown reason, set it on the mantel, and then returned to the party?"

"It's possible," Tab said.

"And when he was called to the telephone, the cat knocked the gun off the mantel and it discharged, shooting your father in the face?"

"Stranger things have happened, Victor."

"Funny Clarence wouldn't have noticed the gun on the mantel when he brought Mr. Orcott the tea and bromide. As I recall, the mantel was empty, cleared away in the hopes of bringing home an Oscar for best director."

"Clarence just overlooked it, I'm sure."

Victor shook his head slowly. "You are a clever one, Tab. What I think happened instead is that you knew Charlotte Masters would want to go home, and you planned to call her a cab, as you had no intention of leaving. You went to use the telephone in the study. The telephones in the reception room and the library were both closer, but you wanted to use the one in the study. While you were in there, you jimmied open the drawer and stole your father's gun. Then you telephoned the cab company, followed by a call to Tony Bolt."

"Why would I call Tony?"

"Because you wanted him to telephone the house in about ten minutes or so and ask for Orcott, and to make it sound urgent, private, and personal so he'd take it in the study, away from the party. You told Tony to keep Orland on the line as long as possible."

"You're guessing," Tab said.

"You then hung up and returned to the entrance hall. You and Sheila, your partner in crime, said you were going out to the terrace to smoke and get some fresh air."

"You think Sheila was my partner in crime? She's not smart enough."

"Granted, she probably wasn't the best choice, but she was convenient, and she was also angry with your father and willing to help. Maybe you convinced her to assist by threatening to disclose her little secret that she was once a star of blue movies, along with Tony Bolt."

"She wasn't much of a star in those," Tab said, "But she seemed to be a natural."

"I'm sure, but that's not something she'd want getting out. So, she agreed to help you. She even told Marjorie about Orcott and Charlotte, knowing it would lead to a fight, just as you'd hoped."

"And why would I hope that?"

"Various reasons. It made Marjorie out to be a suspect if your plan failed and murder was suspected, and it riled up your father. You and Sheila left for the terrace, but you stopped off in the study again first while she went outside. You locked the door to the library, then hid in the closet of the study to wait until your father arrived, removing the gun concealed under your coat. But before you could shoot, Clarence showed up with the tea and bromide. You could probably hear Chowder outside the closet door, pawing and meowing, and you panicked. When Clarence eventually left and your father hung up the telephone, you opened the closet door and shot him in the face. You then locked the door to the salon and placed the gun in your father's left hand. You opened the drapes on the window closest to the door, raised the sash, and climbed out, dropping to the lawn below. In the process, you got your shoes wet and muddy. Remember the footprints?"

"Yes," Tab said, "but yours and Griff's shoes were muddy, too. All three of us were out on the lawn when we were trying to get into the study."

"True," Victor said, "but yours were muddy when you first came in from outside, right after we'd heard the gunshot."

"I told you, I was looking for Chowder."

"A good excuse. Thinking quickly on your feet again. Poor Sheila, though. She's not good at improvisation. Eve noticed she recited where you two were and what you two were doing twice, verbatim—once on the night of the party and again yesterday after I mentioned the cat. As I said, she probably wasn't the best choice for an accomplice. But anyway, where was I? Oh yes, you'd just dropped out the window and down to the lawn. Using a bent wire coat hanger that you had previously tied to the branch of a bush to keep it handy but out of sight, you reached up and pulled the window closed, but you were unable to lock it, of course. You discarded the hanger, intending to retrieve it later, and then went up to the terrace where Sheila was standing watch. The two of you hurried into the salon to join the rest of us, but you dropped a piece of the broken twine in your haste, or perhaps it had stuck to your wet shoe."

"Interesting theory, Victor, but again, you're just guessing."

"Am I, Tab? Clarence told me the drapes on both windows were drawn in the study and the closet door was closed when he brought Mr. Orcott the bromide. Yet the drapes on the window closest to the salon door were open a short while later. We know that because you boosted yourself up and looked through the window once we'd all gotten outside. You would have had to open the drapes in order to make your escape, and you were unable to close them behind you. Still, it was a simple matter for you to pretend the window was locked, at least. You then broke the glass, reached in, told us you had just unlocked it, and climbed inside. You hauled Griff up immediately after to be your witness."

"Once again," Tab said, "an interesting theory, but you have no proof, Mr. Marvel."

"That's debatable," Victor said. "The coroner's report clearly shows your father was shot at a distance of five to six feet, and there were no powder burns or residue on his coat sleeve or hand. And if the gun had accidentally discharged by being knocked off the mantel by Chowder as you claim, it would have been on the floor, not in Orcott's hand. I'm sure if questioned, Tony will admit you put him up to placing the call that night, and Sheila won't be hard to crack. She puts on a tough act, but I think she's a scared little mouse. Once the police haul her downtown, she'll sing."

"Off key, no doubt," Tab said, drawing a small caliber revolver from inside his suit coat.

"You surprise me yet again, Mr. Rockwell. I didn't picture you as the type to tote a gun."

"I don't, normally. But one never knows what one might encounter. I suspected this visit might not go well, and I was correct." He looked briefly over at Griff, who was still seated at the table. "On your feet, Mr. Fenwick."

Griff did as he was told and stepped over next to Victor, keeping his eyes on Tab.

"Good. Hands up, gentlemen," Tab said.

"That's difficult for me to do, Tab. My ribs, you know."

"Sorry about that. But you'll soon be out of your misery. Hands up."

Victor and Griff both raised their hands, Victor wincing as he did so.

"You're the one who rented the black Ford yesterday," Victor said. "Or was it Tony?"

"No, it was me. I used a fake license, though."

"With the first name of Albert, which was your given name before you changed it to Tab Rockwell. And you used a last name of Smith. Not very original."

"But easy for me to remember. Tony's only involvement in this was making the telephone call, as you correctly guessed."

"He didn't know you were going to kill your father?"

"No. He did telephone me just after you left his place yesterday, though. He was worried about what you really wanted and said you were asking a lot of questions. Then Sheila called me and said you were going to come out to see her after lunch. I obtained a fake driver's license from a friend in the prop department at the studio way back when I was underage and wanted to get into bars. I still have it, so I used it to rent a car. I told Sheila I was going to drive over and park at the end of her road. As soon as you left, she was to come down to the car and tell me what was discussed."

"Which she did, hobbling in her high heels," Victor said.

"Yeah, stupid. Anyway, after she talked to me and told me what you said, I figured you were definitely on to something."

"So, you tried to run my car off the road."

"I saw that in a movie once. I figured if I didn't kill you, I might at least scare you enough to stop nosing around. Unfortunately for all of us, it didn't."

"I'll be sure and send the repair bill for my Cadillac to you, Mr. Rockwell."

"You're hilarious," Tab said.

"Thanks. Now that I'm getting older, maybe I'll branch out into comedies. So, now what happens?" Victor said.

"Now, I'm afraid I have to kill you both. I'm sorry, I really am."

"Two more deaths on your hands?" Griff said. "You'll never get away with it."

"I doubt it. I think quick on my feet, as Mr. Marvel here so kindly said. I'll make this look like a lover's quarrel, a murder-suicide. I'll shoot you first, Griff, and then I'll shoot Victor, making it look like Victor killed you and then shot himself. The gun will be found in your hand, Vic."

"It's your gun," Victor said. "They'll trace it to you."

"Nope. I'll wipe my prints off, and I bought it at a pawn shop in West Hollywood yesterday. I paid cash and didn't give my real name. The gun's untraceable."

"It doesn't matter," Griff said. "No one would believe Victor would murder me."

"I beg to differ. I plan to give an exclusive to Agatha Mudd, on the condition she doesn't use my name, of course. All about how the three of us were in a love triangle. Griff had fallen for me, and we had started an affair which Victor discovered. He confronted you about it this morning and killed you in a jealous rage. Feeling remorseful, he shot himself. Tragic. And just in case some nosy neighbor noticed my car in your drive this morning, I'll tell the police I was here to see Griff when Victor came home unexpectedly. I'll say that you, Victor, were in a rage when you found us together, so I left and let the two of you fight it out, never dreaming it would end in death. I'll have tears in my eyes, of course, because, despite what the critics and my father said, I *am* a good actor."

"You'd shoot us in cold blood?" Victor said, staring down Tab.

"Is there another way?" Tab said.

"That's not the line," Griff said.

Tab cocked his head, momentarily thrown off. "Huh? What line? What are you talking about?"

"William Taylor's line," Griff said. "His character, the gangster. When Vic's character says, 'You'd shoot us in cold blood?' Taylor's character is supposed to say, 'Hot blood or cold, don't matter to me. You're finished, Beaumont, in more ways than one, and so is your young friend, here. This gun is loaded.' "

"Good job, Griff," Victor said. "You remembered William's line."

Griff beamed. "Hey, imagine that! And I think I remember mine, now, too. After Mr. Taylor's character says, 'You'd lose that bet. I'm not that drunk,' *I* say, 'Yeah? You smell like cheap booze mixed with formaldehyde, and you look like hell.' "

"I knew you'd get it, sooner or later," Victor said.

"Shut up, both of you. You're quoting lines from *The Lady Screeched. I* was supposed to be the star of that movie," Tab said. "God, I hate you, Griffin. They gave you *my* role. I hate both of you, actually. You're both queer, just like me. But you each have your big movie careers, your fans, and your fame. What do I have?"

"You *had* a wealthy, powerful father until you killed him," Victor said.

"I killed him because he wanted to destroy me and was doing a damned good job of it, just because he found out I'm a homosexual. He knew about both of you, and he hated you for it just as he did me, but because you're both big stars for the studio, he couldn't do anything about it."

"Except ridicule us to our faces and make our lives miserable," Victor said.

"You should have heard how he talked about you behind your backs."

"What he said to us in person wasn't exactly something I'd want my mother to hear," Griff said.

"Yeah, the old man wasn't much for pleasantries, especially when it came to homosexuals. This town and this industry are full of them, and it drove him mad. All my life I had to listen to his rants, to his nasty comments, his snide remarks and crude jokes, knowing if he knew the truth about me, that would be the end. And then he did find out, and he reacted just as I thought he would. It didn't matter that I was his son. *I* didn't matter to him."

"I'm sorry about that, Tab," Victor said. "You should have mattered to him."

"Yeah, well, clearly, I didn't. To be honest, he reacted slightly better toward me when he found out than I expected," Tab said. "I figured he'd disinherit me, which he did, and blacklist me from Icon, which he did, but he didn't throw me out of the house, and he didn't have some goon beat me up or try to have me lobotomized."

"Instead, he asked you to escort Charlotte Masters to the birthday party," Griff said.

"That was a surprise. But he wanted Charlotte at the party. He wanted to be able to dance with her and have a good time, and he wanted her to have fun. He knew I'd be a safe escort, and with me as her date, no one, or so he thought, would suspect he was cheating on his wife yet again. I was tempted to tell him to go to hell and to tell Marjorie the truth, but then I thought of something better."

"You decided to have Sheila tell Marjorie about Charlotte. That way you couldn't be blamed," Victor said, "and Marjorie would let Orland have it."

"Yes, that was my initial idea, and Sheila was more than willing. I got her to ask Griff here to escort her to the party. I relished watching her confront my old man, but then I realized nothing would come of it, nothing would change. So, I thought of something better still."

"Meaning you figured out a way to kill him," Victor said, "at the party, with plenty of witnesses who would testify your father was alone in a locked room when he shot himself. And if anyone became suspicious, there were plenty of other suspects there, too."

"Something like that. You're pretty clever, too, Victor, I must admit. I told my father I'd escort Charlotte on the condition he lifted the blacklist against me. He refused, offering me ten grand instead, and a one-way first-class train ticket out of town."

"And you told him you would accept that," Griff said, "knowing he would soon be dead. But if he'd disinherited you, you'd have nothing when he died. Why not take the ten grand and leave?"

"You know, if he would have just agreed to lift the blacklist, I think that would have been enough. But he refused because he wanted me gone. He was embarrassed by me. He said I was an abomination and a humiliation. So I didn't care about the inheritance, and I still don't. I'm not stupid, I've put away some money, and I have a trust fund from my grandmother. It's not a lot, but I'll be fine. Once you two are dead, that is."

"If you kill us, Tab, you'll get caught," Griff said.

"You will, Tab," Victor said. "Put the gun down. People know you're here."

"You're lying."

"I'm not. I can help you get a good lawyer. People know what your father was like. A jury may decide it wasn't first-degree murder."

"I'm tired of hearing you talk, Marvel. Shut your mouth and say goodbye."

"Make up your mind. It's hard to say goodbye with my mouth closed," Victor said.

"Good one, Vic," Griff said. "Or should I say, Axel?"

Victor grinned and winked at Griff. "Thanks, Jasper."

"I said, shut up, both of you!" Tab shouted, aiming the gun at Griff.

Behind Tab, the kitchen door to the terrace swung open, and Eve walked in.

"Victor, Griff, what's going on here?" she said.

Tab whirled about. and the gun discharged. Fortunately, the bullet just missed her, shattering a shelf of dishes next to the door. It lodged deep in the wall.

Griff and Victor rushed Tab, hoping to get the gun away from him. Vic got there first and wrapped his hand around Tab's right wrist, forcing it up.

With a strong left, Tab landed a solid fist in Vic's gut, sending him reeling into Griff as Victor bellowed in pain from his sore ribs. Both men toppled to the linoleum kitchen floor. Tab raised the gun once more and aimed again as Eve came about. She thrust the hand with the gun in it away with her left hand and kneed him hard in the crotch, while at the same time giving him an uppercut with her right fist. Tab crumpled into a heap on the floor. Eve knelt down, pried the revolver out of Tab's hand, and got up again, backing away. With the gun now aimed at Tab, who was still writhing in pain and agony and holding his crotch, real tears in his eyes, she looked over at Griff and Victor, who had gotten to their feet once more.

"You two okay?" she said.

"Just peachy," Victor said, holding his ribs.

"You don't look okay, Vic," Eve said.

"Nothing a hot bath and a whiskey sour won't fix," he said.

"Nice try, tough guy," Griff said, "but I'm calling the doctor again."

"Call the police first," Victor said.

"Right," Griff said, moving off to the kitchen telephone.

"Thank God you came along when you did, Eve. You certainly took care of Tab."

Eve nodded and smiled. "Your knight in shining armor, or a white and green checked dress, as the case may be. Always at your service, gentlemen."

Chapter Seventeen

Thursday, February 29, 1940
Victor Marvel's house

"Good evening," Griff said, entering through the front door of Victor's house after letting himself in with his key. He was wearing his tuxedo again, which was smartly tailored, freshly cleaned, and pressed, and was carrying a bottle of chilled French champagne.

"Good evening, Mr. Fenwick. My, don't you look dashing?" Eve said. She had been sitting in an easy chair by the fireplace in the two-story-high living room but got to her feet to greet him.

"And you, Miss Spellman, are stunning. Another new gown?"

"Why, thank you, kind sir. And yes, I just bought it last week, as a matter of fact. I mean, we *are* going to the Academy Awards. It wasn't easy to find something I liked that I could actually sit down in, so when I saw this sleeveless deep violet dress at Henri's, I couldn't resist. He promised me it's a one of a kind, but I'm doubtful."

"Well, even if three other women are wearing it tonight, no one will look better in it than you."

Eve walked over and kissed him on the cheek. "Thank you, darling, that's sweet. Too bad you bat for the other team."

"Speaking of my team, where's Victor?"

"Still upstairs, primping."

"Of course he is." Griff set the bottle down on the console table behind the camelback sofa. "I'm pleasantly surprised to see you here, Eve. I figured we'd pick you up on our way."

"Victor offered, but I knew you two would want to be alone tonight after the ceremony, and I live in the opposite direction, so I said

I'd drive over here beforehand. That way we can all come back here and you two can go inside while I see myself home."

"Aw, thanks, Eve, that's swell."

"Don't mention it. Where's your date, Griff?"

"We'll pick her up on the way to the Cocoanut Grove."

"Anyone we know?"

"Doubtful. She's the daughter of my neighbor, though she lives near the Ambassador Hotel in an apartment with another girl. Her name's Mary Alice Applewhite. I've given up on starlets."

"Probably for the best, as long as Miss Applewhite doesn't want to break into movies," Eve said.

"I don't think so. She's an English teacher at the high school," Griff said. "She seems nice."

"Who seems nice?" Victor said, leaning over the small half-moon balcony off the upstairs hall and looking down into the living room.

"My date for the evening, Miss Applewhite."

"Ah yes," Victor said. "I can't wait to meet her. I'll be right down." He turned and descended the stairs.

"Good evening, you two," he said as he came through the arch from the hall a moment later. He was dressed in a double-breasted tuxedo with satin lapels, the same one he'd worn to the Orcott party the previous year.

"Good evening, Victor. Two handsome men. You almost look like bookends," Eve said, looking from Victor to Griff.

"Hello, Eve, and thank you. You look lovely, as always." He walked over to Griff and embraced him with a kiss. "And you are handsome as ever. Did you miss me?"

"Terribly."

"But I only just saw you a few hours ago."

"Seems longer."

"Sweet talker. I missed you, too."

"All right, you two, enough," Eve said.

"Sorry," Victor said. "We have to get this all out of the way before we have to put our heterosexual personas back on."

"Fair enough," Eve said. "You *will* have to be on your best behavior from the moment we pick up Griff's date until you get back here at the end of the night."

"Speaking of your date, I hope she won't mind squeezing into the back seat of my new Lincoln Continental," Victor said.

"As long as she's squeezed back there with Griff, I'm sure she won't mind," Eve said.

"Actually, I think she and her roommate, a woman named Louise something or other, are more than just roommates, if you know what I mean," Griff said. "That's what my neighbor implied, anyway, and it's certainly the impression I got when I met the two of them. It makes it easier, actually. I don't like lying to or misleading people."

"I agree," Victor said. "And that *does* make it easier. No making excuses when the night is over and you and I want to come back here." He glanced at his Rolex. "We should probably leave in about thirty minutes. We have just enough time for a cocktail."

"Sounds good to me," Eve said.

"Me too. I'll pour," Griff said. He picked up the champagne and crossed to the bar in the cabinet to the left of the fireplace. "I brought a bottle of bubbly. Champagne cocktail, anyone?"

"Perfect," Victor said.

"Make it three, my good man," Eve said. "You know, I'm looking forward to tonight, but doesn't it seem frivolous in light of what's going on with the world right now?"

"I know what you mean," Victor said solemnly. "The Germans have bombed several cities in Poland, and I just read where the Nazis have passed a law that forbids Polish Jews to travel on trains."

"It's just a matter of time until the United States gets involved in the war," Griff said, popping the cork in the bottle.

"I don't know," Eve said. "Mr. Roosevelt has promised to keep us out of it."

"We're going to reach a point where that won't be an option," Victor said.

"I agree, and I intend to sign up as soon as that happens," Griff said.

"You'll look smart in your uniform," Eve said, "but I don't like to think of you going off to fight."

"I don't either," Victor said. "So, for tonight at least, let's not think about it anymore."

"Fair enough," Griff said, handing out the cocktails. "Here's to my two favorite people and to Hollywood's biggest night. May the stars shine ever bright."

"Hear, hear," Victor and Eve said as they clinked glasses with Griff and each other and sipped.

"By the way," Victor said, "did you hear they're doing a tribute to Orland Orcott tonight at the ceremony?"

"Uh, yes. He would have liked that, I think," Griff said. "Lots of people saying bogus nice things about him, and all paying tribute to one of the most hated men in Hollywood while pretending they liked him."

"I'm sure if Tab Rockwell hears about it, he'll be furious," Victor said.

"I feel sorry for Tab, to be honest," Eve said.

"Why?" Victor said. "Because they convicted him of manslaughter and attempted murder and sentenced him to life in prison?"

"But his father was so awful to him," Eve said.

"Yes, but that doesn't justify what he did. He'll probably get out on parole before too long anyway. And it could have been worse," Griff said. "He could have been convicted of murder and sent to the gas chamber."

"Worse than that, he could have killed both of us in my kitchen that day," Victor said.

"True, and he would have, if Eve hadn't come to the rescue. Thanks again for that," Griff said.

"You're welcome again. And Tab *would* have been sent to the gas chamber if the jury hadn't been so sympathetic. He had a good lawyer."

"One of the best. Marjorie paid for it," Victor said. "They said Tab didn't act alone."

"Well, to a degree, he didn't," Eve said. "He had help from Sheila and Tony."

"True, though Tony and Tab both testified Tony's involvement was only an agreement with Tab to telephone Mr. Orcott and keep him on the line as long as possible. Tony said Tab told him it would be a tryout of his acting skills, and if he did well, Tab would see to it he got a screen test," Victor said.

"And he claimed he didn't know Tab was going to kill his father," Eve said.

"I believe him. Tony said he kept Orcott on the line as long as he could, but at some point, Orland slammed the phone down and the line went dead," Victor said.

"And so did Mr. Orcott."

"Griff," Eve said.

"Sorry."

"And as for Sheila," Eve said, "she said Tab told her that in addition to having her tell Marjorie about Charlotte, he wanted to play a joke on his father, and she was only too happy to go along with it. When she heard the shot and Tab appeared shortly after, he told her he didn't know what the noise was, but that the joke had failed, and they should stick to their rehearsed script."

"And she never thought that was odd?" Victor said. "Even after finding out Orland was dead?"

"Apparently not, but this is Sheila we're talking about, remember," Eve said.

"True, but I'm willing to bet she's smarter than she acts. Sheila may have been fully aware of the plot. She's lucky she and Tony weren't found guilty of being accessories to murder," Victor said.

"Most likely only because Tab wasn't charged with homicide," Griff said.

"Definitely," Victor said. "She's been released from her contract at Icon, by the way, after her part in Gary Cooper's *The Westerner* was cut. Last I heard, she was making a movie called *Neptune's Naughty Nymph* for an independent studio. By the way, William and Lydia are at our table tonight. They're meeting us at the hotel."

"Oh, I'm so glad," Eve said. "How's William doing? I haven't seen him since the premiere of *The Lady Screeched* last November."

"He's okay. Still thin and weak. I must admit I'm worried about him. You know that trip to Mexico Lydia made?" Victor said.

"Yes. You thought she was carrying Orcott's child," Griff said.

"I said it was a possibility," Victor said. "But it turns out she was telling the truth. William was having some severe pain, and he needed opium to help him get through the film shoot. He didn't want anyone to know at the time, but he said I could share that with you two now."

"Oh. I could tell something was up. He tired so easily during filming. At least he's at the three-year mark since his cancer surgery," Griff said.

"Yes, he is," Victor said. "I wish I could say he was doing better. But there is some good news. Lydia's engaged."

"How wonderful," Eve said. "I'm so happy for her."

"Me too," Griff said. "Who's the lucky guy?"

"A doctor, believe it or not. She met him at the hospital when William was there last year. I think she's bringing him tonight, so we'll all get to meet him," Victor said.

"I look forward to it. Will Marjorie be there?" Eve said.

"Yes, seated at Mr. Rainer's table, since Orcott is being featured in the memorial tribute."

"Wowzer, she's at the head of the studio's table?" Griff said.

"Yes, as a guest of honor," Victor said. "I spoke with her a while ago, and she seemed in good spirits."

"She should be," Eve said. "Her louse of a husband is gone, and since Orcott was murdered, the prenup she signed is void. I imagine she'll be dating again soon, and hopefully she'll choose more wisely this time."

"I hope so," Griff said. "Say, Agatha Mudd will be at the Cocoanut Grove tonight, too, covering the proceedings, I'm sure. Have you heard from her recently?"

"Yes, I had lunch with her last month, and I got to meet her daughter, Sylvia, too. She's a nice young woman. Agatha told me she's decided to go public with what happened between her and Orcott all those years ago."

"I think that's a smart idea," Eve said. "I'm sure the public will be on her side."

"I believe so, and so does she," Victor said.

"Agatha also told me she interviewed Charlotte Masters recently, by the way. Her debut film, *Over the Sea*, is coming out next month, and the advance reviews have been favorable, both on the movie and for her," Victor said. "I think another star may have been born."

"Good for Charlotte," Griff said. "So, all's well that ends well."

"More or less," Victor said. "By the way, my friend Carson at RKO mentioned they've arranged for a screen test for Tony for the new Tarzan movie."

"From what I saw of Tony Bolt at the trial, he'll be excellent in a loincloth," Eve said.

"*If* he gets it," Victor said. "If not, there will be other opportunities, and he's a smart man with a plan."

"That's good to hear," Griff said, finishing his drink. "I still can't believe *The Lady Screeched* wasn't nominated for a single award, though."

"It's not surprising, considering the competition," Eve said. "*Gone with the Wind*, *The Wizard of Oz*, *Wuthering Heights*, *Stagecoach*, and more. We didn't stand a chance."

"*Gone with the Wind* is favored for best picture and almost every other category," Victor said.

"I'm rooting for *Mr. Smith Goes to Washington*. That was an outstanding film," Griff said.

"Mr. Orcott would have your head if he heard you were rooting for a picture from another studio," Eve said.

"Well, then, it's a good thing he can't hear me."

"I'll second that," Victor said. "And I must point out that nominations notwithstanding, you both got rave reviews for *The Lady Screeched*."

"So did you, Victor," Griff said.

Victor shrugged. "Agatha Mudd was kind to me, anyway. But Griff, you've already been assigned another film, this one with a bigger budget, and Eve, I hear you've been offered a part in a new picture, too. A starring role. *The* starring role."

Eve beamed. "Yes, I'm thrilled. And, there's a certain stuntman on the lot who recently asked me out. He's handsome and awfully sweet. I hope you don't mind, Vic."

"Not at all," Victor said. "I think it's marvelous. Our faux romance had to end sooner or later. I'll see to it Agatha does a nice little write-up, placing all the blame for our breakup on me."

"Nothing doing. I intend to take full responsibility for breaking your heart," Eve said with a smile.

"All right, Miss Spellman, if you insist."

"I do. But what of you two, my handsome bookends?"

"As a matter of fact," Griff said, "we have some news of our own. I'm going to move in here with Victor."

"How wonderful," Eve said. "But aren't you worried about what people will say?"

"A little, but hey, it's worked for Cary Grant and Randolph Scott all these years," Victor said. "They could easily afford their own places, yet they live together."

"A happy, handsome couple," Griff said. "I met them both at a charity function last year. They seem very much in love."

"I thought that was just a rumor," Eve said.

"And that's all it will be for us, just a rumor," Griff said. "I'm not worried."

"I'm more nervous about it than he is," Victor said, "but this awful war in Europe, and the thought of Griff enlisting, has made me realize that life is short."

"You're absolutely correct," Eve said. "I'm reminded of a quote by Oscar Wilde: 'There are moments when one has to choose between living one's own life, fully, entirely, completely—or dragging out some false, shallow, degrading existence that the world in its hypocrisy demands.' "

Victor raised his glass. "Well said, Mr. Wilde. And on that note, what say the three of us go pick up Miss Applewhite, and then we can all go to the Ambassador Hotel and the Cocoanut Grove for Hollywood's biggest night?"

Mystery History

- The Brown Derby restaurant, which was shaped like an actual brown derby hat, was a celebrity hot spot, first opened in 1926. It closed for good in 1980.
- The Ambassador Hotel, across the street from the Brown Derby, opened in 1921. Inside was the famous Cocoanut Grove nightclub.
- Don Lee's Cadillac dealership in Los Angeles did exist, and it stood on Seventh and Bixel.
- Sidney Coe Howard wrote the screenplay to *Gone with the Wind.* He died tragically in the summer of 1939 when he was just forty-eight, crushed by a tractor.
- Florence Ryerson, Noel Langley, and Edgar Allan Woolf all were credited with writing the screenplay for *The Wizard of Oz*.
- Dorothy Arzner was a pioneer in women's directing, and she had a prosperous career until she retired in 1943. She had a long-time relationship with a woman named Marion Morgan, spanning forty years.
- Victor Marvel's early years were inspired by the life of actor William Haines, a hugely popular movie star at MGM who, according to legend, was forced to give up acting when the head of MGM, Louis B. Mayer, told him to give up his younger boyfriend, Jimmy Shields, and get married to a woman or he would be fired. He chose the latter option and began a fulfilling, successful career as an interior decorator, with many famous clients, including Joan Crawford. He and Jimmy were together forty-seven years until Haines died in 1973. Jimmy, unable to live without the love of his life, died by suicide shortly after.
- Eddie Quillan was an actor and singer, born in 1907. In later years

he played a variety of characters on *Little House on the Prairie* and other television shows.

- Glenn Miller, the Andrews Sisters, and Bing Crosby were all big names in the music industry.
- Lionel Barrymore, Humphrey Bogart, Gary Cooper, Joan Crawford, Bette Davis, Errol Flynn, Henry Fonda, Clark Gable, Charles Laughton, and Tyrone Power were huge movie stars in the 1930s and 40s.
- *The Westerner*, released in 1940, was a western starring Gary Cooper and directed by William Wyler.
- Frank Capra was a popular and powerful director of the 1930s and 1940s.
- Cary Grant and Randolph Scott, both big names in the movies, have long been rumored to have been lovers, sharing a beach house together for several years, though some dispute that they were romantically involved.
- Madame Vionnet and Coco Chanel were both popular, successful designers of women's fashions.
- The surnames of Shufflebottom and Cobbledick used in this book come from an actual newspaper of the time provided to the author by a friend, Lawrence Simon.
- Supposedly, early pornographic movies were sometimes referred to as blue movies because they were often shot on inferior-grade film, which gave them a blue cast.
- KFI radio in LA first began operations in 1922.
- Los Angeles Mayor Frank Shaw was recalled from office in 1938 after claims of corruption.
- The Hertz rental car company began life as Hertz Drive-Ur-Self in 1925.
- Early California driver's licenses did not have a photograph on them but instead a thumbprint, along with basic information such as height, sex, and eye color.
- The name Orland Orcott, used in this book, came from a deceased relative of the author's, whose name was Overland Orcutt.
- Victor Fleming won the Best Director Academy Award for *Gone With the Wind*. He also worked on *The Wizard of Oz*.
- Mervyn LeRoy was a director who worked on such films as *Gypsy* and *The Wizard of Oz*.
- The highest grossing films of 1939 were: *Gone with the Wind*, *Mr. Smith Goes to Washington*, *Jesse James*, *Babes in Arms*, *The*

Wizard of Oz, *Goodbye Mr. Chips*, *Dodge City*, *The Rains Came*, *The Women*, and *Drums Along the Mohawk*. Of the ten films, five were from MGM or MGM/Selznick.

- The movies up for Best Picture of 1939 were: *Gone with the Wind* (winner), *Dark Victory*, *Goodbye Mr. Chips*, *Love Affair*, *Mr. Smith Goes to Washington*, *Ninotchka*, *Of Mice and Men*, *Stagecoach*, *The Wizard of Oz,* and *Wuthering Heights*. Of the ten films, four were from MGM or MGM/Selznick.
- Chowder the cat was inspired by one of the author's cats, who is polydactyl and was named Chowder at the Humane Society when the author and his husband adopted her. Her name has been changed.
- Prostate cancer, which the character of William Taylor had, is still the second leading cause of cancer death among men in the United States. If caught early, it is treatable. The author underwent surgery and treatment in 2016. If you're fifty-five or over, please ask your doctor for a PSA test.

About the Author

David S. Pederson has written multiple mysteries, all featuring LGBTQ+ characters. He's a two-time finalist for the Lambda Literary Award for Gay Mysteries. His second book, *Death Goes Overboard*, was selected by the GLBT Round Table of the American Library Association for the 2018 Over the Rainbow book list. Two of his poems, "My Candle" and "I Never Knew," were used in the 2024 OCTC stage production of *Love Notes Cabaret of Words & Music*.

In 2024 he was invited by a local bookstore to conduct a workshop on writing mysteries. He's passionate about mysteries, old movies, ocean liners, and reading. He, his husband, and their sweet rescue cats reside in the sunny Southwest.

Website: http://www.davidspederson.com
Facebook: https://www.facebook.com/DavidSPedersonWriter
Instagram: https://www.instagram.com/dave.pederson/

Books Available From Bold Strokes Books

A Marvelous Murder by David S. Pederson. When a hated director is found dead in his locked study, movie star Victor Marvel, his boyfriend Griff, and friend Eve seek to uncover what really happened to Orland Orcott. (978-1-63679-798-4)

Fatal Foul Play by David S. Pederson. After eight friends are stranded in an old lodge by a blinding snowstorm, a brutal murder leaves Mark Maddox to solve the crime as he discovers deadly secrets about people he thought he knew. (978-1-63679-794-6)

One and Done by Fredrick Smith. One day can lead to a night of passion…and possibly a chance at love. (978-1-63679-564-5)

Puzzles Can Be Deadly by David S. Pederson. Skip loves a good puzzle. Little does he know that a simple phone call will lead him and his boyfriend Henry to the deadliest puzzle he's ever encountered. (978-1-63679-615-4)

Triad Magic by 'Nathan Burgoine. Face-to-face against forces set in motion hundreds of years ago, Luc, Anders, and Curtis—vampire, demon, and wizard—must draw on the power of blood, soul, and magic to stop a killer. (978-1-63679-505-8)

Head Over Heelflip by Sander Santiago. To secure the biggest prizes at the Colorado Amateur Street Sports Tour, Thomas Jefferson will do almost anything, even marrying his best friend and crush—Arturo "Uno" Ortiz. (978-1-63679-489-1)

Mississippi River Mischief by Greg Herren. When a politician turns up dead and Scotty's client is the most obvious suspect, Scotty and his friends set out to prove his client's innocence. (978-1-63679-353-5)

Murder at the Oasis by David S. Pederson. Palm trees, sunshine, and murder await Mason Adler and his friend Walter as they travel from Phoenix to Palm Springs for what was supposed to be a relaxing vacation but ends up being a trip of mystery and intrigue. (978-1-63679-416-7)

The Speed of Slow Changes by Sander Santiago. As Al and Lucas navigate the ups and downs of their polyamorous relationship, only one thing is certain: romance has never been so crowded. (978-1-63679-329-0)

Manny Porter and The Yuletide Murder by D.C. Robeline. Manny only has the holiday season to discover who killed prominent research scientist Phillip Nikolaidis before the judicial system condemns an innocent man to lethal injection. (978-1-63679-313-9)

Murder at Union Station by David S. Pederson. Private Detective Mason Adler struggles to determine who killed a woman found in a trunk without getting himself killed in the process. (978-1-63679-269-9)

Corpus Calvin by David Swatling. Cloverkist Inn may be haunted, but a ghost materializes from Jason Dekker's past and Calvin's canine instinct kicks in to protect a young boy from mortal danger. (978-1-62639-428-5)

A Champion for Tinker Creek by D.C. Robeline. Lyle James has rescued his dad's auto repair business, but when city hall condemns his neighborhood, Lyle learns only trusting will save his life and help him find love. (978-1-63679-213-2)

Inherit the Lightning by Bud Gundy. Darcy O'Brien and his sisters learn they are about to inherit an immense fortune, but a family mystery about to unravel after seventy years threatens to destroy everything. (978-1-63679-199-9)

Pursued: Lillian's Story by Felice Picano. Fleeing a disastrous marriage to the Lord Exchequer of England, Lillian of Ravenglass reveals an incident-filled, often bizarre, tale of great wealth and power, perfidy, and betrayal. (978-1-63679-197-5)

Murder on Monte Vista by David S. Pederson. Private Detective Mason Adler's angst at turning fifty is forgotten when his "birthday present," the handsome, young Henry Bowtrickle, turns up dead, and it's up to Mason to figure out who did it, and why. (978-1-63679-124-1)

Three Left Turns to Nowhere by Jeffrey Ricker, J. Marshall Freeman & 'Nathan Burgoine. Three strangers heading to a convention in Toronto are stranded in rural Ontario, where a small town with a subtle kind of magic leads each to discover what he's been searching for. (978-1-63679-050-3)

One Verse Multi by Sander Santiago. Life was good: promotion, friends, falling in love, discovering that the multi-verse is on a fast track to collision—wait, what? Good thing Martin King works for a company that can fix the problem, right…um…right? (978-1-63679-069-5)